WUQUIN

THE HOLY BOOK OF THE ATEESTA RELIGION

NAVEEN MULLANGI

ISBN: 979-8-9986711-3-5

Dedicated to humanity & my unborn brother.

My baby brother, even though we never met and I never saw you, I know that my life would have been much brighter and colorful with you rather than living as an isolated, alone, only child by myself. In a world where death comes to people who are born, you left us even before coming into this world. Even though I do not believe in any supernatural elements, I wish you were there in Heaven, overseeing us. With love from your brother & family - Naveen Mullangi

1

Ateesta is the religion of a character called 'Nathan.'

Nathan is the hero of the novel "I Killed Satan - The Great War of Man and Satan."

'Wuquin' is the holy book of the Ateesta religion. 'Ateestans' follow Wuquin, and they live their lives according to the Ateesta religion.

Wuquin is the only book they follow to know how to live their life as an Ateestan. Wuquin describes how Ateestans live and see the universe and life.

Naveen Mullangi is the founder of the Ateesta religion, which means I, Naveen Mullangi, the one who wrote what you are reading here, founded this religion for the "I Killed Satan - The Great War of Man and Satan" novel.

Naveen Mullangi is the author of the novel "I Killed Satan - The Great War of Man" and Satan and "Wuquin - The Holy Book of Ateesta Religion."

No one knows who the founder of the Ateesta religion is in the story of "I Killed Satan - The Great War of Man and Satan" novel, but in real life, it is Naveen Mullangi who founded the Ateesta Religion for the "I Killed Satan - The Great War of Man and Satan" novel.

Naveen Mullangi named the hero character of the "I Killed Satan - The Great War of Man and Satan" Novel as 'Nathan'.

***

In the story of the novel "I Killed Satan - The Great War of Man and Satan," the Hero character, Nathan, is the Prophet of the Ateesta religion. The only known prophet of the Ateesta religion is Nathan. No one knows who the other prophets are according to the story of the novel.

According to the novel "I Killed Satan - The Great War of Man and Satan," The Wuquin is the holy book of the Ateesta religion, with no names of specific authors other than Nathan, because in ancient times, people opposed rationality and feared intelligence. So, the Ateestans practiced their religion in secrecy. It was after the developments of modern technology and the wide acceptance of rational thinking and various forms of intelligence that the Ateesta religion became socially accepted, and Wuquin was widely read publicly by Ateestans.

Nathan, the hero of the novel "I Killed Satan - The Great War of Man and Satan," learned about the Ateesta religion, read and researched the Wuquin deeply. It is he who completed the final version of "Wuquin - The Holy Book of the Ateesta Religion" at age 26, once and for all, to end of the times, after the end of times too, to be never modified and rewritten, or to make changes to Wuquin again ever in any way, shape or form. This holy book is that version of Wuquin, which was completed by Nathan after he met Father Wulshaan in the Sacred Wulshaan universe. Ateestans only follow what is said in this book and nothing else.

According to the novel "I Killed Satan - The Great War of Man and Satan," Nathan is the Last Prophet of Ateesta; there are no prophets after him in any way, shape, or form. There are no other prophets after Nathan in any way. Do not believe in anyone except Nathan, as the prophet of Ateesta, and Nathan is the only known prophet of Ateesta; the Prophetship ends with Nathan, and that's it. There are no Prophets and Prophetship in any way after Nathan.

Ateestans should only take Wuquin as the standard, base, and whole for everything, and there should be nothing before and after Wuquin. Do not assume about other unknown prophets; no one knows who they are, even the Last Prophet of Ateesta, Nathan himself. Do not speculate about them and disrespect them. They are who they are, and no one knows about them.

Even the legal establishments and texts of legal establishments should only be formed according to the teachings of God Yinta in Wuquin, through the Last Prophet of Ateesta, Nathan only; they should not collide with Wuquin in any way, but must be aligned with it.

In real life, Naveen Mullangi completed working on the "I Killed Satan - The Great War of Man and Satan" novel and "Wuquin - The Holy Book of Ateesta Religion" in his 20s.

Ateesta Religion was created for the Hero character of the novel "I Killed Satan - The Great War of Man and Satan," and it is needed to tell the readers how the hero character sees this world and what he believes in.

This final version of Wuquin, which you are reading now, is the same book that was completed by the hero character Nathan in the novel "I Killed Satan - The Great War of Man and Satan." As per the novel, Wuquin is written by God Yinta through many prophets spanning thousands of years. Nathan is the last prophet of the Ateesta religion.

In real life, Wuquin - The Holy Book of Ateesta Religion is finished by Naveen Mullangi and will not be modified, changed, rewritten, or made changes to it in any way, shape, or form to the end of times, after the end of times, too. And in real life, there are no other known or unknown prophets. Naveen Mullangi, as the Author, wrote the entire "Wuquin - The Holy Book of Ateesta Religion" and "I Killed Satan - The Great War of Man and Satan" Novel. Which means I, Naveen Mullangi, who wrote what you are reading here, wrote "Wuquin - The Holy Book of Ateesta Religion" and "I Killed Satan - The Great War of Man and Satan" by myself completely. I decided to keep Wuquin as it is for eternity, and there will be no changes to Wuquin ever in any way, shape, or form. This is the first and last version of Wuquin.

Wuquin talks about many things that are essential to life and humanity, but a person who is reading Wuquin must have the ability to go back and forth to understand Wuquin completely, as Prophet Nathan did not talk about one topic completely at one time, at one place only, or on only one page. Prophet Nathan wrote Wuquin as God Yinta revealed it to him.

Indeed, Yinta is merciful.

2

Wuquin, an emphasis on thinking rationally with an emotionally balanced common sense and an intellectual, moral approach to life, with health, wealth, taking care of family, and seeking truth as a priority.

Ateesta is a way of life, not just a religion.

Ateesta is the world's first religion that encourages critical thinking.

To know how Ateestans see and perceive God, we must know about who God is in Ateesta. In Ateesta, there is only one true God. He is 'Yinta'. Ateestans believe God Yinta is in our minds. God Yinta gives you good, great, creative, refreshing, rational, and highly matured intellectual pragmatic thoughts that will not give you instant, short-term happiness and satisfaction, but God Yinta, through his thoughts, gives you a long, fulfilled, long-term happy life.

The one who opposes God Yinta, is Satan. Satan is also in our minds. At the beginning of time, according to I Killed Satan - The Great War of Man and Satan novel, Mother Adis, The first energy created Earth purely, but Satan took over Earth and polluted the minds of people with the diseases of stupidity, dumbness, emotional imbalance and tried to make the Earth a Satanic world, but God Yinta fought a war with Satan to stop it. The war between God Yinta and Satan is called the War of Nazreck. In the War of Nazreck, God Yinta defeated Satan.

After the war of Nazreck, God Yinta gave his powers of thinking to humanity to fight the bad thoughts given to people by Satan, also called Satanic thoughts. The great thoughts and thinking power we have now are the results of the powers God Yinta gave to humanity.

Satan always tries to occupy the total space in the minds of human beings through his Satanic bad thoughts. Satan wants to give you instant satisfaction and happiness by destroying your future. Satan makes you unnecessarily unhealthy, cruel, Irrational, dumb, and stupidly aggressive in the process of occupying space in your mind. Don't give Satan that space in your mind. Give all the space in your mind to God Yinta rather than to Satan. You, as a human being, have to fight Satan and the Satanic thoughts that Satan gives you using God Yinta and thoughts, thinking power given to you by God Yinta. You must fight consciously within yourself to give total space in your mind to God Yinta.

In a simple way, God is in your mind. And God gives you good, great, rational, and highly matured intellectual, pragmatic thoughts that will not give you instant kick and satisfaction, but a long, fulfilled, happy life. Satan wants to grab that space in your mind through his Satanic bad thoughts. Satan wants to give you instant satisfaction and happiness by destroying your future and making you more cruel, dumb, and stupid aggressive in the process. Don't give Satan that space in your mind. Give all the space of the mind to God rather than to Satan.

Ateestans know that God Yinta and Satan are not real, which means God Yinta and Satan do not exist in any way in reality. But Ateestans see God Yinta and Satan as names for the collections of thoughts that will impact life positively and negatively.

God Yinta and Satan are just symbolic names for the great thoughts we get in the mind and the worst thoughts we get in the mind.

***

Rationality means that as an individual, you try to see things as they are and improve those things for the better.

Intelligence means learning and the application of knowledge. And use wisdom to improve life in every aspect.

Mind is the software of the brain, and its programmers are evolution, family, environment, cultures, practices, etc, and others that influence the upbringing of the mind.

You might think common sense is common, but it is not common among many people. Common sense means the action you can take on a particular matter that makes sense based on science, past, present, and its estimated impact on the future in the related context and on the other unrelated things indirectly, and also by considering all the variables and constants of that particular matter you are dealing with. Common sense is relative, just like Rationality and Intelligence. Of course, the nature of their relativeness is unique to themselves and varies according to the context.

The word "Ateesta" means 'Sacredly Pure.'

"Wuquin" means 'The thing that makes someone sacred and pure.'

You should determine your own morals.

Ateesta religion gives great importance to critical thinking and questioning everything to know about how, why, where, and other related things that determine the quality of your life and impact your life directly and indirectly.

Ateesta religion believes the time has come to make the ability to make sense and rationality prevail in this world with the help of intelligence and morals.

Ateesata teaches rigorous emotional balance and emotional awareness because emotions hold the power to destroy oneself and others.

Ateesta is a religion for rational, intelligent people who seek the truth in a technical, scientific, mathematical, and philosophical way.

Ateestans are aware that equivalents of the Ateesta religion are outdated, and they do not provide any insights on how human beings should deal with newly developed technologies. And they do not describe how a human being can approach life in a world that is full of science and modern technologies.

Ateestans are also aware that those old equivalents of the Ateesta religion provide some ethics and morals, but newly developed brain-related science and technologies, along with neurological and psychological studies, are challenging those ethics and morals of the old equivalents of the Ateesta religion.

Honor, Strength, and Progress are very important for a human's life in Ateesta.

No matter where you live, what you do, etc., and what your lifestyle is, you must never leave science, rationality, and common sense.

Ateestans also recognize Ateesta as the religion that rational people on Earth and their equivalents outside of Earth should follow. Wuquin is the Holy Book they should read to know everything about the Ateesta religion. There is no other holy book, and other things they have to follow other than Wuquin. They must not follow anything other than Wuquin.

One cannot become an Ateestan by birth. He/she should prove himself/herself to become an Ateestan. You cannot become an Ateestan by birth just because your parents, father, or mother are Ateestans. There is a process to becoming an Ateestan.

The process is hard. To become an Ateestan, you should first read Wuquin, which is the Holy Book of the Ateesta Religion. After reading Wuquin, you must select five books on five topics. Those topics can be on anything you like. You have to read those five books and give a speech or presentation to some people who also want to become Ateestans or are already Ateestans. The speech or presentation should be on what you think about Wuquin and what you learned after reading those five books. That's it.

Half of the speech/presentation time is for Wuquin, and the other half is for what you learned from the other 5 books, and how what you learned will help you in day-to-day real life. Also, the books should not be related to any supernatural belief systems. STEM, philosophy, etc, books are preferred, and they need not be strictly academic. Fiction, too, is okay, but no matter whether those five books are fiction or nonfiction, they should not be related to any supernatural belief systems, and your speech/presentation should align with Wuquin.

No one makes you an Ateestan, but the presentation/speech you give itself and that presentation should last only a maximum of 20 minutes or less, but not less than 8 minutes.

The idea is to show that the person who wants to become an Ateestan is capable of thinking critically and rationally.

With no marks or no one approving or rejecting you to become an Ateestan, it gives you the freedom to express yourself freely, and how great you can use that time to express your thoughts.

So, how well you give your presentation or speech entirely depends on your interest and passion. Even though people are not giving you any marks, approvals, or rejections, they can see whether you have put your mind to work, or not, to give that presentation or speech. That is the whole point.

The two rules for the process of becoming an Ateestan in the Ateestan Yan event of presentations and speeches are that you should not talk negatively about or to anyone who gave the presentation or speech, no matter whether it is good or not.

The time limit given by organizers of the event for each speech or presentation is based on how many people are participating in the event and how much time is good to allot to each person to easily complete the presentations and speeches of all people who want to become Ateestans.

If you have many people on the day of the Ateestan Yan Event, you can allocate less time for presentations and speeches. But if you have only a few people and more time, then you can allot more than 20 minutes for the presentations and speeches. It depends entirely on the number of people and the time available on that day. But no matter what, the presentation/speech of each person should not be less than 8 minutes. So use multiple stages for these presentations/ speeches and split people into groups to make it easy for them to complete all the speeches/presentations.

Ateestans can also upload their full speeches or presentations to digital platforms after giving the initial presentations/speeches physically in front of their fellow Ateestans. This is optional, not compulsory. But in order to become an Ateestan, a physical presentation or speech to fellow Ateestans or to people who want to become Ateestans is a must, at least for 8 minutes. Then, they can upload their full presentations or speeches to digital platforms for other non-Ateestan people to see. The time given here is just based on common sense, not on any fixed rule.

The event people organize to become an Ateestan is called 'Ateestan Yan.'

Try to organize as many small Ateestan Yan Events as possible. It is to reduce the boredom of people during big Ateestan Yan events, and nothing more than that.

But if you decide to organize a big Ateestan Yan event, then have multiple sections in the Yan event to give multiple presentations or speeches at the same time.

Include music, food, nonalcoholic drinks, without any kind of drugs or substances that alter the natural state of mind, and other fun activities that are not dangerous in the event.

So that people will have a good time that day after their speech or presentation.

A person with any kind of disability and a person who cannot see, speak, write, read, or hear can also become an Ateestan. A person who is born with physical and mental illnesses and problems can also become an Ateestan. They just have to express their thoughts about life and how they see it in their own way. No standard rules for them. they just have to show a sign of intention to progress in their life. They can also show it to society and humanity, but it depends on their interest. But if a person is in a situation where he/she can't do this, then too he/she can also become an Ateestan with the help of another person accompanying him/her to explain the intentions of this person who cannot express them by him/herself in any way.

There will be many personal interpretations of Wuquin. Many people follow their own personal interpretations, but it should be done with only one common end goal in mind, which is set by Wuquin here. The common end goal of any interpretation of Wuquin must be these things. They are the progress, no harm to each other, questioning everything, and seeking a justifiable scientific or rational answer that makes sense for everything. If you can't find that answer, search for it yourself and work on it, and after finding it, share it with humanity.

To construct a temple of God Yinta, you must know these things.

The temple must have an equilateral triangle-shaped roof with one sharp point of the triangle stopping above the middle of the front entrance. The temple inside must have images and replicas of important discoveries, inventions ever made by humanity, with the names of the discoverers, scientists, and inventors. The entrance of the Yinta temple must face east (the direction of the sun in the morning on Earth). It symbolizes the encouragement of Ateesta to Ateestans for seeking the truth and enlightenment through their personal journey of sunrises and sunsets, representing their achievements and struggles in life.

One text must be on the inside walls of the temple, along with others. That text is, 'You are enlightened when you achieve all the goals you had in your life or in the process of trying to achieve those goals."

A statue of God Yinta should be present inside the temple. One statue of God Yinta should be outside the temple.

And the structures of all temples of God Yinta must be exactly the same.

No one worships God Yinta in any way. And there are no worship and praying processes of any kind in the Ateesta religion. You just visit the Ateestan temple, and that's it. The main purpose of the Ateesta temple visit is to make you remember the teachings of God Yinta in Wuquin, that's all. Earth rotates, but we need a standard of measurement to do things. So, use the east direction because the east is the direction in which you see the sunlight every morning. That's it.

We build temples of God Yinta facing East just to symbolize rational thinking, intelligence, freedom, and liberty, also love for your nation, brotherhood between men, and sisterhood between women.

God Yinta in the I Killed Satan - The Great War of Man and Satan novel is neither skinny nor thick, and he is a long-haired 26-year-old male born in Master Universe to Mother Adis, the first energy, Mother of Known and Unknown universes.

He has a lover called 'Sumaaraa'. No mortal knows how she looks. She lives with God Yinta in his residence in God's Heaven. She is the only daughter of Beeliaal, the Emperor of Emptiness and anti-universes called Xhehroom Universes.

Ateesta asks Ateestans to see life as it is and improve it rather than getting their hearts broken while realizing the reality they live in.

Of course, it will be painful, but we have to face the truth absolutely to improve reality rather than just living in our dreams and imagination without working on them to make them a reality.

Ateesta religion does not believe in any kind of supernatural powers, forces, or elements. Ateesta does not promote any kind of supernatural worship. In the God Yinta temple, no one should worship or pray to God Yinta in any form. God Yinta just symbolizes prosperity and progress. The temple of God Yinta represents rationality and common sense.

Humans, by nature, want to believe in something supernatural that is a higher power than themselves. It is a normal thing, but not correct.

***

Ateesta strongly opposes any form of worship of any supernatural forces.

Belief in supernatural powers needs no logic and rationality because it is emotional.

After believing in supernatural powers for our own reasons, like getting money, finding peace, gaining something, being happy in life, or for any other reason, and then we try to give the worship of supernatural powers a rational logic, but only after believing in them irrationally initially.

We also give it a constructive ideology so that people keep believing in those supernatural powers.

It is because we don't want to be seen as stupid by ourselves, and we also don't want to take a chance if supernatural powers exist and if they can help us.

Ateesta asks questions about this process of believing in supernatural forces.

When you make something unquestionable, it doesn't matter whether it is a sacred thing or a thing related to supernatural powers, or it could be anything, then it becomes dogma, blind faith, and dictatorial belief. You will kill and do any stupid thing when someone questions it. Don't be that dumb of a person. If something is so sacred, then according to human values and rationality, it must have a big heart and a welcoming nature to allow questioning it. And it should answer those questions through its teachings, at least to some extent, and to the questions questioning its intentions too. But when that very thing which is considered sacred is scaring people, stopping people from questioning it because it is sacred, and it is a great, true supernatural power, then we can come to a conclusion that it might be sacred, but not as sacred as it shows itself to the world. We analyzed this just through our human values and rationality, but this is a supernatural power.

So it must be more flexible and higher in all types of values and morals than humans, right? While welcoming the questions of people and encouraging a questioning nature in humans. If not, is that sacred at all? And is it just a supernatural power with the attitude of a typical egoistic human who dislikes the situation when his/her children question something he/she does?

***

Man is always fascinated by supernatural elements. It is normal.

Again, I emphasize that the end goal of Ateesta is freedom, liberty, and progress. Not the Opposite.

Freedom is more important than peace because insecure dictatorial authorities use the pretext of peace to oppress people and even progress.

Evil authorities do not want people to get economically stronger so that they don't need assistance from the government.

If people are economically weak and need assistance from the government, the government can tax and control people as much as it wants, but people can't fight back.

In general, people are peaceful but not criminals. So you cannot be peaceful while getting robbed, raped, and destroyed. You cannot be peaceful while authorities and politicians use tricks, tactics, and even legal systems and laws to take away what is yours. Fight, fight for yourselves. It is for this reason that Progress, Freedom, and Liberty are more important than peace. But it doesn't mean peace is less important. Peace, too, is important, but it should be the result of the transparency and honesty of society.

Let the men and women do what they want in life and ask them to take responsibility for their success and failure, too. Be afraid of thugs and criminals in the darkness, not of supernatural elements.

Do not make fun of people who worship supernatural powers, but see the intention and their good hearts behind it. Respect their prayers and accept them if they pray for you. There is nothing wrong with respecting other people's beliefs, no matter what you think personally about them or whether you believe in those supernatural powers or not.

Ateesta is Ateesta, nothing else!

Any association, any power, anything threatening your freedom, your life, and the property you own, even if they have the support of the legal system to do it, even then, you must oppose it. Be brutal to people who come to you to assert their power over you and your things. If they find a legal loophole to keep you trapped, use the loopholes in the same law to go against them in every possible way. In places and things, they do not expect you to be there, go into them, find legal loopholes, and use those to kick them down and get them out of your life.

You are Ateestan. You don't need to adhere to their laws telling you how you should live. Go to war with them. Don't be oppressed even if no one supports you. If injustice is done to you, you must fight it. It is your basic responsibility. Then you can get support from people.

Atheism has nothing to do with the Ateesta religion, and we do not support nihilism in Ateesta. We deny supernatural things of all kinds. We don't hate or oppose people who believe in them. They have the freedom to believe in what they want to. But as an Ateestan, you must make sure that those supernatural things and worship, etc., are not damaging your life and happiness, and also not making you do irrational things and harm people.

Ateesta is Ateesta. Ateesta is not Atheism or any other thing than what is described by itself in Wuquin.

Even though Ateestans disagree with supernatural elements, we can learn the good things and leave out the bad, irrational things from the philosophies of supernatural belief systems.

Anything that is hindering the growth and progress of humanity in any aspect should be destroyed and abolished. Those rulers should be ousted, and those political systems need to be dismantled. Any political and economic system that takes away liberty and freedom, the free will of people, must be destroyed completely.

You should know that no Non-Ateestan in power naturally cares about people. So, it is the people's responsibility to make sure that those in power care about them. They should be under constant scrutiny and pressure, accountable, and transparent in all of the ways about how they are working as people's representatives.

There is nothing wrong with working or hoping to get material gains in the world as long as you are putting in the effort. There is also nothing wrong with prioritizing a spiritual way of life without expecting material wealth in life. It is the person's personal choice. But you have to live them or any other way of life honestly to yourself first, and without harming others in any way.

Ateesta has no favorites in anything other than rationality, intelligence, common sense, and morals. All other religions and groups are equal to it.

You do not need to despise and hate the names and entities of supernatural figures in any religion. You can respect them and not believe in those supernatural figures.

All the supernatural powers worshipers are relatives of themselves, even if they do not accept it. They belong to different supernatural powers belief systems, but because they all believe in the theory that some supernatural power created the universe, rather than believing in Human evolution and a rational explanation of how the universe came into existence according to science. That is why they are all relatives of themselves, even if they believe in different supernatural powers.

They all do the same thing but in different ways, but they fight among themselves about determining how those ways should be. Ha ha!

***

The Ateestans search for the answer to who created the universe in a rational and scientific way, rather than believing in the theory that some supernatural power created the Earth and the known universe to us, and is still creating the universe that is being expanded continuously.

Do not spend or give any money or resources to any supernatural worship. Money, the economy, and finance do not care about your emotions. Try to do something extraordinary in life, try to learn a great skill, and become financially independent through it.

The believers who believe in supernatural powers spend money heavily on supernatural worship-related things in their supernatural worship places. So, any supernatural group's tax money or donations should go back to their own group only, not to other supernatural groups in any way. The government or anyone should not take that money for any reason at all.

Also, the government should liberate all supernatural powers' institutions from government management. The government should not take any money from any supernatural worshipers in any form. But they can give them money or resources.

Even though you respect the beliefs of supernatural powers' worshipers, never let any of it take away your freedom and liberty in any way.

Freedom and responsibility are important for an Ateestan. Freedom is the primary right of any human being, and an Ateestan's primary responsibility is taking responsibility for his/her life and behavior.

The Government of any type is there to serve people, not the other way around.

3

Be careful of people who try to use rationality and their personal credibility and their degrees and even Ateesta or any other religions and philosophies to propagate something to people and make them do something that benefits a few institutions and people, and also encourages worship of supernatural powers of any kind.

All other religions are equal to Ateesta and Ateestans, and vice versa.

They may use these to try to make you part ways with Ateesta. Because as an Ateestan, you prove you can be a good, calm, energetic, positive, and respectful person to everyone, and also to all believers of supernatural powers of all kinds, without believing in any kind of supernatural powers, and still be rational and sensible.

It frustrates people who want to see a chaotic society and want to create divisions and confusion between people using group ideologies or religions.

They thrive on this chaos and try to gain power over others and benefit personally, but they make it appear like group vs group or religion vs religion.

Ateesta stops this confusion and chaos and starts giving clarity of thoughts and clarity of mind to people, thus helping to stop all the harsh acts, mindless judgments, and acts on the verge of emotions, hatefully or for any reason whatsoever. You can be a great, honest person with morals and self-confidence without believing in any supernatural powers.

Some people are so sensitive and scared to know the truth that no supernatural power is overseeing their lives, and life or death, and success or failure are up to them. With such people, be sensitive to them. Don't scare them with the truth of rationality, and also by telling them to see life as it is, even though it is much more interesting than believing in nonexistent supernatural powers.

Also, be careful with people who do not have an open mind to listen and discuss things, stick to only beliefs in supernatural powers, and find every possible reason to continue believing in them with blind faith rather than exploring and questioning things. They live in their closed mind till their death and let them live with whatever they believe in. Let them be.

Ateesta religion's holy book, Wuquin, cannot cover everything in human life and every aspect of everything in human life. For them, what Wuquin did not cover, you should explore them and decide for yourself on how to approach and deal with them. It is the nature of the human race to deal with unknown things. But use your rationality, common sense, intelligence, and morals to create a path of how you should deal with those things that were not explained by Wuquin.

Rationality is a double-edged sword. Use it properly with the aim of progress by using the combination of intelligence, common sense and morals.

Never be arrogant or rude to supernatural powers believers and to their beliefs. Be respectful and go your way.

Never disrespect anyone, no matter who they are, and never accept disrespect.

There were no supernatural powers worship systems before man learned to think, speak, write, and create the first language in the world.

All supernatural worship systems came after man started becoming more and more rational and intelligent. The regular people who know so much about the world and the reality they live in rationally at their times have scared the powerful people who are in ruling positions at those times.

If regular people spend their time more asking supernatural powers for things they want and worshiping supernatural powers that don't exist, rather than working for what they want and learning about what they want, then it makes people instantly less knowledgeable about many important things and happenings in their time.

Because they gave the only power they had, which is using their mind to think and work to get what they wanted, to the supernatural powers' worship processes, and they became more wishful and begging-oriented. Many times, by luck, we get what we want with no hard work or any effort from our side. This happens a lot. When this happened, and with time, people confirmed by themselves that a power that is not human is helping them to move forward in life, and they should spend more and more time worshiping those supernatural powers to get what they want, rather than working for them in real life.

The supernatural powers believers made their supernatural powers and their systems look sacred, feared, and interesting, so that any human being would be scared to question those supernatural powers, fearing bad things would happen to the person who questions them.

It is evident that all the supernatural things that are considered sacred have always scared people.

The supernatural things that are considered not sacred are also always scared people.

Do not confuse cultures and their literature, architecture, and other cultural things with their supernatural powers and worship processes. Supernatural powers and worship are only one part of any culture.

You can learn many things from many cultures if the things you want to learn have rational merit. And respect the cultures and their supernatural powers' figures, but still do not believe in those supernatural powers.

If any supernatural worship group describes their whole culture as just their belief in their supernatural powers, and there is nothing important in their culture other than worshiping their supernatural powers, then be careful with them. One single word that you might say that slightly offends their supernatural beliefs, they will not hesitate to even kill you.

Gladly gain knowledge and learn skills from any culture and refuse to believe in their supernatural powers because learning skills that are rationally credible is good and sane, but not believing in supernatural powers.

Because skills and works of cultures are developed by humans only, not by supernatural powers, even though they have their own supernatural powers' figures at the center of their cultures. No supernatural powers came to Earth and created the cultures. Cultures are developed by human beings.

Understand that the supernatural powers' belief systems were designed in a way to create an emotional connection, a higher-than-human sacred feeling in people while they are learning about their own supernatural powers, figures, culture, skills, and works of their culture. It is to form a strong connection to what they are learning, to respect what they are learning, and to learn those things at a faster speed with great focus. It will be hard to teach people the same exact skills and work if they take out supernatural elements in them, because people who are learning those things will not respect those things that they are learning at the same level as when supernatural elements are included in what they are learning.

The supernatural belief systems made the process of believing in their supernatural powers sacred and emotionally highly impactful with carefully crafted prayer methods and different methods of worship, which will evoke an emotion in people commonly that can be fear, calm, peace, happiness, satisfaction, and anything for that matter that differs from what a normal human being feel in general in his daily life. So that those unusual emotional experiences will stick with people, and they get a strong impression of supernatural powers in them, and start believing in them.

You can use the same psychological tactics for anything and make it as appealing as believing in supernatural powers. It just takes fear in people, their desire to get material wants satisfied, the need to have mental peace, for the poor to get rich, and for lonely people to get social approval and publicity, and also by creating a fear in people that bad things will happen to them when anyone questions supernatural powers.

Everyone who believes in supernatural powers and everyone who does not believe in supernatural powers has problems in their lives. Bad things and good things happen to everyone. We just try to link them with supernatural powers because the supernatural powers belief systems have programmed us that way since our birth.

Imagine people spending time learning about government expenditure and what their politicians and leaders are doing. It will be a nightmare for corrupt establishments, and it will change the world in less than a day if people spend more time knowing things about their country, corruption, and government than spending time on the worship of supernatural powers. Just imagine what would happen if people did this for one week. Just for a week, imagine how many governments around the world will collapse. You do not need to stop worshiping supernatural powers entirely if you are a believer in them, but just spend a week knowing about your country, politicians, and leaders, and what they are doing and how they are spending your tax money.

Ateestans can form military forces, strong armies with the most advanced weapons, technology, and intelligence, and can take over a country and install a new government in that country, which will free all people from religious violence and any type of political oppression or anything that is taking away the liberty and freedom of people, for that matter.

Ateestans have the fundamental responsibility to eradicate religious violence or any type of oppression through the military anywhere in the universe. Do not kill yourself in the process, but kill the oppressors. Allow any religion if it gives freedom and liberty to people, and eradicate any religion if it is taking away any kind of freedom from men, women, and children. Their books and their Gods can do nothing to you if you are fighting against their oppression of people, according to their books and Gods.

If they are oppressors and dictate to people to live according to their ways of religion and Gods, books, ideologies only, but thinking of it as sacred, still, it is not sacred. It is still oppression.

Any religion, with or without believing in supernatural powers, needs at least one country for itself to survive in the world. So, make sure Ateestans have a country on Earth to live in with the majority of the Ateestan population. Make sure it is the most advanced developed country with zero crime rate and absolute freedom for its citizens.

Trishone, a country mentioned in the I Killed Satan - The Great War of Man and Satan novel, is an absolute Ateestan major population country. It is the money capital of the world. Wizbome, too, is an Ateestan majority country, but the Krise religion is almost 30%, and they polluted the country with superstition and mindless worship of supernatural powers.

They are good people, but their way of life, which has slavish qualities and asks for putting total blind trust in their Krise religious beliefs and their God Krisaan Regor, made them oppose many developmental changes in the country for nothing more than their supernatural beliefs were getting violated and by stopping them they are satisfied psychologically according to their religious beliefs.

But man is an emotional animal more than rational. Because we came from animals, but only man has the ability to be rational on this planet now. Any dog or animal (we respect them too) can be emotional and intelligent in its own sense. However, only a man can be rational, and man is the only animal that can understand the complexity of rationality completely. And the matters that rule the world and their own life.

We cannot let the precious gift given by evolution in the form of rationality and intelligence go to waste just because our animal emotions dominate us. Use emotions as fuel. They are not bad, but they are also common in every other animal, but not the rationality and human intelligence.

The human imagination has no limits in terms of good and bad things. The proper systems in place to control people to not let them commit crimes and also do not suppress their freedom in any way are important, and also, systems should not let people go rogue. It is more important than believing in supernatural powers.

Ateestans do not believe in supernatural powers because they don't exist. The concept of supernatural powers is no more complex than quantum world science.

The believers in supernatural powers might even use quantum science to convince people that supernatural powers exist. They don't, but quantum science is a science. It is not a supernatural power.

It is super dumb to believe in supernatural powers now more than ever before, because we are uncovering the mysteries of the quantum world and mastering artificial intelligence and other advanced technologies and science, yet we are compelled to believe in supernatural powers that are not real and true. We are asked to believe in those supernatural powers because they are part of the civilizations, cultures, and fashions, and also our ancestors told us so.

The supernatural powers have been part of many cultures for thousands of years. So you see a trace of supernatural powers and figures in everything those cultures have. It can be languages, songs, dance, literature, music, architecture, etc. You can respect the supernatural powers and figures of those cultures and learn from those cultures without believing in the supernatural powers and figures in those cultures.

Music, singing came hundreds of thousands of years ago. They are not started by any supernatural power, and no supernatural power has any right to ban or limit, or prohibit them in any way. The age of music and singing is much older than the age of the supernatural powers that came later through their messengers or Prophets, ha ha! The difference is literally hundreds of thousands of years. Actually age of the Human lineage is much higher, literally millions of years, than the age of the Gods. Supernatural powers are the result of our human imagination; they and their teachings came from us, and through us. All the supernatural powers teachings, books on Earth, and in the universe came from Humans, written by Humans. People are following their fellow Human Being or Human Beings' teachings that were recorded thousands of years ago by Humans. And now they are fighting with each other to make others follow certain teachings or books. Human Beings are following the teachings of Human Beings in the name of the Gods and fighting among themselves to decide which Human teachings they should follow, hahaa!. Ateesta solved this problem.

Supernatural powers worshipers assume that if something bad happens to us, Ateestans who do not believe in those supernatural powers they believe in, then it is because those supernatural powers they believe in got angry at us. But like us, they too get many problems and bad things happen to them in life, too, but they believe in those supernatural powers. And still face the same types of problems and bad things in life as Ateestans because life is rational, even if you are not.

***

Do not get into the stupidity of considering exposing evil things is more evil than those who actually do evil.

Ateesta religion alienates the supernatural elements in all religions and their cultures, and only encourages Ateestans to study their cultures and other things. It is very hard for any culture or religion to stand in front of Ateesta and prove itself by showing they have many other things in their culture other than just their supernatural worship processes. Because we still respect them even after not agreeing with their supernatural powers beliefs when it comes to supernatural powers worship processes of any kind.

We look at their culture and how they contributed to the progress of humanity, and their attempt to create a peaceful world with harmony and coexistence by keeping their supernatural powers worship processes aside in the calculation. Only then can we see how positively their religious group impacted the world. Ateesta sees itself in this way, too.

There will be strong attempts made to suppress Ateesta with many fake allegations and accusations, but stay strong and remember what Ateesta teaches.

The way to live is by navigating millions of things in life, like money, religion, family, and your personal interests, the way you see life and millions of other things should be sometimes flexible, sometimes rigid, sometimes both, sometimes not both, and sometimes something else.

Develop a deep understanding of life, how you want to see the world, and how you want to live your life. This needs a super broad view and consideration of things.

You learn it slowly as you move forward in life, and there are many elements of the unknown in the process, and you face and deal with them along the way.

***

Those unknown risk elements are the things that make your life interesting to live.

And you should move smoothly in that direction. There is no one correct way to live life. You can live as you want as long as you are moving forward with the goal of progressing in getting things you want in life and not harming others and letting others harm you.

Acknowledge that those supernatural powers systems are designed to give a way to live life to normal people and to have fun in life, because not every person has the mental capacity to derive their own meaning from life and to give a meaning to life, which makes sense. So, supernatural powers' belief systems are placed in proper manners to give a blueprint to live a life in a particular way for those who cannot think and decide for themselves on how they can live their life.

Any interpretation of Wuquin should result in the progress of humankind, not the opposite in any form.

Ask yourself, did the first humans, when they were learning to make weapons, hunt, and discover the foods to eat, did they know about supernatural powers of any kind at that time? Also, were they already praying to supernatural powers at that time?

Or do you think the beliefs of supernatural powers and worship processes slowly developed as man developed tools, started learning about the Earth, and expanded his knowledge, intelligence, and imagination skills?

You will be a fool if you let astrology or any other thing decide your future rather than your hard work, talent, skills, and network. You decide what your future is based on how you react to things that happen in your life. Other than that, nothing else can decide your future.

***

Teach teenagers how their hormones affect their lives and behavior. Tell them not to get confused when they observe changes in their body and thoughts. Tell them the science behind it, not the propaganda of any kind. Ask them to embrace their true nature and take care of their health.

Ateesta and Ateestans respect all religions and believers and non-believers of supernatural powers. Ateesta doesn't hate anyone and does not oppose any individual or group. We request and encourage everyone to think and think critically and question everything.

Man, by nature, wants to believe in something that is higher than himself. So, believe in rationality, the power of intelligence, and God Yinta in your mind.

Don't do the overaction, and don't have arrogance and a stupid ego. Always be reasonable and humble.

The criminals in society are more dangerous than animals in the forest. You should not let your guard down, but act like you have your guard down to get along with people in general.

Again, you might think common sense is common, but it is not with many people.

Even though we do not believe in any supernatural elements in our Ateestan culture, you should still respect them. And embrace and learn from all cultures, literature, music, etc.

Before becoming an Ateestan, you belonged to a culture and a religion. It doesn't matter whether you follow it or not. If anyone attacks that old culture of yours and the religion you belong to in any form, then defend it.

If anyone attacks your family or community based on the culture or religion you belong to, then even though you don't believe in supernatural elements of your culture and religion, still fight against that attack and protect your culture and religion, defend them in every form, even if it asks for violence.

Otherwise, all the rationality, intelligence, and morals in your mind will not protect you from the forces that are attacking you and seeing someone who is born into your culture and religion as their enemy, and assumes you are against what they believe in based on the culture and religion you are born into.

Because they don't see the difference between your personal beliefs, how you see life, supernatural elements in your religion, culture, and what culture or religion you are into. Those who attack you based on your culture and religion assume and believe your personal beliefs and preferences do not matter, and what matters is just what family you were born into and the culture and religion of your family. Then, based on that, they will attack you and even kill you, and don't care about your personal views, like whether you believe in the Gods of your religion and whether you like your culture or not, etc.

Those people who hate your culture, religion, and the community you are born into will destroy you, your culture, your family, your identity, your entire existence as an individual, your groups in society, and your family's woman, too. So defend your old culture and religion and protect them even if you don't believe in the supernatural elements of them. It is because the group or community you are born into should be safe first in order to keep yourself, your family, your children, and your woman safe. And after that, you can become an Ateestan and learn more about the world as an Ateestan.

First, make yourself and your family, your children, and your woman safe, then go with the exploration of life rationally, and philosophically as an Ateestan, and achieve great things in life.

There is no Heaven and Hell. There is no Afterlife. Make the most of your life while you are still alive, and do something meaningful in life.

Even if we hypothetically consider Heaven and Hell to exist, even then, we can live happily on Earth by being rational, conscious, and good, just like in Heaven. And if we don't do that, the Earth itself feels like Hell with all the crime and mindless hate.

***

So instead of focusing on unknown things, focus on using your life greatly to live every moment happily, just like in Heaven. So that if Heaven exists, then you can live your eternal life happily, and you lived your mortal life too happily. What's wrong with it? If you are not happy on Earth and if there is no Heaven and Hell after death, then you waste your life for nothing. I'm not saying Heaven and Hell exist. It is just a hypothetical scenario to give you different perspectives. Ateesta does not believe in any Heaven and Hell. Because they don't exist. The immortal thing in the universe is your higher purpose in life and the universe itself, not you.

Did dinosaurs worship supernatural powers before human beings? If yes, then what happened to them? Why did no supernatural power stop the asteroid from destroying them? And why do you think that the supernatural powers humans worship now will stop the asteroid that might hit Earth in the future? (even though we don't have any evidence of any asteroid hitting Earth and creating a total wipe out of humanity-level catastrophe, but just to think hypothetically). If any asteroid is going to hit Earth, then we humans only have to somehow save ourselves by sending rockets or other vehicles at the asteroid and destroy it before it reaches Earth. So humans have to save themselves, and no one is coming to save us.

The First humans didn't have any supernatural powers telling them how to make fire, cook food, and hunt. They used their mind to figure them out. All supernatural elements came as man got more resources and had more leisure time to imagine things. So the imagination power of humans improved, but it has been used to mass control the people and to make them fear authority because human beings were told by their rational minds that everyone is human and equal.

Regular people know that if they do something wrong, then people in power can kill them, but then they can also kill whoever is in authority if people in authority do something wrong, too. So no one is above them.

To stop this way of thinking and take away the rational way of thinking from normal people, they created many systems of supernatural powers beliefs that are unquestionable by any man because supernatural powers are above humans. And supernatural powers-related teachings told people to honor and respect the persons in power, no matter what they do by without questioning them. And they inflicted violence, guilt, fear, and other things on people to discourage them from questioning and fighting injustice done to them.

The worship of supernatural powers also helped to control crime to an extent because people who believed in supernatural powers feared Hell if they did something bad, to conveniently help rulers in power to rule smoothly with less crime in ancient times, but people were also encouraged at the same time to go against other people who did not believe in the same type of supernatural powers as they believed in, to conveniently help rulers in power in fighting against their enemies in ancient times.

This controlled many types of crimes but also encouraged and increased other types of crimes, which are explained and supported by so-called supernatural powers in their teachings against people who did not believe in them. You should think about and also debate how the belief in supernatural powers helped control crime, and also increased crime. You should study this effect.

When a person's character is not good, then nothing can stop that person from doing bad. When a person's character is good, then nothing can make him do something bad.

It doesn't matter what he/she believes in and does not believe in. But the things that a person consumes in any form in his/her life, the life that person is living, the people he/she meets, and also his/her own mind's nature will result in the actions that person takes in his/her life, and those actions have consequences. They can be good or bad.

Whether belief in supernatural powers decreased or increased crime, and which types of crimes, is a big topic that cannot be discussed here entirely, but you have the brain and the power to express your opinions, so use them and discuss this.

No one knows which supernatural powers the first humans worshiped or prayed to at their time, while they were learning how to hunt, trying to survive in those harsh environments hundreds of thousands of years ago. Just human beings started worshiping supernatural powers. Before modern human beings - Homo Sapiens, the Neanderthal and the earliest forms of the human race knew no supernatural powers worship. They still survived, and we are here now. I'm writing this book, and you are reading this book.

You might not associate yourself with the form of supernatural powers worship group that you are born into through your family, and you might not even believe in those supernatural powers. But geographically and culturally, you still belong to that group.

If you were born in a family that follows a certain kind of supernatural powers worship processes, or if your families are natives to the land you were born in, then you might still not believe in those supernatural elements and beliefs of your family, or also from other religions and cultural groups' forms of supernatural worship processes, too but you still belong to your family's culture, and if you are native to the land you were born in, then you also belong there geographically primarily.

So people may address you with a name or multiple names according to the religious and cultural group your family belongs to, and also, if your family is native to the land you were born in, then people may use a name or names to address you with your identity in a cultural and geographical context.

If the name or those names they use to address you are respectable, then you must accept them. You should not hate and talk bad about them. Because it is your identity, and your ancestors gave you that by fighting in countless wars and making countless sacrifices.

You might not believe in supernatural beliefs, powers, and worship your ancestors did, but respect the heritage and titles they are giving you, even if you do not use them to describe yourself if asked by others.

Be a happy and cool person in general.

***

If people don't have freedom of all kinds, freedom to live life as they want, and even to worship supernatural powers, then that country needs to reestablish freedom for its citizens.

Otherwise, Ateestans should bring freedom to those countries.

No, Wuquin and Ateesta do not contradict themselves here. Even though Ateestans do not believe in supernatural powers, they respect others' beliefs, and they know that everyone is entitled to live their life in the way they like. And as Ateestans, we seek liberty, freedom, justice, and truth.

If supernatural powers believers of any religion are struggling even to see their own religion's Gods, then help them. Quash all the money they have to pay to see their own Gods. For which everyone is equal in front of any God in any religion from an Ateestan perspective.

It is possible for an Ateestan to come into the office and give the people liberty, freedom, justice, and truth, or when Ateestans take over a country that is run by corrupt leaders and form an Ateestan government.

As an Ateestan, anything that discourages your critical thinking, rational way of looking at things, and asking for blind faith based on unquestionable stories and teachings is just making you a fool. No exceptions.

The process of believing in supernatural powers is designed in a way that looks and makes you feel sacred. And with the sacredness attributed to the process of making you someone who believes in supernatural powers and the things they ask you to perform physically in the form of prayers, other processes, and the stories they tell you that affect you mentally and with the peaceful approach to this process of making you a believer of the supernatural powers and by offering you health, wealth and other things without any efforts if you put the blind faith and worship supernatural powers is totally carefully crafted, designed and executed processes.

This process of making a person a believer in supernatural powers engages with that person on all levels, which are physical, mental, and spiritual, and that process creates a strong, positive, sacred impression in that person. From then on, that person will see and feel everything related to those supernatural powers in a highly sacred way that no one can question anything about those supernatural powers anymore for any reason whatsoever.

Anybody can use this carefully designed process to make people believe in anything. It is because it does not need any reason. It just evokes strong, unusual emotions and feelings with the taste of calmness and sacredness in people, which they do not feel in their daily lives.

The unusual flow of strong emotions and feelings a person experiences during the process of becoming a believer in supernatural powers, the person thinking of that process as sacred, will make that person a strong believer in those supernatural powers. That person will experience unusual feelings and things when he/she pray regularly to his/her believed supernatural powers, too.

This process is the same for all supernatural belief systems. It was followed by all supernatural belief systems. It is also followed by people who want to convert you into their supernatural belief system, from your supernatural belief system, the one which you belong to through your family, or culturally or geographically.

Converting from one supernatural belief system to another supernatural belief system is the peak of stupidity, and if it is done with the intention of getting material gains in life, then it is more than stupidity.

So don't be that fool and realize that in life, for anything to achieve, efforts are necessary from your end. Or at least luck (Scientifically), but not blind belief in supernatural powers.

Any kind of hate or fear injected into you, any materialistic and afterlife promises or anything that was promised to you without your work and thought into it or at least by luck of permutations and combinations (mathematically if all people who don't believe in any supernatural powers participate in a lottery by buying tickets then also someone will win. You don't need the help of supernatural powers to get lucky. It is bogus and false.) Then those promises are made to convert you into their supernatural belief systems, nothing else. They might say their supernatural powers may help you with your hard work and luck like an add-on, but no, it is not possible. Why should their supernatural powers help you and you only?

Why don't the supernatural powers you believe in help the other believers who believe in those same supernatural powers you believe in, and why don't they think about whether the other supernatural belief systems' supernatural powers help their own believers when they are competing against you? Because all of them, too, believe in some kind of supernatural powers, right? So, why are you particularly special to the supernatural powers you believe in, and why not the others who also believe in the same supernatural powers as you? Are they saying your supernatural powers favor you for some reason over others? Or are they saying the supernatural powers you believe in are more powerful than other supernatural belief systems' supernatural powers? How does that work, and how can we measure that power rationally, if not mathematically?

4

Some people might use your own culture to appeal to you to convert you to their own supernatural belief systems. Be careful with those poisonous snakes. They will take away your property, money, women, children, and all the valuable things from you in the process of converting you.

There are no ghosts and demons or any other kinds of evil spirits or entities, etc., so stop being scared of them anywhere, even in the darkness. Approach physics and science to explain any unexplainable thing if you encounter any.

If you get scared of any ghost or any demon or evil entities, immediately, while in fear, think according to the law of physics. That is, according to the laws of physics, it is impossible for ghosts, demons, and other evil forms to exist. It they exist, we would've quantitatively and qualitatively, too identified them by now, but nope, they don't exist. We already have all the technology to recognize an evil entity, and it is not a question of technology we have now and whether it is advanced enough to find ghosts or evil entities but sheer rational logic of thinking how many people are killed by ghosts and demons since the first humans started hunting on Earth will give us the clarity. As knowledge of man increased, his imagination power increased with evolution, and he formed many fears, habits, and stories to help him and his kin to survive.

Anyone can break the laws made by humans, but no one can break the laws made by nature. We just discovered those laws of nature through exploration. If you ever get scared by ghosts or demons, then just learn a little bit of physics, psychology, and how the universe works. I'm sure you will never take any ghosts, demons, etc, seriously. If you follow this, then even though still you feel scared when you are alone or in darkness thinking of ghosts and demons, but then again your mind will immediately try to go into logical mode and will start thinking more realistically, like is that an animal, or a thief, or any criminal. This approach will help you a lot in protecting yourself. After learning physics and psychology and how the universe works, you will feel dumb about how you got scared of ghosts, demons, etc. Supernatural powers believers use ghosts, evil entities, and demons as a reason to believe in good and God related supernatural powers, so that those good supernatural powers help them in facing those evil supernatural powers. All this is just a rich fantasy, that's it.

If anyone says ghosts, demons, and other supernatural elements exist, then imagine how much money you can make by discovering them for the first time in human history. Imagine the Nobel Prize and all the other awards and money you can get. Ask the person who told you that they exist for an address and how you can catch one. When someone tries to scare you by saying ghosts and demons, etc., exist, or if you get scared in the darkness or while alone, please be careful that it might be an animal or criminal, but certainly, it will never be any type of good or bad supernatural power.

If there is a problem about a thing that is in conflict, even after approaching it logically and rationally, then sit and talk about it. Discuss it and come to a resolution for that problem, rather than becoming dumb and aggressive about it and making a wrong decision emotionally. Always focus on rationality, inner calm, and peace rather than intense emotions and carrying the life based on those rash emotions.

***

If you have time, then never make any decision instantly and act on it when you are excited, motivated, depressed, sad, or feeling good. Always take time to think about the outcome and how you can achieve a positive outcome. Consider all possibilities of doing it. Calculate the probability of its failure and success after making a decision. Now that you have approached a problem logically and rationally, you will have clarity on your decision. Analyze whether it is correct or not through your gut feeling and intuition. Now, listen to what your gut feeling and intuition are telling you. Keep your rational decision and your gut feeling, intuition side by side, and now rationally analyze both of them and make the final decision on whether to act on it or not, or how you can make it possible.

You will be under tremendous pressure and stress while dealing with problems, particularly when it comes to your appearance, health, family, and finances. So you have to always make sense inside your head. Try to think clearly and find the reasons for the causes of problems instead of just feeling sad and taking extreme steps just because of your emotions. Use your emotions as fuel to solve your problems. It doesn't matter what emotions you are feeling; use them to your advantage and have control over them. Your solution to the problem you are facing might help other people, too. So remember the five pillars of the active mind and stop being dumb.

If you are sensitive-minded, then you must start practicing and learning maths and physics. They will toughen your mind, give you the mental strength to take pressure and stress in many heartbreaking situations in life. No matter what you are interested in, always practice basic maths and study basic physics. They will help you in many ways you can't even imagine.

For Ateestans in Ateesta Religion, The Five Pillars of Active Mind are Very Important.

5 Pillars of Active Mind:

1. Consciousness: being aware of what you are doing all the time. So, there is no excuse for the good/bad things you do and the crime. Be

good to everyone. Even in your darkest times, you must believe that the situations and things that put you there can be changed with your consciousness. With your inner awareness and continuous work towards light and prosperity, you can come out of the darkness in your life.

2. Intelligence: Intelligence has many forms according to the person and his/her interests. Always strive to improve the process of how you think. Always try to Stop Being Stupid. Always seek individual freedom. Freedom to do what you love and freedom to live your life as you want without harming anyone and yourself. Any kind of harm to oneself and others is banned. To protect yourself and others, you can use violence, but in those cases, you must see the rest of the pillars of the active mind, Wuquin's teachings, instead of going irrational in emotions.

3. Fight Injustice: Use intelligence, strategy, and other inner and outer tools of all kinds to always stand up to injustice. It doesn't matter how big an authority is doing it; question everything and try to understand things that have a negative or positive effect on your life directly or indirectly. Do not make society a place where an intelligent person becomes a villain rather than a hero. Also, be aware of the world's dangers in all forms, shapes, and ways. Work rigorously to protect yourself and your loved ones from those who are trying to harm you and your family.

4. Respect your family: take care of them and fight for them till your last breath. If they are not good to you, then just stay away from them and shine in your life rather than living in Hell. Make society a better place by taking care of yourself and your family first. And then help people for learning to take care of themselves financially, mentally, physically, and in all aspects of life, death, and in everything in between and outside.

5. Common sense: Always behave with common sense and morals, and don't be stupid. Always be rational and behave with common sense. Walk away from negative people. At the societal level, in the context of life-altering things, always be rational, and even if it pains

some people, still go with rationality and common sense.

Believe in energy and the law of conservation of energy, even if it seems irrational, because everything that is scientific was once felt irrational until it was demystified by science.

Extremism is not good when it comes to anything that can be even politics, society-related matters, etc. No matter what you believe in, unless the thing you are fighting for must be like that according to science.

Don't be too conservative, and don't be too liberal. Strike a good balance between both that makes sense.

Your behavior determines your social class, not your birth, not your name, not your skin color, not your race, and nothing except your behavior in society. Nobody is more socially high class than you, just because they have a particular name or were born in a particular community, or for any reason, for that matter.

Royalty comes from your character, behavior, attitude, and personality, not from your blood or anything else, like the family, race, or community you were born into.

No Ateestan should behave in a way that decreases the honor and respect of the Ateesta religion, Wuquin, and Ateestan culture.

Take all the actions and precautions to protect fellow Ateestans, as intelligence and rationality are rare and attacked all the time by emotionally motivated, self-satisfied, illogical reasoning, and blind faith followers and believers of supernatural powers and their so called teachings.

If you recognize the stupidity of haters of Ateesta, then ignore them. If you want to answer them, do it rationally and logically with morals if needed. They will come up with all kinds of blame games, try to instill fear in you through sentiments involving other religious-related matters, and also use sympathy and psychological games, etc., at the time you are talking to them, but they also do the same things when you stop responding to them.

No one should play politics in matters of honoring and preserving the dignity of the Ateesta religion and Wuquin.

Never disrespect other religions, and also never tolerate disrespect to Ateesta and Wuquin.

Hypothetically, If you worship a supernatural power, then actually you are not getting anything physically to you like any products or things you want in life by the direct or indirect result of worshiping those supernatural powers, but the people who are propagating to you to worship those supernatural powers say you will receive all the glory, all the things and money in the future and also mental peace.

But just think, to make you worship a supernatural power, they don't need to invest money heavily specifically for you, because all they need is a place to talk to you and show you some things to make you believe in those supernatural powers, that's it.

And from there, you will visit those places of supernatural powers worship again and again for the rest of your life, and you will also give money to those places.

So your belief in supernatural powers makes you give your money to those who are propagating it, and in return, you get hope and mental assurance that everything will be good and you will get all the material things, mental peace, and happiness you want in your life.

It is not a fair exchange of money and time for you if we look at it rationally, as you are not getting anything in a measurable, quantitative form from those places and people who are propagating those supernatural powers.

***

You are not getting any measurable quantitative products from those supernatural worship places. Let's say that is okay, but you are also not getting any measurable qualitative services from those supernatural worship places. Psychological services with words framed in a sacred manner, for giving mental assurance that are like everything will be good in your life, and you will achieve great things in life, etc too are not effective and also delusional too many times.

So, the supernatural powers' worship systems give highly unequal returns to those who believe in them, and those little returns, too, are also always mostly only with words of mental assurances in different forms, promising health, wealth, and other things, if at all, at least, that's it.

But you can get the same level of sacred hope and sacred mental assurance even from your family, if someone who is older than you and has some kind of authority over you in your family tells you very strongly that your life is going to be great and what you want to do in life, it will happen and they know it somehow. Even your friends or strangers can give you a strong hope, like that, when they tell you very strongly and confidently that you will be successful in your life and will overcome your problems. Try this. This will have the same exact strong psychological effect on you, if not more.

In that positive energy, you will definitely overcome your problems and achieve success if you just get the words of assurance from your family or friends, just like you get from supernatural worship places' blessings and people who propagate them, using supernatural powers' teachings, and books. Add the same level of depth and a little mystic touch to your words, that's it.

The person who is telling you that you will overcome your problems and will achieve success should make it sound sacred, calm, and very strong with great confidence; that's it. This should be done every time, no matter whether you see success or failure in life.

The state has nothing to do with any religion. The state cannot be for or against any religion.

***

Inner calm and peace should be your first priority to have a great life, and for your mind to function properly, even under stress, to meet deadlines. Even if stress and deadlines are self-imposed or external, take them with an open heart and work hard to reach deadlines rather than getting stressed out in a negative way and getting ill.

Love and peace go both ways. You cannot love someone or groups of people while they are actively trying to destroy you. Save yourself first and come out of that being lovable to everyone and the peace trance. See the reality and take action to survive. Violence for supernatural powers is the height of stupidity. But always fight back if you are being attacked. To suppress that violence, one has to be more violent toward them than they are. One-sided peace can never stop violence, but greater counter-violence can achieve peace.

Any God, any good or bad supernatural powers or elements, has no value in the world if human beings stop believing in them, worshiping them, and talking about them.

Humans made Gods. It can be by the stories they write and their imaginations, or through the great people they get inspired by. Ultimately, human beings have made God, a supernatural power, too.

Human beings made ghosts or evil entities, a type of bad supernatural powers, used to increase the respect for God-type supernatural powers. But in fact, none of those supernatural powers exist.

The nature of supernatural powers presented to the world by their own teachings and by their believers is very egoistic.

The supernatural powers are super egoistic.

If not, then why do supernatural powers only help people who worship them and pray to them? Why don't supernatural powers treat everyone equally and help everyone, the people who worship them, and also people who don't?

What difference does it make for the supernatural powers if just they receive the worship offerings or prayers from people, quantitatively or qualitatively?

Nothing, it just satisfies their ego.

If someone doesn't believe in supernatural powers, then they get no help from those supernatural powers and will not go to Heaven of those supernatural powers, but if they believe in those supernatural powers, then they will go to those supernatural powers' Heavens and their evil deeds will be forgiven.

This is just sheer stupidity.

If supernatural powers behave this way, then they are no more than political parties on Earth, who will do anything for votes. On Earth, political parties try to gain votes by making promises of money and other facilities to people.

In this supernatural powers case, these supernatural powers are asking for your blind faith and belief so that you will go to Heaven for believing in them, and to Hell if you don't pray, worship, and accept them. They are using all the tricks to get you into their boat, right? Heaven for believers, Hell for nonbelievers, forgiven for evil deeds to believers, rot in Hell and burn eternally for the same evil deeds to nonbelievers, hardships and problems for nonbelievers on Earth, great prosperity for believers on Earth, etc.

There is no emphasis on hard work and using your mind to learn things and improve your life; there is no encouragement for true own achievement in these supernatural powers teachings.

No supernatural power teachings encourage man to think critically, why?

Also, if you believe in those supernatural powers, you will also experience the psychological comfort and feelings of being forgiven for all the bad things you do in your life.

This is a carefully crafted mental illness. When a mental illness or anything, for that matter, becomes a standard in society for centuries, then it becomes normal. The people who do not believe in or follow those carefully crafted mental illnesses become weirdos.

We say science and technology are like magic, but we don't realize that the magic itself is science.

When you are trying to achieve something in life, there will be anxiety and doubt about whether you will achieve that in your life or not. You will think a lot about whether that great thing you are looking for in life will happen or not. This is also the same for the first humans in caves every day, millions of years ago, whether they could hunt successfully, eat, or go hungry.

This anxiety is the basis for our wishful thinking and wanting something to happen in our favor, and we are not satisfied with just the self-confidence to give us hope in these anxious situations. So, we need some powers higher than human to give us assurance that the things we want in our lives will happen, even delusionally. That is why we have supernatural belief systems now. This helped reduce the anxiety of the masses in hard situations and was then used to control them to organize societies gradually. It is still being used now. This also led to the popular belief that if they worship a supernatural power, then good things happen to them. Millions of years ago, the cavemen were anxious about whether they would have a successful hunt on that day or not. In that anxiety, they hunted; if they were successful, they were successful. If they are not, then they are not. A successful hunt depends on many variables that are not in man's control. But when they successfully hunted the animal for food, they ate it. On the day the hunt went wrong, and they didn't have any food to eat, they slept with hunger.

But a successful or failed hunt depends entirely on how the animal has behaved while being hunted, and how the humans approached the hunt with their strategies.

When they were successful, they felt happy.

And in the next hunt, when they gave the same amount of hard work and invested the same intelligence as in the past successful hunts, but still, when the new hunt went unsuccessful, they asked themselves why it happened.

The process of going through the hunt again rationally and analyzing their strategies and animal behavior seemed painful to most of them, as they were already disappointed and hungry. They needed an explanation to tell themselves and the calm the anxiety.

They needed a positive assurance from someone that they would be successful in the hunt next time, and if they were not, again, they needed an explanation to take away the blame from them, which is very painful mentally and physically.

So, they came up with supernatural beliefs slowly based on what they thought in their minds to cope with those successful, unsuccessful hunts. And they started coping mentally with great appreciation for their collective imaginations' supernatural powers, if they were successful in the hunt. And when they were not successful in a hunt, they told themselves that some evil supernatural power made the hunt unsuccessful.

Many times, they were successful in hunting, and their beliefs in supernatural powers became strong. Many times, they failed in hunting, which gradually strengthened their belief in evil supernatural powers. Then, the leaders of the tribes and others used these beliefs for their own power and influence.

They cultivated superstitions like only when a particular leader is leading the group, the hunts will be successful, otherwise not, etc, like that.

If something bad happens to a person, then people who propagate supernatural powers worship say that the person's trust and faith in the supernatural powers is not high enough, which is why bad things were happening to him. And that person should start praying, worshiping more and do the other things in the worship processes to get the blessings of supernatural powers.

If something good happens to that person, they say that the supernatural powers always help and love those who believe in them. This is a process of mental adjustment. We try to find reasons for both the bad and good things in life through supernatural powers. We will always come up with irrational reasons about why something happened that can be a good or bad thing, rather than focusing on the problem we are facing rationally. All this process is just psychological and mental adjustment within ourselves to the situation we are in to move forward by telling ourselves a comfortable reason, that's it.

If you are a person with good intelligence, rationality, and good common sense, you will inspire insecurity in people who believe in supernatural powers.

People are afraid and scared of intelligence. They don't like someone who is challenging their age-old views of life and their beliefs, which intelligence might alter those outdated views forever, and they see that change as very painful and will go to any extent to stop it.

Use Satan in your mind as the fuel to survive where no goodness is helping you. But don't give Satan control of the direction you go, but only to God Yinta. Use Satan as fuel to survive in harsh situations, but use and throw Satan. There is nothing wrong with it because Satan will absolutely destroy your life if he gets a chance, without any hesitation whatsoever.

Even though Ateestans do not believe in any supernatural powers, they can use any cultural or supernatural powers related teachings and things if they are rational and good with common sense, and make people feel good and comfortable. You can say this to anyone without any shame or guilt. Good is good, and bad is bad, no matter where they are coming from.

If you have heard a word or words millions of times from your family or culture, you can use those words while describing things.

Also, if you are used to them, then you can say that word or words from any culture, supernatural powers systems to yourself, even inside your mind, you can tell them or repeat them to yourself without any problem.

It is because, even though you do not believe in the supernatural powers related to those words, your life is constructed with the related cultures of those supernatural powers. So, it is quite natural for you to get those words out of your mouth in certain situations, unknowingly, and also in your mind when you see or experience something.

You must not hate anyone or anything extremely. It is because life is fragile, and persistent hate makes a person or group insensitive and numb to reality. They will die a bad death.

Ateestans should respect other cultures, but also Ateestans should create their own culture, customs, and traditions that differ from all existing cultures and religions. But they should only be, according to Wuquin. You must not use even Wuquin and its teachings to demean the Ateesta religion in any way.

Ateestans would follow their own culture as a society, individually, as a family, and in groups, etc.

Ateestans must create their culture with customs and traditions, including music, languages, dressing styles, appearances, laws, architecture styles, food, cuisine, celebrations, rituals, entertainment, other arts and aesthetics, etc. But they all should be respectful to the Ateesta religion and Wuquin.

Ateestans must also form their own cultural names for people, places, things, etc. Those names should sound great, grand, and respectful.

When people hear Ateestan music, see Ateestan cultural clothes, art, etc, then people should recognize that they are coming from the Ateestan culture.

Ateestans should also form countries on the basis of their religion if the countries they are living in are discriminating against them in any way.

But Ateestans must also respect the country and land they are living in. They should also fight for the country they are living in.

With time, Ateesta will become natural to the land Ateestans live in, and Ateestan culture will create its own cultural world in the countries and places where it is being practiced by the majority of the population.

But for any cultural thing of Ateesta, it should be respectful to the Ateesta religion, Wuquin, and God Yinta.

Never let anyone live in your country illegally, and never trouble anyone living there legally.

Do not bend your neck or bow to anyone who is abusing their power. Burn the world of your enemies to save your families and your groups. Respect and honor are important to everyone.

***

The group here refers to the collection of individuals. That group might be formed for any reason whatsoever.

In any country, intelligent and rational people are rare. Protect them to make your country a superpower and save them from harm for the advancement of your society.

Oppose any theory, concept, religion, or anything that takes away the liberty and freedom of people. You must also be a responsible individual in your life.

Your old religious beliefs and supernatural powers beliefs, beliefs in superstition, etc, affect how you think on a subconscious level. Try to refine this and make this process as rigorous and realistic as possible with rationality, morals, and common sense.

If anyone says history doesn't matter, then you must understand that that person is unworthy of your respect.

We die, but what we did to the world won't. Make sure what you do for the world is progressive and strengthens the liberty of people.

When someone slaps you, don't show the other cheek; instead, cut the hand that slapped you.

Peace goes both ways. You cannot get attacked constantly, take the loss, and be peaceful.

Also, peace is always used as an excuse to take away the freedom of people and crush their confidence from the inside, so that no one will protest and start a revolution against corruption and injustice.

Don't worry, Neanderthal humans did not go to Heaven or Hell. They are just dead like any other life form on Earth. Just because, as Modern human beings, our brains evolved and gave us the power and talent of imagination, observation, and analysis skills through which we gained knowledge and thus made our intelligence stronger doesn't mean we, modern human beings, are so special that we get to go to

Hell and Heaven after death. But not our ancestors like Homo-erectus and Neanderthal.

The Homo erectus and Neanderthal didn't even know about Heaven and Hell or the Afterlife. If hypothetically Heaven and Hell exist, then did they go to Heaven or Hell, or not?

If yes, then did the millions of ancestors of human beings in the process of evolution go to Heaven and Hell, also?

When our first humans had only the choice of hunting for food or not hunting for food, did they go to Hell for hunting? (You have the absolute freedom to choose the food you want to eat. This question is just to see things from different perspectives.)

See how logically formed, imaginative stories mixed with some emotions fell apart. Supernatural powers believers may come up with some logic, explanations, and theories after this, but they do it out of their love and respect for their supernatural powers beliefs, and also to make you believe in those supernatural powers they believe in. I encourage you not to believe in any supernatural powers-related explanations about human evolution because it is not correct rationally or with common sense, either.

I'm not negatively criticizing any supernatural powers believers and any supernatural powers worship, particularly. When I say the word 'any,' it means anyone and everyone who believes in any kind of supernatural powers, but I want them to think critically, rationally, and explore things.

No matter what supernatural powers believers say about love, peace, and other things. You can be all those positive things without believing in those non-existent supernatural powers. Actually, believing in any supernatural powers makes you feel good when you are with your group of people who also believe in the same type of supernatural powers you believe in. But also, many times, it makes you hate other types of supernatural powers' believers. Ateesta takes away that hate and negativity among people and makes everyone respect each other.

Your religious and supernatural powers beliefs affect how you think indirectly, directly, and subconsciously, without you even realizing it consciously. And even if you don't believe in supernatural powers, still growing up in a family or community that believes in supernatural powers is enough to have that cultural effect on you. Try to actively cut that type of supernatural powers beliefs' influence on you in the process of thinking rationally.

So that you enjoy the advantage of rationality, intelligence, and common sense to the fullest.

With new technologies, it would be very hard for humans to survive if they are discouraged from thinking critically and are just asked to follow whatever is written in some super old supernatural powers' teachings. It is because those old supernatural belief systems are mostly memory-oriented, which asks people to remember a few things and also ask them to follow them without questioning them. But Ateesta is a thinking religion that encourages thinking critically, rationally, and questioning nature.

New technologies will replace human knowledge-based work to a great extent, but critical thinking-based Human-specific work will never be replaced by any technology. But humans will lose that critical thinking ability if they still follow super old supernatural belief systems. So Ateesta will replace those old supernatural belief systems, and in the future, where critical thinking and intellectual skills are needed, Ateesta will culturally produce those highly talented Human-unique, creative, intelligent people who cannot be replaced by any new technologies in masses.

There is no supernatural Heaven or Hell but when there are teachings of supernatural powers that say someone can go to Heaven if they worship that supernatural power, do good things, live a good life and help others etc, and also go to Hell for not doing them and not believing in them then people will start behaving like maniacs in an organized manner as time moves on because those supernatural powers teachings, Heaven and Hell will become central parts for people to decide about the things they want to do and don't want to do in their life rather than thinking about those things realistically, as, are those things do good or not rationally and morally, by not considering those supernatural powers teachings, going to Heaven and Hell for doing them, etc.

Ateesta encourages Ateestans to live a good, moral, rational life because it is the best way to live life, and that's it. There is no supernatural Heaven or Hell or anything for them. Ateestans live their life righteously, rationally, and morally good just because it is what people should do, that's it. Not to go to Heaven or for anything. There is no reason to be good other than being good.

Some corrupted people use anything to gain power, even the beliefs of people who worship supernatural powers, including a political, economic system, philosophy, or religion, anything for that matter. Most of the time, they propagate them not because they believe in them but because they see an opportunity to gain power over people and appear larger than life by using those things. Be careful with them.

There will be times when you will be pressured by someone you love to believe in a supernatural power and to worship it. Do it for their happiness or at least pretend. There is nothing wrong with it.

If you are an Ateestan and if you believe in supernatural powers and worship them, still please be reasonable and don't do extreme things. Don't be stupid and kill yourself, your children, or anyone in the process.

Be Brave. It is what makes your life worth living.

But don't be dumb while trying to be brave.

Common sense and rationality prevail, while blind faith kills and is used to organize dumb people so as not to let them go out of control of the dictatorial systems, and knowing the truth.

If you know people who think that they are intelligent, but in reality, if you know that they are cunning and stupid, then they are very dangerous. Keep them away from you and your family.

***

Keep children safe from all kinds of predators, and also teach them manners. Teach children how horrible bullying is and how you, as a parent, can support them if any bully says something or does something to them. Tell them that bullying itself is not good. Tell your child not to bully anyone, and if they do, properly teach them manners and how bad bullying is. They are children, they should be taught good things by their parents, educational institutions. Deal with this sensitively and with great common sense. Protect them, mentally, physically

You must always think about yourself in your life as 'The kind of man I want to be' or, if you are a woman, 'The kind of woman I want to be.' Because human birth is the most valuable thing in the entire universe, and you should not waste it.

Always be careful of betrayals because they can undo years of your hard work and destroy your life entirely.

Be with a little skepticism about anything and anyone, but still be with them and work with them. There is nothing wrong with it because you'd be better off by being careful first than to be sorry later.

As a man, embrace your masculinity and use its power to move forward in life.

As a woman, embrace your femininity and use its power to move forward in life.

Always wear clean clothes, not necessarily costly. Hygiene is more important than the cost of clothes.

Be always careful of what you wish for in life because sometimes, when you finally get it, you often don't really like it after the initial excitement fades away. And many times, the things you hated and rejected the most at the beginning will become the things you will love a lot as time goes on. So, find a common ground for these types of things.

Do not get into debt slavery by buying unnecessary superficial things to impress anyone, even yourself. Buy only if you need it, not for any other reason. Be a little frugal and careful, and be cautious with money. There is nothing wrong with it. If you have money, anyone will take it from you if you give them, but no one will give you money if you don't have any.

Always learn to use debt and other things to your advantage rather than becoming a slave to them. Learn about them according to your time and the situations you are in to use them as an advantage rather than suffering because of them.

No matter what, never put yourself in a position where you completely suffer financially, mentally, and physically. Always keep safe reserves of resources for your minimal survival, at least for without struggling to live your daily life. So that you won't be on the road the moment you lose your job or even everything you have for any reason.

Do anything to survive without harming others. There is no menial job in the world.

Severe punishments should be levied on authorities who abuse their power over the people. It is because of the reason that justice through the legal systems takes a very long, time-consuming process, these corrupt authorities abuse their power a lot and get away with it. There should be processes to investigate these matters in shorter times, in a fixed period.

In the spirit of nationalism, don't go blind and become blind-loyal followers of any leader and political party. Same with liberalism or any ism or system for that matter. Always love your country and be patriotic, but also ask for transparency.

Don't be a blind, loyal follower of any leader and political party in the name of liberal values. Always question, scrutinize, and ask for accountability and transparency.

***

Association is important. Be with idiots, and you will become another idiot. Be with intelligent people. You will learn from them and will become one. But becoming an idiot is a faster process than becoming Intelligent.

You can walk on a bad path for righteous reasons. But make sure you are not affecting good people in a negative way.

Expect the worst, give your best, and be prepared to face anything.

What we don't know, we don't know, and when we know, we know. Make sure what we know is the truth, and not any other thing.

Be careful of sweet talkers who try to convert you to their supernatural belief systems. They will do anything to convert you and turn you into a blind, loyal follower and worshiper of their supernatural powers.

The science that improves life regardless of its origin has the same value if it is proven accurately. No matter where it comes from, a big corporate company or a normal person. If they disclose every advantage and disadvantage of the thing they are proposing.

Adapt to newer technologies. Learn them and improve the lives of people.

Be careful of corporate-sponsored propaganda science and research.

Be a happy, chill person in general.

It is good for your health. What is in your mind should not affect your cool mood in general.

Always strive to become a better person than you were yesterday; otherwise, what are you gonna do?

First, survive when you have no strength. No matter how many insults you get. But after getting power, do what is necessary, but not in a rage. Do it in thought so that you don't lose what you gained.

***

Please don't be a complete cynic and a naysayer. Be open-minded.

If you are a rational person, then there is a great chance that people will get scared of how you think and how you see things. So behold and don't get scared. They might attack you, so be careful even when you don't offend them. Be careful with irrational supernatural powers' believing people while discussing religions and politics, etc, sensitive topics with them. Even if you slightly offend them, they might even physically attack you.

Whatever it could be, a religion, cult, or anything that discourages you from performing critical thinking is making you a fool, but a loyal one, and making you feel good about it.

First, live for yourself, not for anyone. The people whom you love, tell them the same thing too, and after they love themselves, then ask them to love you.

Progress should be your highest priority, along with common sense, rationality, and morals. Nothing else!

Be brutal with groups that are causing problems for people and countries. No matter who they are, religious/nonreligious, no matter what they are fighting for. If they are bringing continuous destruction and loss of life, then do what is necessary, even use brutality to stop their madness.

Don't be dumb while trying to be intelligent.

Please don't be a stupid person by confirming that Satan or Demons, Ghosts, etc, came into a person when they are not behaving properly or not healthy. Take them to a hospital for treatment. Respect and behave good with them.

Think consciously and actively to feel the peace inside of you. Try to get the feeling of peace, happiness, and calmness inside of you consciously by thinking about them in real time. Let me walk you through this. You are ready to sleep, and on your bed, or somewhere at work, or in the middle of doing something, or it could be anywhere, and you might be doing anything. And in that time, mostly, you will be trying to solve a problem in what you are doing. But just take a few minutes off from it.

Then, actively consciously in that moment in real time take a deep breath and think like "Hey I'm working to solve this problem or working on something to complete it but it should not affect my mental peace and clear, calm, positive happy state feelings of mind of mine because the problem I'm facing will be resolved eventually or I will find a solution to it and the work I'm doing will be completed even if takes some extra time.

So, all these things are usually there in life. They are not new. So, keeping all those aside, now, I don't have anything to worry about super seriously and lose my peace, calmness, happy state, and cool feelings in my mind. So, I'm feeling good. I'm calm and clear in my head, and I'm feeling calm, cool, happy, and I'm in a positive state of mind now. Yup!"

You should think like this actively and consciously. If you are not facing any extra problems or any work-related burden, etc., then it will become much easier for you to feel those calm, cool feelings in your mind, which will put a calm, bright, happy, subtle, energetic smile on your face. It is a great feeling and state of mind to experience, try it.

For a quick refreshment, just take a few seconds off from what you are doing and quickly analyze and consciously think that 'I have nothing to worry about. So cool!' and then feel the peace, calmness, and blissful feelings instantly. It is because many times we just feel irritation inside of us because of others, or even for no reason. This will remove that unnecessary stress and dirt from our minds.

You can use this think-consciously technique to list, categorize, and evaluate the problems and situations you are facing, too. Then, you can go through each problem and explain it to yourself to calm yourself down, control stress, and think about solutions rationally rather than just getting stressed out.

***

Do not normalize any type of violent crime.

In the Ateesta religion, you have only one true God, that is God Yinta, and he has been in your mind since the beginning of time for you.

Satan is also in your mind. Satan came into your mind at the beginning of the time of your life, just like God Yinta.

Because the energy that helped you to take birth and to live on Earth is the First Energy of Mother Adis.

Mother Adis symbolically represents the Matter, which is the building block of our universe. So by birth, you get God Yinta and also Satan into your mind because they both are present in the creation of Mother Adis and in the total matter of the universe before the development of life forms happened on Earth.

The summary of this concept is that, as human beings, we basically get animal nature and also rational nature by birth, but which one we use the most, why we use which nature, where, and how we use them in a balance between both of them is what matters.

Optimization of both animal and rational natures is necessary because animal nature is natural to all life forms on Earth, but a deep, strong rational nature is unique to mankind.

Of course, it is unique to mankind until we discover other human-equivalent life forms.

Mother Adis, God Yinta, Satan, etc, are not supernatural powers, and they are not real. We use those names to symbolically represent things in storytelling.

The energy of creation and destruction is both inside of us.

Even though the Ateesta religion does not believe in any supernatural powers, you can actually believe in God, which means a type of supernatural power in any religion.

No, Ateesta is not contradicting itself here.

It is because, by nature, man is hopeful of the future. And very rarely, only a very few highly intelligent and rational, matured people can accept the reality that absolutely there are no supernatural powers of any kind that are looking over them, making sure they are safe, and no supernatural power cares about them in any way because the supernatural powers of any kind simply just don't exist in any shapes or forms or in any way.

To accept this, one needs a tough, rock-like heart.

Then, on top of that, only a very few rational, courageous, intelligent, and daring people will come to an understanding that life is what they make out of it.

If they work hard and do what is necessary, then they can get what they want in life. No supernatural power is going to help them in any way. After realizing this, they plan, use strategy, and work carefully toward what they want to achieve in life based on reality.

So, it is a very hard, rigorous, painful, and heartbreaking process.

Sensitive people cannot handle this much intensity of rationality and absolute reality. They get scared, feel helpless and hopeless, and will fear everything and anything if they start thinking with this absolute truth and realistic approach to life.

So, for these types of sensitive people, even though they are intelligent and rational, there should be a little irrationality in their lives to move forward with the hope that the future is good for them, with the help of a supernatural power they believe in. And even though many people look tough from the outside, they are still sensitive when it comes to supernatural beliefs and the uncertain nature of the future. It makes them feel uncomfortable. But when they think, and if someone assures them that their future is good with the help of a supernatural power, then they feel comfortable, secure, and strong.

These kinds of sensitive people can believe in a supernatural power, and they can even perform the usual worship processes. There is nothing wrong with that because these types of people just can't function without feeling and trusting that they have the assurance of a good life from higher-than-human supernatural powers.

If you are that kind of person, then you can absolutely do it too.

But with consciousness and no extremism. You should be aware that, rationally, the supernatural powers worship you are doing does not change anything in real life, but you are doing it for your own self-confidence and to feel positivity. You can also assume that, since you don't believe in supernatural powers of any kind, but, you are praying or worshiping them, because you want to give yourself mental strength.

Even if those supernatural powers exist hypothetically, all that those supernatural powers want for you is for you to be good and live your life happily, right? They will look at your approach and will be proud of you that the rational nature they gave you is being used well and you are dealing with blind worship and rational worship perfectly, thus making you a human being with a great understanding of approaching complex things with a rational consciousness rather than just having blind beliefs.

If you are aware that praying to supernatural powers makes you feel the assurance of a great life from a supernatural power (even though it is a form of delusion) and calms your anxiety and emotions, makes you gain confidence and mental strength, then it is perfectly fine to continue that worship of supernatural powers.

5

All Ateesta also wants for you is, you to be strong and confident, believe that the future is going to be great, do your work, and put great effort into your dreams and goals, and eventually, want you to achieve them.

If you rationally approach supernatural powers worship with a psychological understanding of the nature of your emotions and the logical mind, then you will strike a balance between your rationality and the amount of irrationality you can allow in your life for your own comforting supernatural powers worship.

Then, you will not go extreme and do dumb things, and also not lose your rational nature and intelligence. You will approach the supernatural elements worship with a great amount of rationality and reasoning with pure awareness and consciousness about what you are doing, why you are doing it, how you are doing it, and also still keep a strong rational maturity and your mind's intelligence strength intact.

You will perfectly balance and manage the rational nature of man with thinking, analyzing, and seeing things in different and new perspectives for the progress and development of your life and seeing life as it is with the Irrational nature of man through supernatural powers worship to calm your emotions, anxiety, to control the fear of uncertain future and negative thoughts.

In general, an Ateestan will take advantage of negative thoughts and criticism. They see the accuracy of those negative things and their probability of happening. They prepare themselves to face them when they finally happen or to prevent them rather than just getting scared. So Ateestans with strong rational and mental strength can handle the truth of the non-existence of supernatural powers. They don't need to worship any supernatural powers to calm themselves and gain self-confidence, courage, and hope for a better future because they already mentally have enough strength to process the real nature of life by realizing that no supernatural power is there to help them and it is up to them whether it is success or failure and life or death.

In general, any government, no matter what they say and show how much they've spent for people and no matter what type of government is ruling the country, that government always wants its citizens to be alive and well to pay taxes but not well up to the point that those people start questioning everything that their leaders are doing, scrutinizing everything happening in the government and analyzing how their tax money is being spent.

So, governments, no matter what type they are, always prefer to have most of their citizens weak both physically and mentally, and they try to keep only enough money with the majority of people to survive. In this way, people always struggle with their weak mentality and low confidence in general. Their weak physical bodies with diseases and illnesses plague them with many personal problems, and their weak financial conditions will never let them come on the road and fight against any injustice done to them in any way.

When people struggle with many personal and financial problems, they just can't think about their country and in which direction it is being taken by their leaders.

Only a few people who are in favor of the ruling governments will prosper in all of the ways. They will use various ways like media, coercion, psy-ops, etc, on the common normal people to confuse and cover the anger of people toward governments.

***

Ateestan governments will change this and liberate people from all forms of oppression.

Ateesta encourages people to get healthy and wealthy to support themselves. So that they don't need to depend on the government for their basic needs, governments use the dependency of people on them for basic needs as an advantage to suppress them in many ways.

First, stop paying taxes and ask the politicians who told you that they were there in politics and government to serve the public, to show how they used your already paid tax money with 100 percent transparency. Ask them a million questions, and they will answer; they have to answer; that is their responsibility.

Only after getting all the answers, then only you have to pay taxes, but any type of taxes should be very minimal. In any case, they should not go more than 1% (one percent). You must fight to keep it as low as possible because low taxes will naturally result in low corruption if people pressure the government and their leaders simultaneously for transparency. After paying taxes, ask the government to send you the details of how your tax money is being spent in a very simple form so that anyone can understand it. If they can collect tax money from everyone and have an efficient mechanism to do it, then they can also send you a document personally with 100 percent transparency about how your tax money is being used.

The government, politicians, and leaders should be scared to use mental and physical suppression in any form on people. The people should get very active in discussing and talking about their country and its economic situation.

No one is an ideal woman, and no one is an ideal man. Everyone is ideal in their own life. Stop looking for an ideal woman and an ideal man to try to be like them.

Everyone is selfish inside and has their own agendas, and don't be a fool to deny this. You are an ideal man or woman if you try to improve yourself in various ways. This idea of finding an ideal woman and asking other women to be like her is just suppressing their own identities and expressiveness. It is stupid. What if the woman who is being projected as the ideal woman is being pushed forward in society by men who want to suppress women or other groups with their hidden agendas? It feels like a nightmare, right? So, stop this stupidity. Learn from great people, but don't become their blind, loyal followers. Same with men.

You can get inspired and learn from others, but do not follow them blindly.

Be enthusiastic and a person full of life, not a perfect, calculated, accurate, rational machine mimicking a human being. We are imperfect, and that is what makes us human beings. If we are ultra-perfect, then we don't need machines. The only difference we as humans can make in this world is to find our imperfections, correct them, and improve ourselves. Live an imperfect, brave, courageous life even if others see you as an irrational person. It is ok if you have your own rationality that makes sense to you personally. Sometimes, even if it looks insane to others and doesn't make any sense to them, you must continue doing the thing you like if it makes sense to you rationally. Be a human being, not a rational machine.

Use rationality to improve your life, but while thinking of yourself as a rational and intelligent person, which you are, please don't become a narrow-minded rational machine.

If you want to achieve something that humanity has never done or tried before, you need to operate on your own rationality, and you should try to do it with people who can understand you, because in those things, even great rational people can talk negatively to you and discourage you.

Be very careful with alcohol and other mood and energy-altering drugs. If you cannot control those habits, they will ruin your life and literally waste your life, potential, and energy. You will be a loser or some mediocre, successful person at the end of your life.

***

Do not ever touch alcohol and other mood and energy-altering drugs of all kinds. You have the freedom to take legally allowed drugs and alcohol, but Ateesta encourages you not to touch alcohol and other mood and energy-altering drugs of all kinds.

If you are naturally high with your ideas, creativity, and mindset, then you don't need any drugs or alcohol. And you will be high 24/7.

Enjoy things that don't destroy your health.
Always try not to die an artificial death.

Reading, learning, studying, writing, and speaking are the greatest things in the world. Don't take them for granted. Read books and read as many books as possible. The degrees you get by spending dollars are okay, but the books you read, the things you learn, and how you use your mind to help the world are important. You can learn the same things at home through books and technology that you learn in a university by spending hundreds of thousands of dollars. So, if you go to college or university, always talk to people, explore things, and learn about people and life. Never ever take education for granted. Have an emotional connection with it, no matter how rational and intelligent you are. Respect it above everything because it is the only thing that has the power to take humanity forward.

Construct buildings and houses as you like with clarity and without getting into a debt burden if you can't manage it. The style of construction can be what you want.

Death is inevitable and the ultimate truth that every life form has to face. We use millions of ideologies, philosophies, and many things to cope with it positively or negatively, or to avoid thinking about it.

Try to the maximum extent to avoid death unnecessarily or for artificial reasons. Die naturally in old age. If a new technology can prolong your life, then gladly accept it and live.

***

If you are poor, you live in one reality. If you are middle class, you live in one reality. If you are above middle class, you live in one reality. If you are rich, you live in one reality. If you are wealthy, you live in one reality. If you are a millionaire, you live in one reality. If you are a billionaire, you live in one reality. If you are a multi-billionaire, you live in one reality. If you are much wealthier than that, then you live in one reality, and the hierarchy goes like this. Your limitations are mostly programmed into you by the socio-political and cultural class you are born into and raised in, and their teachings.

Always try to improve your hierarchy level to the upside. Nothing wrong with it. There is no need to demoralize and demean the money when you are working hard and smart for it.

No matter what, the government should stop causing damage to people's property. And if it is done for any reason by the government, then it must compensate them accordingly.

Do not allow the government or authorities to use stupid tactics and the power of the government to suppress the resentment of people when the government attacks the properties of citizens.

In that case, people have to be very cruel to the government, authorities, and leaders who are behind it. People should not forget about it, no matter what they say, and offer money for the destruction they caused. In a democracy, those leaders and parties should become absolute zero.

It is because attacking the properties of people en masse is a great violation of the freedom of individuals, the freedom to live, and the rights of citizens in any country. Even if it is not in their constitution, they must hold authorities, leaders, and the whole government personally accountable even after they leave their offices and come out of their power positions.

Racism, xenophobia, and any kind of discrimination, and comedy and humor are subjective. See the intention behind something that you find offensive and ask the person who made that remark or joke to explain it, and then, after hearing their explanation, you have to inspect and scrutinize it, and after that, come to a decision whether they are being offensive or not.

Even though comedy and humor are subjective, be careful of people who use them to propagate something harmful and hateful while using comedy as a disguise.

Embrace comedy and humor. Use them to spread awareness of important issues rather than targeting people who make it.

Don't let supernatural powers, believers, and stupidity come into matters of your health, wealth, education, marriage, and other important aspects of your life and damage them.

Particularly, be very careful with people who have superstitious beliefs. They are more dangerous than supernatural powers believers who worship supernatural powers for prosperity in life, in a non-harming way to others and themselves.

In a broad way, physically, all humans look the same, but their psychology and mental capacities vary greatly.

Focus on learning skills, gaining knowledge, and applying them rather than spending your energy fighting for skin color, being racist, and other unnecessary things.

The depths of human aspirations, the courage, and valor of man are unparalleled. Nothing can stand in front of a man when a man decides to achieve something. The purpose of his/her existence, which was determined by himself/herself, becomes greater than his/her life itself. That courage and that attitude are what we need in our brave Ateestans.

Always respect yourself, no matter what you do, where you are, or any of that, if you are not harming others in any way. First, respect yourself as a person.

Take care of your mind, brain, and body because without them being healthy, you will be dead or incapacitated.

***

To be specific and clear, there are no supernatural powers that we can call God or Evil in any universe. There is nothing supernatural of us before we start getting formed in our mother's womb, and there is nothing for us after our death.

Always do anything to protect yourself, your family, your loved ones, and your country. Be patriotic.

Don't do drugs or any extreme things like that. Always avoid smoking, and never drink and drive. Enjoy but not recklessly, especially men. Your masculine strength is not calculated based on how edgy you live your life. But in that process, you die a meaningless death.

You have to take risks to do great things in life, absolutely, but make sure those risks make sense. There is a great difference between driving a car at 200 miles/hr on the race track as a professional and on a real road as someone with hormones rushing through the body, where the public is present.

So know that difference with your common sense. No matter whether you are a man or a woman, always try not to drink, smoke, gamble, or do anything that you know absolutely destroys your life, even bit by bit, spanning decades.

Man does not need to be loyal to any ruler, politician, or government except to himself and his family, other human beings, and life forms. Man does not need to be loyal to supernatural powers of any kind.

You can eat food of any culture and religion if it is healthy and not polluted. Food has no religion. Food habits might be different. If you expand any philosophy or theory on this, then logic goes both ways.

You must have an emotional connection with rationality because it will help you when you are in deep trouble, because of your stupid/

meaningless actions, or for meaningful ones too.

The ultimate result of Wuquin and Ateesta should be the progress and prosperity of mankind, and also whatever other kinds of life forms like/similar to us, we discover in the future.

To all the things Wuquin did not talk about, to approach them, deal with them, or decide about them you must follow these guidelines: You must keep it respectful, keep it rational and keep it morally correct, and also suppress violence as much as possible and try to make sense rationally and intellectually according to the times you are living in. In times when it is not possible to deal with them, as explained above, then you can use violence to suppress violence. Violence made to make peace and for righteous reasons is equal to meditation in Ateesta.

Never shy away from war and violence if it is serving a higher purpose to you as a country, individual, or group. Even if you don't care about supernatural beliefs, there will be many who are ready to kill and die for their supernatural beliefs. Never show mercy on them if they attack your women, family, and your very existence as a community, and if they forcefully try to convert you to their supernatural belief system. Be very cruel to those forces. There is nothing wrong with it.

Ateestan countries must build for themselves the greatest war machines the world has ever seen. Conquer the world and rule it. But build an economy based on trade and business, not entirely on war. Never fight among yourselves.

Do things that make you feel good. If they are not harming you or anyone, not inspiring any dumbness in you, and not crossing certain limits of irrational beliefs, then it is ok. Also, do things that make you feel good, even if doing what you love seems a little irrational to others, because it is your life, live as you want.

Follow any ideology or philosophy you want, but the end result should be your happiness and progress from your perspective.

No matter whether you are an Ateestan or not, you don't lose anything by following rationality and the five pillars of the active mind, other than improving your mind and your approach to life for a happy life and a great future.

Believe in supernatural elements of any kind, only after seeing concrete scientific rational evidence completely. Otherwise, no.

If you believe in fortune-telling, there is no greater fool than you in the world. You make your future, and people can shape it. Other than that, nothing supernatural can make or break it.

Give all the rights and privileges that men have to women and leave everything to their choice and preferences, vice versa. No woman is less than a man, and no man is less than a woman. Coexist peacefully. But men, protect women from the evil forces in society, mentally and physically.

Men and women are the same in every aspect, and at the same time, they are very different by nature and have their own uniqueness. But men, remember, the nature of the birth of a female is very sacred, and without them, there is no life naturally. Protect them in every way from all the propaganda that is trying to turn them into just working machines as they did with men by giving them the same mindset through years of stereotypical slave education, through a system that is established to make loyal workers and workers only, not thinkers and creative, brave, courageous men and women who will have a higher purpose in their life.

Learn anything from anywhere if it helps you, even if you oppose that very thing or person.

Love and love failure make you dumb. Be careful. Love, but don't torture yourself just because the other person is not loving you back. Free yourself from that cage and be happy.

***

Even though you know the reality and are a little skeptical, you still generally should have a positive attitude and optimistic hope about things, and work for them. Don't be miserable and waste your life without enjoying your life and being happy.

Keep the mind and body clean.

The supernatural powers worship beliefs and faith should not be spread by false promises and weapons. If it is done that way, then it will lead to its own death by Intelligence, Philosophy, Technology, and Rationality. Instead, the supernatural powers beliefs should make you think critically, explore, learn, and make you love the whole of humanity while still being supernatural in nature. Just like we expect parents to love all of their children equally, the supernatural powers should love all of humanity in the same way, right?

If you finally had enough and saw enough unnecessary emotional bursts and unnecessary negative emotions in yourself and at home, also irrational and illogical financial and health-related decisions at home and if your family doesn't understand a word you are saying with rational and science approach to things and if all they cared about is what other people are thinking and society is telling them to do then try to make them understand about rationality and emotions and how rationality helps to take better decisions and how negative emotions drain a person and family. Explain to them how a calm and clear approach and discussing things freely, even by disagreeing with each other, leads to better decisions and good relations between family members. Tell them not to care about what others think and start thinking about your family, its security, health, and better productive use of money. They will definitely say to you that they don't need to learn from you, in a harsh tone. So, if you think they don't appreciate your suggestions, then quietly approach your life rationally and be productive. When you finally start achieving some success in life, then they will start believing in you and consider what you are saying and what you are thinking about different things. They know many things you don't know, and you know many things they don't know, and you both don't know many things, too. So you both will put your minds to work and make qualitative decisions together by learning from each other and learning new things. But in order to do all these things, first, you need to be responsible in your life, disciplined, and try to use your life to do great things.

If you always do what society tells you to do, then that is blindly following the slave path. Society will take the credit for your successes, and you will bear the responsibility for your failures. But you should take the responsibility for both. Actually, you should tell society that it is the reason for your successes, and you are the reason for your failures. Then society will say no, you are responsible for your successes, and your failures are just bad luck, and you don't have to worry about them. Even if they don't, it doesn't make any difference, but play it.

Make sure you and your family use the advantage of rationality, freedom, liberty, and critical thinking. As the last prophet of the Ateesta religion, I, Nathan, sincerely wish you get the benefits and blessings of rationality, intelligence, common sense, and critical thinking.

Use every useful thing in the world for the betterment of your life, rather than opposing them just because people of different faiths invented those things. If it is useful scientifically and rationally, then make use of it. But also make sure not to let irrational things dominate your mind. Always think.

Don't lie to gain respect, and get yourself into problems, and into debt to maintain that respect you are getting from others. Gain respect for your attitude, personality, and the man you are or the woman you are, but not based on the job you have and the money you are making, because they can go away at any time. Even if others are giving respect to you according to the money you have and the job you have, then too, you just maintain it, but don't get attached to it emotionally. If your money or job goes away, then don't get depressed that others are not respecting you. So, from the start, build respect for yourself based on what kind of man or woman you are, not on the Jobs and money you have.

You can lie, but only for the greater good, you are not causing any harm to anyone, and also, you are not deceiving yourself, not making yourself bankrupt, and not making yourself fall into problems. Just lie to keep your pure moral respect, and if you need help, ask for help rather than dying with the imagination of respect on you, in others. And imagining that respect for you going away when you ask for help, inside your mind, that no one remembers after you die.

Even if no one understands what you are saying, showing, explaining, etc, don't lose your sanity and patience. Improve your work, and don't worry, eventually, people who are smarter will understand your work, and by the time they find your work, you will have many versions of your work and so many solid things to show. But never tell those important things to people who steal those things and put their names on your work. Be careful with whom you share your work and secrets.

There is nothing wrong with being frugal if it gives you security and hope for the future.

You might take a holiday from your work, but your rationality and common sense should not.

Common sense is not the sense that is common in people, but the sense that should be common in people.

Don't be stupid, and don't be stupid thinking you are being intelligent.

Other people's moods and emotions are infectious, and it doesn't matter whether they are good or not. So stay firm and don't get infected with their emotions while communicating with them, or seeing them, or in any way. Make sure you are safe if you smell something wrong.

Empathy is important but be empathetic not entangled in others' affairs.

Avoid unnecessary interactions with stupid people. They drag you down to their level. Use strategy and tactfulness while communicating with them and get things done. After that, go on your way.

If you have to make a decision, then don't take it based on your emotions. Calculate your intuition and consider it. Also, you have to use rationality, good knowledge about what you are dealing with(if possible), strategy, proper timing, and execution, along with considering all the variables, constants and fixed facts. Then, you can make a qualitative decision about what you are dealing with. The probability of success will go up when you consider all these things rather than just doing something out of emotion. I'm not explaining this process with an example here, but you can take a problem or something you are dealing with and use this process. Explore it and experiment with it with your thinking.

Ateestans are religiously obliged to own land compulsorily. It can be a small lot or acres, but you must have land of your own. This land will save you from becoming homeless, and your family and you will at least have a place to stay when everything is falling apart in an economic sense or in a family finance context.

One health rule for all Ateestans is that you and your family should sit together once every month and share things about your health with each other. If needed, you should get some medical tests and plan to save money for getting at least basic medical tests that detect illnesses at their initial stages. You must always look out for each other when it comes to health, no matter how your relationships are. So that you can prevent any serious illness at its initial stages, saving your life and so much money in the process. You can also use this Family Yan to discuss other things, too. But don't make it a painful thing. Keep it fun and meaningful to children and everyone, rather than a boring task. Don't be narrow-minded when it comes to health, especially.

When your children/wife/husband doesn't get love from you, they try to get it from outside. So, take good care of them.

Even after loving them madly and taking good care of them, your wife/

husband can still cheat on you. In those times, don't harm them in any way. Just move on and live your life. It is painful, I know.

Don't lose your beautiful children, wife/husband, and your family because you got addicted to alcohol, drugs, gambling, etc. Don't be that person who takes the life out of people who love him/her because they have no one in the world except you.

In Ateesta, homesteading is good and encouraged if you can work hard by yourself to save money and live a stress-free life. And also, keep yourself and your family safe in the wild. But make sure that in the process of homesteading, you are not losing opportunities and becoming isolated. Stay free but connected with the world.

You always know when the screen time is unnecessary, yet you have it just to pass the time. Consider it a sin and stop it. Have screen time or digital time in any technological context only if you have a valid reason, that is, to study, work, have entertainment, etc., but not mindlessly. Without even knowing, you will spend thousands of hours of your time on the phone without doing anything productive, and much later in life, after 10 or 15 years, you will realize how much time you wasted and how mindless screen time, digital time, etc, wasted your life. No matter how much you cry, regret, and feel bad about it, there is no going back. So, please go out and do something productive. Get a job or do something on your own and earn money. Please don't waste your life on your phone and computer or any technology if you are not using it with a purpose, productively, and with a reason. Be conscious of the technology and learn it, but don't waste your life in the consumption cycle mindlessly.

A mad belief in yourself with a solid basis of logical nature is important in achieving your goals, even if it seems impractical to others. If you follow your own proper way of doing things, be optimistic about what you are doing, and see success as one of the outcomes, then it is okay. But you should not forget the teachings of God Yinta in Wuquin.

Faith can indeed move mountains, but you should first try to move the mountains and take the failure of not being able to move the mountains. Then you can learn from that failure, and you can actually move the mountains.

Remember, you can keep yourself and your family safe, secure, and happy only when you take care of them well, and expect the problems that might come from all 360 degrees, and be prepared for them. Also, be a little cautious by looking after yourself and your family. Better be careful now than regret later.

Young people are full of energy and do dumb things in split seconds, with high energy when they are with their friends. And they get themselves in trouble. So, rather than letting them drive cars and bikes at 150 miles per hour on public roads just for fun, please teach them and make them aware of the amazing things they can do with that energy in sports, art, STEM, and other amazing things. Passion for cars and bikes is never wrong. But be careful on the road. You can always buy another vehicle but not another you. Cars and bikes, etc, passion is sacred, so be responsible with your passion and its culture.

Tell them how great they would become by spending their energy on many meaningful things, the great challenges they will overcome, and the awesome adventures they can have in life by pursuing meaningful things. Because they will waste their life by spending their valuable energy and mind on stupid things, and go to jail, waste their life, die, or get seriously injured. Young people must know that if they are unhealthy, then none of the people who encouraged them to do stupid things will be coming to take care of them after they get injured or become unhealthy. And you, your family will suffer because of your mindless actions in a rage. Please don't do that.

Friends are awesome. There are great people who will help you become a great person, so become friends with them. Not the ones who will ruin your life.

Many young people think that when they go out at night and do something bad, drive at higher speeds, or commit a crime, then, by morning, everything will become normal. And they can go back to their normal lives as they do every day.

Somehow, young people think whatever happens at night finishes at night, and there are no consequences. But no, you might die after crashing at high speed, and you cannot come to life the next morning. The crime you committed will not be forgotten by the law, and no, it will not become normal in the morning. Everything you do at night will come to haunt you in the morning, it can be a good thing or a bad thing. Please don't get yourself into trouble with the law unnecessarily in a meaningless way and waste your time by going to jail.

Everyone is already connected with the universe that is why we are here physically and mentally, but in order to get the ability to understand the language of the universe in a rational way, you have to learn a lot about the universe technically through the intense study to understand who you are as a person and also to know about the universe and how things are made literally in the universe through the intense study of physics, chemistry, and mathematics, etc. That is why Ateestans love science, which is integral to Ateesta.

After death, there is nothing mentally or physically. The Death, that's it.

Make the most of your time when you are alive by not wasting your life, particularly on screen time, digital time, etc, unnecessarily, by not being productive with it. We don't know what happens after death rationally or scientifically, at least at the time I'm writing this. If you know somehow clearly and rationally with scientific evidence, then you can change your thoughts about this.

In the context of Wuquin, storytelling symbolically, there is no specific beginning or end to God Yinta. There are no stories of God Yinta specifically, too, because he wasn't born and will not die. But we can try to explore who he is through Wuquin. We see God Yinta not just as a God but as the universe itself because he told us to go out and know more about this universe, how it came into existence, and how everything works in the universe. So, God Yinta is the manifestation of the universe in a way, but he is not a God to whom we should pray and worship. In fact, praying to God Yinta is stupid. Instead of praying to him, you can sit in silence, close your eyes, and use your mind to get clarity in thoughts for the things you want to do in your life or to become calm.

Horrible people say and do terrible things like rape, murder, kidnapping, etc, regularly in the world, and the concerned legal systems work to control those things. Still, regular people actually never take those crimes ultra seriously unless those crimes affect them or the people they care about. At the societal level, they see those bad things happening in society as just bad things happening, and that's it. They do nothing about it or superactively pressure the government or authorities to take action swiftly to make the crime rate go to zero. But when someone proposes some action plan or something that will control those crimes or asks regular people to think critically about those crimes and sensitive things, regular people find a thousand reasons to stop thinking critically or not to think at all about those horrific things. It is because thinking critically and rationally involves significant pain and mental strength. Most people do not have the mental strength and courage to face the pain of reality. So, in return, the normal people accuse someone who proposes solutions to problems and to make the crime rate zero as extreme, unnecessary, and offensive. But when a rape crime or gruesome murder happens and it becomes popular then they ask for swift action on the criminals and criticize the law and government.

This is one of the classic ways that the masses escape from responsibility and the absolute truth. Politicians and business people know these types of dark things about regular people, and they use the psychology of people to survive and thrive by using these mass mental and psychological games and secrets.

Politicians and authorities are not bad by default. But if they are bad, it is hard to stop them from abusing their power. So, create proper systems for monitoring them clearly and transparently.

No matter what, Ateesta encourages nations to achieve a Zero Crime Rate.

***

Stop behaving with a slave mentality inside. Question. Question everything and anything. No matter whether the thing you are asking questions about and exploring is considered sacred, untouchable, or dirtiest. It doesn't matter. Question and explore. That is how progress and prosperity happen.

Handle things and people who scream and threaten when you question things. Those things can be anything. When they don't have any answers or at least something that makes sense from a perspective, and ask for only blind faith, then they get angry, and they might even try to kill you. But you are not dumb. They are. So handle them at the same level of toughness and continue your exploration. Your legal systems should support this process rather than coming at you with some vague laws that they made to secure the support of some particular groups to politicians, political parties, or systems that made those very laws. So that those specific groups or people whom you are questioning will, in return, support those politicians, political parties, and systems, and those politicians will further help them to gain more support and to come into power in your country indefinitely.

When a man is truly gracious, talented, good, and well-behaved, no one on Earth can discriminate against him/her. If they do, they are siding with Satan intentionally.

6

Hypothetically, let's analyze the supernatural powers' believers' ' God loves you and wants to give you a great life' theory a bit in detail by keeping ourselves in their God-believing mindset, but as a rational outsider. It goes like this: Someone who says he is lord or God without showing clear, rational, and scientific proof is mostly Satan trying to deceive people by doing good deeds publicly. God must tell his believers that even though he is God and has all the powers to change things as he wants, he as God still wants his believers to work hard in life and stand on their own feet rather than he as God encouraging his believers to mindlessly worship him and beg him to get everything in life through stupid worship processes.

At least God must tell and encourage his believers to ask him for great thoughts, initial support while doing new things in life, and help to get the momentum initially in things they want to do. God should not tell his believers to mindlessly worship him so that his believers get everything they want in life and in the afterlife just by worshiping him, because it is not true. It is a superstition, not a rational belief in God.

See, many believers pray to their Gods for the things they want in life. They could be peace, happiness, money, or whatever they want, and they also pray to their Gods to go to Heaven in the afterlife, and not to go to Hell. But why does no one pray to God for a better beforelife, which means for better things happening to them before their birth and the start of their life? Is it illogical? Or their Gods can only change and improve their believers' current life and afterlife, not beforelife or before their birth?

See how the total afterlife and going to Heaven or Hell concept falls out when we go to the beforelife, and think about where we are in the beforelife, like we think about going to Heaven or Hell in the afterlife. Supernatural powers believers will come up with some pseudo-scientific logic or some emotionally slightly logical response about the beforelife, after reading this. But think, did they emphasize greatly the beforelife and about the beforelife as they did with the afterlife in general for thousands of years? And why do they only talk and say that their God will give you a good life and a good afterlife through Heaven, and why don't they talk about why God gave you the specific life you are living right now, and where are you before your birth in the beforelife? In Heaven or somewhere else? And why don't the Gods change the past or promise to turn time back and change the past and give you a great life from birth itself? Why does God only promise to change your current life and promise you Heaven in the afterlife?

Gods have all the powers, right? Why can't God turn time back and give you a better life from your birth when you start praying to that God from a point in your current life much later? Why only promise about great things that will happen to you in the current life, when you start praying to God, and when you die, you go to Heaven? Can't any Gods give you a better life from your birth by turning time back when you start praying to them?

Can't God even change your painful childhood and the sad things that happened to you in the past when you start praying to him? Why does God only promise great things in the future, in general, and in the current life about the things that will happen only? Why no God promise great past and life that have happened already? Doesn't any God have the power to change the past, at least for a few minutes? Why do Gods only make promises about things that will happen or about things in the future, and not about what has happened?

Can't God change bad and sad things that have just happened in your current life by turning time back just a few minutes? Why do the Gods generally focus mostly on the future and things that will happen in life rather than equally focusing on the past, beforelife, and the current life, afterlife?

If God tells us important things that we should know before we come into this world, when we were still in the beforelife, then we will become good people in the current life, right? Then going to Heaven in the afterlife would be easy, too. But instead of that, why does God always want his believers to worship him and beg him or pray to him for a better current life and afterlife, while totally ignoring the beforelife?

There is nothing greater than human beings in the world, even if they fight among themselves, and even after you find any alien life forms. Protect humanity and all races of humanity.

Just the blind believers of supernatural powers with blind faith and weapons in their hands get hysterical when someone criticizes the supernatural powers they believe in, and they believe that they were appointed by the supernatural powers themselves to defend the supernatural powers. How ironic and stupid!

So, the supernatural power they believe in wrote in its teachings telling its believers to defend its teachings and figures when someone criticizes them, but why can't the supernatural powers just answer some criticism or questions? What's wrong with it? Why should it be like.. no one should question the supernatural powers and their teachings? Isn't it dictatorial?

Are supernatural powers dictators or Gods?

It is a supernatural power, right? Then it can guess some common, frequently asked questions by people and at least answer them in its teachings.

Do the supernatural powers not even have the tolerance to take a little criticism? What kind of supernatural power is that? Doesn't that supernatural power have at least a little emotional maturity to handle criticism? If not, then I'm 100% sure, many great men and women have greater character than that supernatural power.

And remember every time you make a meaningful contribution to humanity it doesn't matter how small or big it is or to other life forms on Earth, every time you do something positive it doesn't matter whether it is a very small thing or a thing that can change the world for better you should know that you are with God Yinta and God Yinta is with you in that process of doing good.

Every time you behave stupidly and do bad things just out of emotion, you are drifting away from God Yinta, and moving closer to Satan. You can use this book to learn more about God Yinta. God Yinta is the Universe, and the universe is God Yinta. If you want the story of God Yinta, then you are asking for the story of the universe and how it came into existence, which you have to research and discover for yourself through science.

How do you know your God Yinta is helping you, which means the so-called universe is helping you?

The answer is through your thoughts, pristine, clear, conscious, intellectual, rational thoughts. Through those thoughts, God Yinta will talk to you and tell you what to do. But it is not easy. It takes a lot of work to develop that ability, so keep using your mind consciously for everything rather than doing everything in automatic mode.

You will be under tremendous pressure and stress while dealing with problems in your life, particularly when it comes to your appearance, health, family, and finances. So you have to always make sense inside your head. Try to think clearly and find the reasons for the causes of your problems instead of feeling sad and taking extreme steps just because of your emotions and the pain you are feeling. Use your emotions as fuel to solve your problems. It doesn't matter what emotions you are feeling; you must use them to your advantage and, with the help of rationality, gain control over them. Your solution to the problem you are facing might help other people, too. Remember the 5 Pillars of Active Mind, Ateestan philosophy, and stop being dumb.

I don't want you to harm yourself and others in the process. And also, I don't want you to get extreme and irrational, too. But if any kind of supernatural powers' worship is bringing you and your family together and if it is helping you and your family and community, then in the name of God Yinta, please do it.

God Yinta will feel happy if you are using those supernatural powers worship processes to get hope and strength by not harming yourself and scamming others in any way.

It is because the life.. life is cruel. And in times when you are at the lowest point of your life, and if no one is with you to support you properly at that time, then those times can break you mentally and physically, too.

Nothing in the world can give you stronger psychological, mental strength in those low times than supernatural beliefs and worship. Your rational nature and intelligence will help you absolutely, and they alone can make you come out of those problems, but they cannot give you the great hope and super strong emotional assurance that you need to make yourself feel positive again. But a little irrational belief in supernatural powers, worship, and prayers to those supernatural powers can give you that big mental psychological strength to face the darkness in your life. And that strength will have effects in the real world too, through your actions based on that strong positive hope, assurance you felt by praying to those supernatural powers. So, in that context, you can pray or worship to supernatural powers to get that strong positive hope, assurance, but ultimately rationality and intelligence should be your weapons to fight against those problems you are facing.

There is nothing wrong with it because you are not scamming or harming anyone in any way. You are just believing that someone will help you, and in this case, that someone who is going to help you is a supernatural power, and that supernatural power might help you through a thought you will get, a human being, or through an animal, or it can be anything or anyone. It makes sense if you look at it in this way. Again, Ateesta is not contradicting itself here, and it is not contradicting itself by saying it is not contradicting itself. You should have a broader understanding of life, the universe, and things in it to understand this and the intention behind this. Sometimes your survival is more important than anything. Survive!

If you don't want to pray to other non-Ateestan supernatural powers but still want to be a little irrational and feel the strength psychologically and mentally that your future is great because a supernatural power will help you and guide you, then you can do this. If you want to pray to a supernatural power, you can do this.

If you want to pray to a supernatural power to get strength psychologically and mentally, and want to feel the strong positive assurance that your life will be good, then rather than praying to other supernatural powers outside of Ateesta, you can pray to God Yinta like you pray to other supernatural powers.

In ways or processes that are familiar to you, you can pray and worship God Yinta. But you do this consciously and rationally, that you know God Yinta does not exist and he is not a supernatural power, but you are praying to him or worshiping him is just because for you to get the strength psychologically, mentally, and feel the strong positive assurance that your life will be good that's it but with a touch of mysteriousness to calm the mind and emotions indirectly by consciously doing this. This positive assurance feeling will calm the minds of sensitive people completely than logic, that's it. You can celebrate festivals and do other processions too, based on God Yinta and Ateesta, but do them rationally and consciously, not with any sort of blind belief and blind faith in any supernatural elements.

Symbolically, what you are doing here by praying and worshiping God Yinta rationally is, you are just asking your mind to give you great, clean, pure thoughts to improve your life. That's it. This is much better than blindly worshiping supernatural powers. Psychologically, a man has to concentrate his emotions and feelings of devotion and sacredness on something to feel good, and to feel that a holy power is helping him/her. So, that is what we are doing here but rationally.

Be honest, but make sure your honesty doesn't finish you and your life. Also, not being honest, too, might finish you and your life, and make you a bad person. Find the balance to survive the power dynamics of the environment you are in. Do not be honest with dishonest people and groups.

Don't feel bad that you are not a billionaire or millionaire. First, focus on being clean and hygienic in life in all aspects, and get a cool and chill attitude. Greet people respectfully and have honor for yourself first. Be respectful. Money is very important to live, there is no doubt in that, but also your attitude and what kind of person you are. If you are a narrow minded a** hole no amount of money can make you happy just because you have big mansions and cars etc But if you are a cool chill person in general with good income, even as an introvert or extrovert, You can live a decent happy life which is much better than a wealthy guy who has a narrow attitude and irritable natured in general. So be a cool and chill person in general. If possible, make sure people feel energetic and great while being around you. After being a cool and chill person in general, Focus on money and earn as much as possible. No shame in that, too.

No one can do any harm to you mentally unless you accept what they want you to feel. Even if they do something to make you accept the pain and torture they are trying to inflict on you mentally, then you must act like you accepted it, but inside, you don't. When the right time comes, crush them, take the opportunities, and move higher in life.

It is because any person or any institution that wants to harm you for any profit or any reason, first they try to make you accept those things that harm you, not by force, but by convincing you mentally first. If it is not possible, then they might get physical, but one leads to the other anyway. So, know the truth first before accepting anything, doing anything based on what you have accepted mentally. Also, don't harm yourself by thinking that others want to harm you or control you. Find the truth first, but don't assume the truth.

Free your mind from weakness. Free yourself from your self-imposed limitations and pain. Endure the pain and face it. While taking the pain, you fight the problems and kill the problems, not while avoiding them. But be wise in selecting the problems you want to fight on.

I, God Yinta, am giving you the freedom of thought, freedom to live, and skills to survive in this harsh, beautiful world. I, God Yinta, am giving you the truth. The truth is that what is true is the truth, and sometimes the truth changes, and sometimes it doesn't. So seek the truth and know your self-imposed limitations and pain. Then you will not be a slave to anything. The truth always depends on the context you are in, while taking all the variables and constants into account.

Believe in your efforts, not in any supernatural powers.

You can keep your home and property as you want. No one in the world, whether it be the government, city authorities, or any Parasite Home associations, etc, can dictate to you on how you should keep your property and live your life.

Take this very seriously because oppression of people and taking away the freedom of people start from the power-hungry leeches who would do anything to assert their dominance. Take a gun into your hands or protest to change the law itself to make yourself free from those leeches' traps. If they keep troubling you on how you should keep your property, then ask them to pay money to you first to comply with the rules because they want to see those rules implemented on your property, not by you voluntarily and also you live as you want in your property and it should not be disturbed by others in any way.

Never pay any fines or any money to home associations or their equivalent parasites, whoever they are. Form a group or a big community on these issues, and with the power of your votes and strength of unity and power, you can negotiate with any law or politician. Scare them and warn them by telling them how many votes and how much support they are going to lose if they go against you and how much campaigning you will do against them as a big community or city or village or as an area collectively when elections come and tell the politician or person who is behind all the problems you are facing that he/she will disappear without even getting a few thousand votes and support politically. You can use this tactic in any form if the person is not a politician, and if it is a company or some hate group. Crush the arrogance and power of them totally and make them ineffective in all forms. You can form other power systems to negotiate with politicians and governments if they are not democratic, but you must always try to match the power of those with whom you are negotiating.

Use the political systems of countries to bend the higher powers to your will, in a democracy with votes and unity for your cause, and in dictatorships through violence against the evil authorities, specifically, evil powers that are supporting those evil authorities, not against normal people.

Value yourself first. Don't be a mindless consumer of anything because you think it makes you look rich or cool or whatever. Be conscious of money and spending.

Don't get in trouble with the law without a strong reason. Even if you are not guilty, did nothing bad but make a scene with police officers or law enforcement authorities, etc, they can always find a way to file a case against you. Initially, comply with the law and police officers, but do not admit to something you haven't done. Do it with respect, no matter how much those officers try to irritate you.

You, too, have rights, but make sure to use them efficiently with proper knowledge of the law or get a lawyer. So initially, do not behave rudely with any law enforcement authorities, and do not admit to anything you haven't done, in fear. Once the moment when authorities try to take you to the police station or somewhere passes, then everything cools off, and your lawyer will take care of everything. And you will never have unnecessary cases on you in this way. No matter which country you live in. Use the law, and bend it according to how it can help you. And if you don't know how to do it, then remember that the law enforcement authorities know how to use it against you. So always be patient, smart, and conscious of how you deal with law enforcement authorities.

Always be in touch with a lawyer or someone who can get you out of trouble using the legal system.

If you can't afford a lawyer, then get into a contract with a lawyer every year as a group of people or community, and ask that lawyer to take care of you and your group/community when you get stopped by a cop and in other things that will help you immediately if a lawyer steps in. This will also help you in avoiding unnecessary trauma because if police or other authorities know you have a lawyer, that lawyer will come after them with a big fat lawsuit and problems if they trouble you unnecessarily and with cunningly made-up stories, things. They will stop the cunning games with you.

This will give you immediate safety and security if those bad police officers or other authorities are unnecessarily aggressive, passive-aggressive, or cunning with you. Use the same law they use against you to keep yourself safe.

This is silly, but don't live your life by random quotes you read somewhere without any context. Always understand the backstory, particularly if those quotes are from supernatural powers' teachings of any kind. The blind believers hide many things and show only those things that will get respect and use them to try to convince people to convert them into their supernatural belief systems.

Money is a tool to get things done. Do not get attached to it emotionally, only rationally. Earn as much money as possible without emotional attachment to it. And always be wise with money, with no exceptions.

Even if you are not at all interested in money, it is better to earn a lot and do something good with it rather than just sit idle. But you can also save and invest properly according to your risk tolerance. Again, be rational with money, not stupid.

Aren't we insulting our First Human Ancestors, who led harsh lives for hundreds of thousands of years just to eat and survive, who hunted great mammoths and lions for food and to keep themselves and their children safe, by believing some supernatural force made the universe?

Is it not disrespectful to our human ancestors to believe that some supernatural powers created human beings out of some supernatural powers' magical creation, and also believing that all the things that our human ancestors went through in the process of evolution is a lie?

Our Human Ancestors went through many unexplainable painful sufferings, which made the humanity that we have now possible, and just because we believe in some supernatural powers now from a few thousand years after the modern humans learned to speak, write and communicate and created languages, we now are denying Our Great Human Evolution and our human ancestors suffering and their pain, struggle for the hundreds of thousands of years in the wild.

You just try to think about how our human ancestors would feel if they knew that we were denying them. Their children are denying their entire existence now because they have some stories of supernatural powers they believe in, and by believing in those supernatural powers, they get every good thing in life. Imagine how they would feel if they knew this.

Deal with haters of the Ateesta religion and Wuquin with rationality and logic, not by emotions. People who hate the Ateesta religion and Wuquin will find as many reasons as possible to continue hating them. People who love the Ateesta religion and Wuquin will find as many reasons as possible to continue loving them.

Let everyone wear what they want, but ask them to keep it respectful to themselves and to the place they are in. Same with food.

Productivity is important, but the purpose of your productivity is much more important.

Always study philosophy and discuss it. Philosophy should be your best friend, along with rationality and common sense.

You decide whether you are happy or not. Your happiness cannot be determined by anything external. You must become a person who can debate in favor of or against the Ateesta religion and its philosophy, supernatural powers worship, atheism, or any other things, and philosophical concepts. You must have that total 360-degree understanding of things. This is crucial for you to know who you are, and in the process, you will know how to approach everything in life and life itself.

According to the I Killed Satan - The Great War of Man and Satan novel, only rational people who studied the universe and the world rationally and scientifically followed the Ateesta religion. Even though the 'I Killed Satan - The Great War of Man and Satan' novel is a story, you must be rational and calm down when attacks on the Ateesta religion and Wuquin occur verbally, and learn from them. Through those verbal attacks, you will improve your understanding of the world, people, and human nature. Verbal attacks only.

Personally, stop engaging with trolls digitally or through any other technologies. It is the best antidote to bullying and trolling on digital platforms. Respond with your success in the real world rather than with rage through the keyboard. If trolling becomes your career, be careful because people enjoy the trolls and move on. People will follow someone else who can make more fun by trolling than you. There is nothing wrong with trolling as long as it has credible points, but try to create new content and new art too, rather than always trolling what is already there. Trolling can be done positively and negatively. Do it positively, not as evil psychopath who is hungry for engagement and go to any low for it with virtual signal cunningness.

Build a world with reason and rationality as paramount, with emphasis on common sense.

Sex is beautiful. Do it with consent.

You are the worst creature ever if you betray the people who trusted you. Also, do not say a word if you can't keep it.

Beware of evil people who use the Wuquin and Ateesta religion to make money and scam people. Again, do what Wuquin encourages, which is critical thinking, if you encounter any of those people. Believe only what the Last Prophet of Ateesta says and Wuquin, no one else.

Everyone is the same in Ateesta. No one is above or below. Everyone is unique. There is no discrimination in any form based on the color of skin, race, or anything for that matter, even based on the intelligence and achievements of people.

There are no supernatural powers or things in the world of any kind that we cannot explain rationally. Also, believe in your efforts more than any supernatural powers.

There is no afterlife, rationally and scientifically, as I write this. Use your life fully when you are still alive.

People are so distracted in the world by phones, TV, movies, etc, and all the other things appearing in front of their eyes everywhere. It is because of this constant distraction effect on their ears, eyes, and all other senses that when people finally sit in silence and meditate, they get to experience the calmness in the mind and how the mind processes everything in silence. People are perceiving this calming effect from meditation as some supernatural experience because it relieves them from all the things that stress them in life. And they are seeing this as life-changing, and the greatest thing that connects them to some supernatural higher power or to somewhere sacred or to someone far out in the universe who is very sacred. But people should understand that it is just the mind experiencing the calmness from all the things stressing it out. Many institutions and people are using meditation and other things like that to make money by mixing meditation with supernatural elements, which creates a mysterious interesting calming effect on mind. Be very careful of them.

You get the same calming effect in your mind if you sit in silence and meditate without involving any supernatural-related beliefs or elements in the meditation process. But since supernatural elements capture our interest and create a strong emotional impression on us, when mediation gets combined with supernatural elements, it gives strong, mysterious, sacred feelings and great confidence in ourselves too, because we feel the positive assurance that our life will be great from supernatural powers' support mentally. Basically, it's a small positive delusion with no harm, mostly.

***

If you don't love the land and country you live in, even to protect yourself and your family from other nations who want to destroy it, then you are not even a man. Be protective of your nation and respect it because your life, freedom, and family depend on its independence from all the evil things that want to take over your country and control it.

Always use all your advantages to succeed. They can be money, influence, handsomeness/attractiveness, etc., without degrading yourself and giving up precious things like your love and sex, etc. Also, make sure you do not regret what you achieved in your life, because if you regret the very thing you got from doing all the hard work, then what you achieved will be a waste.

Ateestans on special occasions can wear clothes with a combination of Red, symbolizing their bravery, and White, symbolizing peace, and Black, symbolizing they are not afraid to fight against injustice. Please don't waste money on these clothes if you can't afford them. God Yinta, will be happier if you buy something useful to you with that money than these clothes. Buy these clothes only when you can afford them and have enough money.

Better to live under a dictatorship that cares about the country and gives citizens their freedoms of all kinds than in a democracy that curtails the freedoms of citizens through all the complicated laws and processes.

Ateesta does not favor or oppose any form of government, but encourages those governments to give all types of freedom to people.

Remember, freedom is important no matter what.

Every able and mentally fit citizen should have a gun and weapons with them to save themselves and their family from trouble. You don't mess with anyone, and they don't mess with you. If you do some stupid violence, you'll pay the price.

Individual rights above all.

Law is made by humans, and those sets of humans who make laws cannot decide how millions and billions should live their daily lives forever against their will.

Ateestan Governments should construct prisons in the middle of the deserts.

CRIME IS NOT TOLERATED.

You can do anything to save yourself from criminals and give an explanation later, but saving yourself first is more important.

Morally good and intelligent leaders should rule the country. With efficient governance and services to people with as few taxes as possible, with more efficient, productive spending of tax money.

Be positive, optimistic, and also pragmatic and practical. At the same time, give importance to your intuition and study the negativity too to have a 360-degree angle knowledge about what you are doing, and then make decisions. If you are not in a position to get that info, then make the best decision based on the information available to you, and accept the success or failure by working hard for success. This journey is personal, and you have to carve your own path by taking responsibility for your success and failure. And also study all the available things to do what you want to do efficiently and win at it. There is always darkness in this journey; instead of fearing it, embrace it and face it with courage and with all the tools available to you. Never accept defeat.

Be careful of people who use the names of Ateesta and Wuquin, mimic Ateesta, and say what they want to say in the name of Ateesta. Take this holy book, Wuquin, written by Nathan, as the primary document and the only document from Ateesta. Nothing else.

What you don't know you don't know. So don't make fun of it in an ugly manner.

Equal rights, responsibilities, and accountability. The social and political scenario between men and women should be determined by themselves at the societal level. If you want an excuse for something, you have to make adjustments with the opposite sex. Be careful of political leaders, wanna be social influencer personalities, and idiots who think they are trying to achieve equality by undermining the uniqueness of men and women by manipulating men and women for their own gains.

Be respectful, no matter in what supernatural powers anyone believes in but if the teachings related to those supernatural powers teach hate towards other different supernatural powers believers and asks it's own believers to hate them, kill them or trouble them in any form just because the other types are not believing in it then despise those teachings and throw those teachings away. If any supernatural power, a power that is higher than man teaches to hate, asks to kill people just because they are not believing in that supernatural power and living their life according to how it said people has to live through it's teachings then even if that supernatural power is real hypothetically, We, human beings don't need that kind of supernatural power. And people who believe in that kind of supernatural power and its teachings become unknowingly unnecessarily cruel, cunning and selfish but they think those things are sacred because their supernatural power related teachings told them, the believers, to be like that to its non believers so it is justifiable even if it seems wrong when they look at it in a broader humanistic perspective with morals.

Any ideal supernatural powers should ask us to love humanity, all the life forms on Earth, the universe, them, and ourselves, and should encourage us to live according to how we want by not harming anyone.

Taking away your freedom in the name of rules set by supernatural powers or beliefs, and filling you with hate towards other human beings for the reason of not believing in a supernatural power that you believe in, is never sacred and will never be sacred. No matter who says what, even if hypothetically a supernatural power that said that comes to Earth and tells you to follow its teachings, still you must tell it, "No, they are my fellow human beings, and I'm not killing them just because they don't believe in you. If you want them to believe in you that much, then work your magic in a good way, and tell them to follow you. Do not ask me to become a criminal because this is not a war. On Earth, even in war, if I kill someone in an immoral way, I still become a war criminal, but you are asking me to become a criminal and a killer for you, just to win your love and blessings? What kind of love is it? Is it love and affection or a business deal? You are a supernatural power, Goddamn it, not a human being. But you are a politician clearly."

Everything in life is usually permanent, which means that as human beings, we die because we are mortal beings, but the things we buy, construct, and work our whole lives for mostly don't die. So, you must make good choices about what to work for and what to do in your life. Yes, they might get destroyed, but most of the time, they outlive us.

Many people believe in supernatural powers because others believe in them. And they feel socially secure and confident about it, as now they are socially acceptable. But they don't realize that a part of supernatural belief systems is programmed to make men and women predictable and kill the rebel nature and freedom-seeking nature in them to control them. It also kills the uniqueness of an individual by injecting the same beliefs and training them to think in a certain way about themselves and the world in masses. It cultivates a nature in people to make them always try to blend with others to avoid any conflict, and it kills the questioning and rational nature in them. It makes a man an emotional robot, which is the opposite of the technology robots that operate based on logic. Of course, now those technology robots are learning about emotions. But many human beings are still stuck in emotional supernatural superstitious beliefs, and they have become supernatural powers believing emotional robots.

Do not give the power to anyone to command your mood and emotions. Think critically and rationally, and use psychological knowledge and science in a broader way in dealing with human nature-related things. Determine your mood and happiness by yourself, not based on what others want you to feel.

If you want to preach about the Ateesta religion and Wuquin, then preach only what is in Wuquin. And your interpretations should be positive, and you should have only progress as your end goal.

Mostly, pseudo-scientific techniques and supernatural belief systems promise gains of all kinds without our efforts. And even if they come up with a logic like supernatural powers worship will help your hard work win, then ask yourself, is it making others lose to make you win?

Then don't you think that the others are also just like you, as humans who are trying to live a better life?

Why does that supernatural power favor you only and make others lose? If the reason that particular supernatural power makes you win is because you believe in that supernatural power that your competitors don't, then are your competitors not worshiping their supernatural power as strongly as you do to your supernatural power or is your supernatural power making them lose? Because they also belong to another supernatural power belief system, right? Or is it the same, no matter whether your opponents in any competition belong to your supernatural belief system or other supernatural belief systems?

If the supernatural powers take a side and help you, then those supernatural powers are nothing more than a human in supernatural powers form. So even if those supernatural powers exist hypothetically, they are still not as good, sacred, and divine as you think. If supernatural powers can't see all life forms equal in all aspects, and leave the winning or failure to themselves and their efforts, then how can those supernatural powers be all great and unquestionable?

Be careful with pseudo-science, pseudo-rationalists, and hypocrites who try to use anything for their own survival.

If you are poor, then you must be rational, positive, tough, and strong both mentally and physically to make it in life and come out of that poverty. Use poverty as fuel and to increase your strength mentally and physically, learn from it and use it to get new, fresh, creative ideas, but never plan to stay there for long. At least try hard to come out of it, not just through money, but also from your poor mindset.

There are no supernatural powers and supernatural Gods in any way, shape, or form. God is just a grand placebo effect and nocebo effect, Satan too. All the texts that talk about the supernatural elements related to God are just to make people believe in that Supernatural God and just to put the God Placebo and Nocebo effects, the Satan Nocebo and Placebo effects in people's minds strongly and impactfully by showing their those so called supernatural power written texts as evidence, in this way they will try to lock your rational mind and make you a blind believer of supernatural powers. To make this placebo and nocebo effects work well and build strong systems of unquestionable faith based on them, sometimes the people behind writing these so called supernatural powers teachings used the lives of real people, great people, bad people and blended them into a scripture-style writing, and sometimes kept them purely supernatural in nature, and sometimes mixed both and added other styles too, according to the time and circumstances they were written in.

Any God, hypothetical God, supernatural God, or whatever God in any way who encourages domination of one gender over the other and says that little girls (Kids) have to get married in childhood for any reason whatsoever, dismantle those teachings and destroy those who say it. No girl should be restricted from picking up a book and reading it. If God says something like that about Girls in his supernatural teachings, then fight that God, no matter who that God is and who is praying to that God; that God is not God, that is Satan posing as God, even if we take it symbolically, if not supernaturally. Kids, both boys and girls, have every right to read and learn and become what they want in their careers and life. God Yinta will fight with those false Gods on behalf of the Kids, too. You must oppose this ugly practice.

Do not sacrifice your life, which means don't kill yourself or destroy your life in any way for what you believe/follow in your life, because sometimes the thing you are fighting for or want might not worth it after the heat of the moment passes or a certain period of time passes because things change with time always, and if you think a cause is worth fighting for, then fight for it by being alive and well, not by dying. So that you can tell yourself you are fighting for what is good, and that if it needs any changes or alterations in your approach or in the process of fighting for it, you are ready to make them. All this can happen only if you are alive, not by your death. Live and achieve, but don't die.

Follow the law of the land to avoid initial opposition from the judiciary and legal systems. Then, try to bend them, modify them, and make changes to them to your comfort by force, or in any other way. Just use the law of your land or the land you are in to your advantage.

Never give importance to anyone so much that they can make you angry, depressed, sad, and ultimately, in extreme situations, make you kill yourself. Just chill and be happy with yourself.

Think, you will find a solution that works.

Otherwise, what do you do by dying? Don't be stupid. Think and do trial-and-error processes. Be happy if it works, and be happy even if it doesn't. Learn, move on, and give your best when you still have the chance to succeed and to avoid regret later. If you try 100 percent and it doesn't work, then you'll be sad, but if you don't try properly and fail, then you'll be sad and regret it later for not using the opportunity properly. Sadness is manageable, but regret is very hard to cope with.

No supernatural power is coming to save you. Save yourself.

There is nothing wrong with executing men/women who attack children in a perverted way. Ateesta encourages it, but only legally.

Sometimes, the truth is relative. Sometimes, the truth is absolute. You have to find the truth and its nature according to your situation. Some truths are fixed no matter what, but some truths are always changing. You should also find the nature of the truth you are seeking to know.

What we don't know, we don't know, and when we know, we know. Make sure what we know is the truth, and not anything else.

Any sensible culture with a rich history always has women

supporting it. Actually, it is because of those women who are praying to those supernatural powers in those cultures and following the traditions of those cultures that those cultures thrived, survived, and now we are seeing all these cultures every day, everywhere, in any country. But when women decide not to follow those cultures and not to adhere to the traditional way of life and not to follow the rules of the cultures, then those cultures will die because men mostly don't follow any traditions or cultures as strongly as women and they mostly only follow what is comfortable to them in their traditions and cultures personally, even though they respect their cultures and traditions a lot. So if you want your culture to survive, then give women freedom, let them get educated, and let them work. Along with that, men, you too should wear traditional dresses of your cultures regularly, and tell women that they are the representatives of your cultures and respect them. Otherwise, if you impose all the restrictions and all the limitations on women, stating culture and traditions as a reason, then one day women will revolt, and your cultures and religions will start dying from that day.

If any supernatural power worshipers claim they can cure diseases just by praying to their supernatural powers, then they lose the basic moral right to visit a hospital when they get any illnesses. You can't tell people to come to you for praying to supernatural powers to cure the diseases they have and endanger their lives, but you use scientific medicines secretly for your health problems instead of asking your supernatural powers to cure you.

Anybody who says that their supernatural powers beliefs are important to them than science, then they also lose the basic moral right to visit a hospital when they get any illness. Go to your supernatural powers and ask it to cure you.

You can also try to cure diseases safely if you have established ancestral cultural medicine practices with strong evidence of success, but not with supernatural powers prayers, and irrational food, and liquids, etc., by saying that the supernatural power in them will cure diseases. Go to the law and complain about those people who do these kinds of fake supernatural healing things, etc, without any evidence-based methods.

Citizen science should be encouraged. And they should be given a chance to prove their work. Instead of mindless opposition just because it is not coming from big corporations and people with fancy degrees.

Always enjoy and feel the strength and security that comes from being united and forming a community by talking and discussing, or just having fun.

The technology has the power to make a person more attached to it than to the things that person has to do in his/her real life. In ancient times, even with fewer distractions from technology, the people struggled a lot to even survive because of the bad economy and the lack of sufficient technologies that make life easier. In those times, faith in supernatural powers and worship gave them the distraction they needed in life from all the stress and problems they were facing, and worship of supernatural powers gave them the hope that their future would be great.

It is the same now, too, but the hope they get from the worship of supernatural powers that their future is great is being meddled with by technological distractions.

So, the stronger the technological distractions, the stronger the calming effect of prayer becomes with time. Supernatural powers worship, and meditation are making a person feel calm and clear from the abyss of technology distractions and personal problems, thus making that person feel his/her life has changed while they are meditating in peace and with clarity of thoughts, which further gives them better judgment over things and makes their thinking process efficient. But the result of great calmness in life and even materialistic results in their life are not directly because of the supernatural powers they are worshiping or mystical meditation itself, but just the mind is becoming calm and active with good focus, that's it. The clean processes they were following for supernatural powers worship and meditation are giving them calmness and clarity in their thoughts. So you can remove the beliefs in supernatural elements, which are not rational, and do the same meditation or prayers, and can have the same effects by believing that your efforts will yield great results, gaining strong confidence in yourself, rather than believing in supernatural powers and worshiping them to give you hope. But if supernatural elements are involved in the process, the taste and flavor of prayer and meditations change and become psychologically sacred and strong, positive in our minds.

7

Most of the supernatural powers worship processes create an emotion, and that emotion can be any emotion in a human being, thus making that person or groups of people feel the same things, the same emotions. And through this process, a strong bond is created emotionally in the minds of people between supernatural powers and people who worship those supernatural powers, and also between themselves. It is key in any supernatural belief system, and to sustain itself.

If you think your race, skin color, or community, etc, is superior, then it is superior. If you think your race, skin color, or community, etc, is not superior, then they are not superior. It depends on how you see yourself and your group. Your value does not depend on how others see you, but only on how you see yourself.

People generally attribute the great achievements of a person to supernatural powers rather than to that person's hard work and thinking capabilities, decision-making skills, and risk-taking ability.

So that they can avoid doing the hard work, or thinking critically, or learning skills that are very painful to learn, they just pray to some supernatural powers and hope to get lucky and succeed along the way.

No matter what, just live. Live for yourself, live for your family, and live for no reason but just live. Don't die. Think about your mom, dad, and family, or at least the fun you can have if you stay alive. You don't know how life changes at any second. So, don't be so sure that you will be sad all your life or you will be in the same problems. It will change. It is the nature of life, and no matter what you are going through, it can be good or bad; it will change.

Be cruel to cruel people, brutal to brutal people, cunning to cunning people, and honest with honest people. No, if they are bad, you are not becoming bad. you are using the shield of badness to save yourself from them so that you don't become an idiot loser while being a good person.

Never bend to the protests and oppression against you by people who support supernatural powers and people who are trying to suppress rational thinking. Be careful because those supernatural powers' believers can tell themselves any reason to attack you and kill you and justify it, if you don't believe in the supernatural powers they believe in.

If anyone is torturing you physically or mentally, never take it. Fight back. If you are not in a position to fight back, then wait till you find some other job or work, and leave that place and those people. Be strong. Anything will affect you mentally only if you allow it. I can understand there will be some situations where you feel like you don't have a chance to stand up for yourself, then make the fight public, and make their power, which they are using against you, which they think of as their strength, as their weakness. And fight back.

If you realized somehow that you can't achieve your dreams, or you can't live your life as you want, which happens a lot to many people, then just stay alive and have fun. Having fun doesn't mean that you have to drink alcohol, etc, daily and do every stupid thing that comes into your mind. It means you don't have to worry about anything now, and you can do some work to survive and live. You will be happy after the initial acceptance of this stage inside of you, even if it feels super painful. You can have good fun in life if you are alive and even if you leave your dreams and goals even then there is still a chance that if you are alive somehow an opportunity even if it is super small may come your way and then there is still a chance you become a decent figure in that field. But if you are dead, then technically, there is no chance of any of that. So stay alive, kill your dumb ego and self-depreciating nature, or anything for that matter, to stay alive. Life will change, and that is the nature of life. No matter what, just have fun and live, don't die for any reason whatsoever.

Also, don't die in the hands of a murderer or criminals, fearing that if you fight back, and if they die, then you might go to jail. First, save yourself and do anything to save yourself. Never die. Kill in any situation if they are trying to kill you directly or indirectly through mental torture, or any physical torture. Never let anyone take advantage of your goodness, but be good.

Don't be jealous of any person's success, and don't be happy about any person's failure. Use jealousy as your fuel for success and to inspire you. Use the failures of others as lessons to study.

God Yinta in your mind will always give you the forces of confidence, intelligence, rationality, courage, bravery, and consciousness to fight the wars in your life. God Yinta knows the balance between your emotions and your rational nature. Ask God Yinta in your mind to help you. He will definitely help you.

You must always remember that a person or a race who have great rationality, intelligence, and greater control over their emotions will always enslave other people or races who do not have them. You remember this daily.

Rationality always prevails over irrationality, stupidity, and the rage of emotions.

Always look after yourself and then others. Because if you look after yourself well, then you will live a good life, and if everyone looks after themselves, then they can also live a good life. In this way, if you take care of yourself, your family, and your loved ones, and if everyone does the same thing, then the society will function in good order, determined by itself with good values and good people. Society is a collection of individuals. If you take care of yourself first, and if everyone takes care of themselves, then society will prosper eventually. You can and should help others, too.

Being happy all the time is not a sin, and there is nothing to be afraid of in that. You are wasting your life if you are not happy.

The swords of Ateesta should start coming out from one side as the Ateestans are getting attacked. Do not hesitate. It is the only way to protect yourself in a world where the law is not strict and fringe elements roam freely.

Stop meaningless coping and start asking questions. Because old traditional religions are coping systems built in different forms and ways. They just train and encourage people to make psychological and mental adjustments in themselves to life situations that are good or bad, and also when they are neither good nor bad. Instead of coping mentally and psychologically, ask questions and see the reality. Try to live in reality and improve it. If something good happens, the traditional religions tell you which supernatural power is behind it, and how they should see it, and how happy they should get, and in what way they should celebrate, etc. If something bad happens, the traditional religions teach why it happened, and how you can accept it, and why you should accept it, and how you should see it, and how much more supernatural powers worship and prayers you have to do to come out of that failure, sadness, etc. All they are doing is making you adjust to the situation mentally, psychologically, and physically, too, sometimes, and also by assuring you that the future is great for you, if you increase the supernatural powers worship time and prayers.

Never make fun of any religion's stories and teachings.

***

You can enjoy the emotions of yourself and others if they are positive and not harming you or others in any way.

You can form good relationships with other countries' nationalists and patriots. You can discuss and debate many things rationally without fighting and hating each other.

The world should make sense to you, at least from your own perspective to yourself. If not, you should force it to make sense.

What difference does it make whether you believe in supernatural powers or not, unless you make sense in your mind? If you are an Ateestan, then you are just an Ateestan. You are not someone who hates supernatural powers, believers of any kind, but just someone who seeks evidence with credibility, according to science and rationality, about the existence of supernatural powers. But not someone who spreads hate on believers of supernatural powers. You can criticize and question the supernatural powers and believers, but don't offend them with pure hate toward them. You can question everything, and you can talk to people who want to share their views, and you can tell them what you're thinking, but be civil.

Do not commit any crimes. You will be a criminal if you commit a crime, but when you do something that changes the world, you will become a leader, not a criminal. Become a leader, not a criminal.

You cannot suppress your emotions to zero, but you can control and balance them consciously. You can use them to your advantage, better your life, and achieve ultimate happiness and peace.

The more rational, intelligent you are, the more things you know, and the more fearful you get in life. So, control the fear and balance it.

Channel the fear and overthinking to analyze and learn about obstacles. If you are a person with the capability of great imagination, you can use it to take advantage by imagining and preparing for all the problems you might encounter in life, and you can also get suggestions and solutions in your mind to solve them. Use your imagination to your advantage rather than just getting scared. Sometimes this imagination power comes in the form of overthinking.

Be honest in general. Never trust anyone completely. Always be prepared to face anything and a betrayer, too. Betrayers can destroy anything, no matter how big and powerful you are.

Everything that was promised to you in Heaven by supernatural belief systems is mostly already on Earth. You don't need to postpone your happiness to die and to go to a non-existent Heaven to be happy.

You are a sinner if you commit a crime or an immoral act. Otherwise, you are not.

You should study power, politics, and propaganda to survive in this highly competitive world and to navigate it properly. Otherwise, you will be crushed because of your good innocence. Keep the innocence in you, but don't be stupid again in any emotion. Your sense should prevail, and proper tactics should be used to save yourself from endless addictions and unnecessary spending.

But also don't be just a rational robot genius. Be a human. Visualization before doing something, meditation, and other various techniques should be used by you because they are not irrational. They are techniques of how we put our mind in a winning and trying mode, rather than just being lazy and using rationality to reason out everything to not do anything in life. Don't be a rational naysayer.

Never ever ever have regrets in life. Just try, it doesn't matter whether you succeed in it or not. You can at least tell yourself that you tried, but it didn't work, and after that, you do not suffer inside yourself until your death, when you suddenly realize later in your life that you wasted your time when you had the opportunity to make it and work hard for it, but you didn't.

Imagine yourself at 90 and attached to a wheelchair permanently. You sat in front of your house, and suddenly, after seeing something or someone, you remember the things you wanted to do in life, but you didn't do them because you behaved irresponsibly and wasted your time when you had it. All of a sudden, you realized how much you loved that thing you wanted to do in your life, and you wasted your time completely. And now there is no going back in time, and that's it. You see your family and your children. And you will think about how you would've given them a great life if you had succeeded in that thing you wanted to do in your life, and even if you didn't succeed in that thing, at least you would tell to yourself now that you tried and gave your best, but it didn't worked out for you. But you just didn't even try, and there is no going back in time now. This will haunt you till your death.

You will remember the people asking you to come to practice with them, or the plans you made to learn and train at something, but you didn't execute those plans. You will remember the places that you would've gone to, daily, to practice the thing you loved. But you didn't do any of that at that time. But now until you die, you will suffer inside of you. You will try to stop your tears by thinking about it 24 hours a day and scolding yourself for being an arrogant, useless time-waster you are when you had time.

Then, you will tell your children not to take the time and age they have now for granted and to use them to do great things in life.

So, if you are reading this and if you have energy in your body to do what you want in life, then please try to do it. So that you won't have any painful regrets that you can't correct, no matter how much you try later in life, in your super old age.

Many times, great inventions, discoveries, and things come from people who have had tough childhoods, different backgrounds, or painful lives. So, don't lose hope at all.

Be careful if you are an Ateestan. The mindless supernatural powers believers might attack you, injure you, or even try to kill you, and will try to pass it off as some supernatural power got angry and killed you. Be careful with those types of thugs.

No supernatural power can take humanity forward, but their own creative thinking, inventions, discoveries, courage, and risk-taking.

Ateesta is Ateesta. Don't mix Ateesta with something else to create confusion and negativity, or use it for personal gains and unnecessary controversy. Be careful of evil media-related stunts. They will try to label Ateesta as bad and other things to prevent people from knowing about it and learn from it. Because when people start thinking, then societies change drastically in short times, for the better, and many institutions and individuals who do not like it when people start thinking will come against Ateesta and Nathan.

If someone is using people's blind beliefs in supernatural powers for their personal gains, then question them and seek answers. Clearly verify their explanations with facts, even if you rationally cannot support what they are doing. But if their approach is legal and morally correct, with a genuine background and current work being clear, then you don't need to trouble them again and again, because they are not scamming anyone. They are just believing in supernatural powers, and they have the freedom and choice to do it.

Be careful of propagandistic interpretations of the Ateesta religion and Wuquin. Use common sense in interpretations of the Ateesta religion and Wuquin, with progress as the end goal.

People get scared by intelligence and rationality. When they know you know more than they do in many things, they automatically get insecure and might even brand you as evil for being different. So, be careful about where you show your knowledge and skills. They might even call you Satan, too. It is a classic trick.

No matter how rationalistic and intelligent you are, do not lose the pure innocence inside of you that makes you a human, a person who can love someone deeply with an endless ocean of love in the heart for the person whom you love.

Have an Internal Locus of Control rather than an External Locus of Control.

Ateesta religion should open your eyes at least, and should make you think.

Ateestans should always be very active as groups and individuals in politics, art, and business, etc, to gain strength and influence.

Emotions are like cunning dictators that make you think they are dead and have no power over you. But at the right time, they will come out, take over, and try to destroy you and everything by making you emotionally confused, and your rational thinking skills and intelligence, consciousness, weak. So be careful.

No life form on Earth believes in and worships any supernatural powers except man.

You have to live a good life as a good person, but sending someone to eternal Hell or eternal Heaven just based on their 100 years of mortal life is mindless when the age of the universe is taken into consideration and calculation.

In order to tell you how serious Ateesta religion takes murder and rape and other violent crimes, as the founder of Ateestan school of philosophy, I can tell you that if someone without any reason, without any mutual aggression and without any harm done by you to them in any form, came and killed/tries to kill you or seriously attacked you or people you cared about or attacked women in any form or tries to attack you, randomly then you must hunt the criminals who did it.

In those cases, criminals see the long durations of time that the justice systems and legal processes take as a joke. It gives them more confidence to commit more crimes, rapes, murders, and escapes.

If rape or any serious crime happens to you, your family, or to people whom you care about, then you must personally take the justice part as your responsibility and hunt the criminals who caused you the irreversible damage and pain.

Any criminal with arrogance who thinks they can rape anyone and kill anyone. And their victim families will not do anything to them, and legal systems will never catch them, even if they get caught, they can still come out of jail easily, they must fear you and your family. BUT YOU SHOULD FOLLOW THIS ONLY IF YOUR COUNTRY DOES NOT HAVE ANY TYPE OF LEGAL SYSTEM, OR WHEN THE CRIMINALS ARE OUT OF CONTROL. This is called the Ateestan Family Members Self-Protection Plan (Ateestan Family MSPP). You can form your own Ateestan religious courts, legal systems, and deal with those criminals and justice-related matters.

If your country has a legal system, then make it very active, strong, and effective.

For every hundred thousand population in the country, there should be a separate Rape Court and a Murder Court.

These rape and murder courts, per every hundred thousand population, will deal with rapes and murders related matters only, nothing else. They will deal with the cases in a legal manner and will deliver swift justice to victims. It will also reduce the burden on the judicial system. When the courts dealing with rape and murder become very active, then no criminal will escape the wrath of the law, whether they commit rape, murder, or make false accusations of any kind.

When the honorable judge is granting punishment to a criminal, the victim and the victim's family should have a say in the severity of the punishment. However, the say should only be about increasing the duration and nature of the punishment, not decreasing it in any way.

The minimum prison time for Rape is 240 Years.

The minimum prison time for Murder and Attempt to Murder is 240 Years.

The above punishment duration should be implemented immediately, even though human beings now have a maximum life span of nearly 120 years, scientifically approximately.

***

In the future, if new technologies allow human beings to live longer, and the person who committed the crime can afford that treatment, then they also have to serve 240 Years for rape and 240 years for murder, without any relief because for any reason, whether it can be good behavior or anything.

If someone is proven not guilty later, they can be released from prison legally. Just commit no crime.

No matter who they are, whoever it might be, if they commit a crime, the Ateestan government and legal systems are not going to let them go. They will, no matter what, face the wrath of the government and justice systems. That criminal will be taken out of society forever and will never be released from prison, that's it.

If your country and other countries follow this to deal with these types of extreme violent crimes, then within a short time, just in days, the crime rate will drop significantly, and in a much shorter time, it will become completely zero. Everyone will become civil and nice because everyone now knows that they cannot escape the law if they commit a crime like rape or murder. Everyone will try to solve every problem using paper and their mouths again.

The government should mass advertise this and how cruel this will be with criminals. The government should tell that no criminal will escape from its legal system's wrath if they commit murder, rape, etc, violent crimes. These mass advertising campaigns should go on permanently.

When your country can spend extreme amounts of money on meaningless things, why can't it spend money to build court buildings and hire judges and officers to make the crime rate zero? Rather than finding all the excuses not to do it.

Just because you are weak physically, financially, or in any way, you do not need to fear anyone if you are not doing anything wrong, no matter how strong they appear or are. Everyone knows that guns and swords don't need to know who is holding them. In society, you must be civil, and society also must be civil to you.

The country should be as safe as you or any woman or any kid waiting for a bus on the outskirts of a city or even in the middle of the desert should return safely to their home without anyone raping, killing them. Criminals should not be able to assume that they can escape after committing a crime, but they must know in their minds and hearts before thinking of committing a crime that the legal system will come for them, no matter what.

You and everyone in your nation must know that they must not kill or rape anyone. If they do, the legal systems will grab them no matter what or who they are.

But criminals should also expect people from the victim's family, whom they raped or killed, will be coming for them **if that country does not have a sound legal system.**

You should follow this only if your country does not have a sound legal system.

Instead of just as a family silently deciding to follow this, you can declare this socially that if anyone attacks you or your family, then you have adopted this Ateestan Family Members Self Protection Plan (Ateestan Family MSPP), and you proceed according to it.

You can do this declaration socially with other families who are adopting this self-family protection plan. Not just as families, you can declare you are adapting to this self-family social protection practice as a street, a village, a town, a city, a state, and as a country too. The criminals should know that no matter what, if they commit murder, or rape, etc, in any shape or form, then they are going to suffer at the hands of that victim's family **in the absence of sound active legal systems**. But to not make a mistake in the absence of a sound, active legal system, determine who committed the crime clearly and scientifically, rather than by emotions and in the rage of pain, even in the absence of a usual secular legal system. Ateesta religious courts should take care of this. If you have a secular legal system, then make it very strong.

Again, don't be emotional and don't do anything before knowing about the criminal completely. Never attack anyone who didn't commit the crime, even if technically they are considered by legal systems as a criminal and charged with the crime, and sent to jail. Or you assumed and imagined that a particular person or persons did it with limited evidence or creativity on your part. Only courts should take care of this, they can be secular courts or Ateesta religious courts.

The government must publish the names of criminals who have been proven guilty in cases of murder and rapes publicly, with their photos and addresses on a website.

Want to avoid all this mess? Simple, don't commit murder and rape, and other crimes in any form, that's it. Any false allegations should result in 240 years of prison time for those who make them. Not even a second less than 240 years. False allegations take away justice from real victims. False allegations conspirators must face the stringent, cruel consequences from the legal system primarily. Show no mercy on criminals, false allegations conspirators. You must treat them like a plague in a human's body. You must make sure these leeches don't take advantage of any laws and social customs or anything, and do extortion and blackmail, etc. False allegation conspirators' names must be published to the public through a website and daily announcements on all TV, digital, and print platforms by the legal system. But even for False allegation conspirators, if a crime is committed against them, then they are just like everyone else; they can go to the legal system and seek justice for themselves while facing the consequences for what they did with False allegations. Approach the whole process with great care and clarity combined with common sense and rationality, intelligence, and science through either secular courts or Ateesta religious courts.

No matter who you are, everyone is the same in the justice and legal systems. Criminals use their community, gender, education, or anything for that matter to escape from the consequences of false allegations and crimes committed. Criminals have no social attachments other than being criminals and trying to escape from the consequences of their crimes. Also, make sure you and your family members don't die in the process. A permanent tattoo should be put on the forehead of the criminal, as "Rapist" for a rape convicted criminal and as "Murderer" for the murder crime convicted criminal, and as "False Allegation" for the False allegation convicted criminal, after that criminal serves 40 years of prison time.

Criminals are humans, too, and they have rights, too. But the rights of normal people and the rights of their victims are absolutely more important than the rights of those criminals who commit rape, murders, and kidnaps, etc, highly destructive crimes. These crimes take the lives of people away from them and also destroy their future and families. Criminals should not be able to use any rights or anything, for that matter, to escape the punishment from the legal system.

Ateestans, save yourselves first and make sure you are well off financially and in terms of health and family relationships. Then only you will get the time and soft power to rule over the world in the long term.

At the societal level, never let another Tesla die in poverty. Always honor researchers of all kinds in science, technology, engineering, and mathematics (STEM) fields, etc, provide them with basic necessities, and give them respect. Their discoveries will give you an advantage over everything that is known and unknown to Mankind. Use those findings for your businesses and other things. Nothing wrong with it.

When facing an existential threat, never show your back. Fight, fight like a Lion. Eradicate, decimate, and destroy your enemies to the core. It can be at the individual or societal level of Ateestan. Never ever show mercy to enemies who came to destroy you. In one way or another, destroy your enemies completely to ashes. When Ateestans enter the war, the universe should shake. The destruction Ateestans cause while facing an existential threat should threaten the existence of planets and the universe itself. In a situation where Ateestans are completely going out of existence, then the same should happen to the universe and planet that the Ateestans are on/in. Your enemies need that fear in their hearts. Otherwise, at the time when they can kill you, they will kill you and take over everything that is yours, just because they can overpower you at that time.

Always avenge the enemies of Ateestans. Never forget. No matter who those enemies are. The war machines of Ateestans should teach mind-bending lessons to enemies of Ateestans at all levels. Every Ateestan woman is a Lioness on the battlefield. Every Ateestan man is a Lion on the battlefield. Rule the Kingdoms of All Known and Unknown Universes. The Lord of Lords and Emperor of Emperors, the God of Gods, God Yinta, is with us. No one can go against us, and if they try, then they will be reduced to dust. If anyone comes against Ateesta and Ateestans, then look at them as fringe extreme elements. Teach them a lesson in a way 1 trillion times stronger than the intensity of the heinous acts they commit.

I know this feels a little harsh to you, but the bullets and weapons of your enemies are much harsher.

At the time of war, remember, you are an Ateestan. And your God, Yinta, is the only hope for you and your fellow Ateestans. Burn everything to the ground that is coming against us.

No Mercy to The Enemy.

If the enemies want forgiveness, then they should not have come against us in the first place. That is the only way to give mercy to enemies.

8

Ask your government why there are no modern ticketing systems for raising different issues with the government. When big corporations are using software ticketing systems very effectively to solve issues, millions of them in days, then why can't your government use this technology of ticketing systems at least for a set of issues that are very critical, like roads and water, etc?

Ask your government to start implementing these ticketing systems for the public in a very simple manner, and hire more manpower to manage and solve issues.

Love the person who loves you. And never beg for love, that's it. If a person who loves you for who you are comes into your life, then they will be with you because they love you, not for your money or anything, and even if you lose everything, they will still be with you and support you to conquer the world.

If you run after a person who does not love you with their full heart, then you will see all the conditions of them to be with you, and they might leave you if they lose interest in you and find someone better than you in terms of material things.

I know it is super hard to control feelings and affection for someone if we love them intensely. Still, you must always be with a person who loves you when you have everything and also nothing.

You should love that person with great intensity and feelings, so that the person who loves you gets to experience the things mentally and physically that only a few lucky people get to experience. If they get that unusual intensity of love and feelings inside of them because of you, then they can clearly see the difference between you and others slowly. When certain situations arise, they may start liking your intense love much more and enjoy it suddenly, a million times more than they did before. You and that person will experience many great unexplainable things inside but that person whom you loved so intensely, after may be months or years, will suddenly and randomly realize after seeing other people and their love lives, or after facing certain situations, will come running to you and tell you how much they appreciate your love and care and will start seeing you as everything, literally everything in their life from that moment. So, love someone who loves you and love them so intensely, and also make sure that the person you love is also appreciating your love and care. This is for romantic relationships only, not for biological or other types of relationships.

The worst sin in life and in the entire universe is loving someone with great intensity who doesn't love you back.

If you love a person who doesn't love you back, then you love, you suffer, you smile, and also, you die, that's it. Some people make philosophies out of this to keep doing it, but just don't go this route. Also, don't hate them too. Just be a good person to everyone, but love those who love you back, and spend your time with people who love you, rather than chasing someone who doesn't love you just because you love that person with all your heart. Give that heart of yours to people who love you, and like you, and also love them back. It is much better, trust me on this. The world should be filled with love, but with mutual love and respect, not with the love of one side chasing and desperation.

To construct a house, you need a lot of money, time, and manpower, but to destroy it, you simply need a few seconds. Never underestimate the power of destruction and the patience needed for progress. Simplify the bureaucratic processes.

It is not by the number of years we live that the world recognizes us, but for the things we did when we were alive. Do great things not to get recognition but to achieve and live a meaningful life; recognition is just a bonus.

If you are a worker or an employee of any type, then your past and your experience should be expressed and revealed by you and only you. You must not be forced in any way by anyone to take any digital/ other type of account on any platform to prove your experience through some agency, thing, or someone else. It is your life.

You are the person who is going to work for a company or institution, not that agency or anything that certifies your experience in any shape, way, or form. It is the primary violation of freedom and liberty to force any worker or employee to take part in any platform that records their data to prove their experience or history, other than proving their experience and talent to the employer with their skills and knowledge for the job.

A company or institution can take IDs of workers and employees to confirm their identity, but no organization or company can force employees or workers to take or give any funds or any other types of accounts, where through those accounts or platforms, the government or others can access your information and work details and duration of employment history, etc, in any form. You must oppose those types of systems that will be used by the governments for spying and by companies to control employees in toxic environments, and make it hard for employees to move on from those toxic workplaces if they want to.

The private, financial, and personal lives of individuals should not be exposed to corporate or to any other entities in any way. People should fight to keep it that way. Anyone should know about the work you do and the money you earn only when you tell them.

Fight against corporate authoritarianism. Never let any government, employer, or anyone know where you worked in the past or about your personal life without your consent. In some countries, some types of funds are being used to track employees' data and employment history and restrict employees from working on their hobbies and interests in their personal lives. If the employee is suffering financially, this prevents them from taking another job, too.

It is a serious violation of the fundamental freedom of a human being. Companies in many countries are forcing their workers and employees to take some type of fund account or similar accounts so that they can control the financial life of an employee, because those types of accounts are usually only created and accessed by employers.

It is also to make those employees or workers depend on the money that they are earning from one job only. This prevents people from doing other jobs, working on their other interests severely, and restricts their financial life and making them depend on only a single job or work earnings, thus making them financially weak and obedient to those employers, no matter how much they abuse these employees and workers.

Extra incentives/pay must be given to employees/workers to compensate them for making them not taking other jobs.

Employees cannot even close those account numbers assigned to them, even in their lifetime. Those account numbers will record the workers/employees' jobs, their salary details, and their work locations completely, and if the government or any employer wants to trouble a person for raising their voice against any wrongdoings in society or company, then they can target that person easily with this data.

Many governments act like they are asleep in these matters, but in these matters, the governments act cunningly, and they will never ask companies/institutions not to force their employees to subscribe to those types of accounts if they don't want them.

Governments use these things to control the freedom of people. And they know it restricts the freedom and financial freedom of employees. Employees have to work on only one job, no matter how talented they are, and they have to suffer financially by not getting enough money for their talent and skills. And they propagate that it is bad and unethical to do two jobs, even if you are that talented and skilled, because there are many people who are unemployed. But those companies work on multiple projects at the same time, and those companies' owners own multiple companies, but expect employees/workers to do only one job. They will come up with all the corporate, rich-sounding words to create a scene and effect. All the rules, ethics are only for normal people, not for those companies/organizations, in many ways.

But the corrupt governments never tell clearly what they are doing to decrease unemployment with day-to-day reports. They give only broad, vague explanations, hiding behind legal processes and other things that normal people are not aware of in bureaucracy and government.

They also accuse talented people who move out of their country of being unpatriotic, while those talented people are restricted in many ways from increasing their income, and if the corporate system in the country that they are in is designed to keep employees as slaves to it through some types of tracking accounts and other platforms that record the data of employees. Create opportunities and pay them well so that talented people stay in your country.

These biased groups expect intelligent people and talented people to stay where they are and die so that their country will be developed and their ego gets satisfied, but intelligent and talented people are not like normal people who struggle to live and earn. They go where they are appreciated most. And there is nothing wrong with it.

What papers can't mouth can. What mouth can't papers can, when those both can't, then your hands can.

Always keep evil corporate companies' arrogance and dictatorial policies in check. Never bend to evil corporations. You must bend them. They are not doing any charity. They are doing business and using your financial vulnerabilities to their advantage. No matter what they say, they are cruel and cunning, along with the corrupt governments. But also respect their achievements. You cannot find fault with a horse if it kicks you because it is its nature, but you have to be careful with it and use it properly.

Corporate is not bad by default; only bad is bad.

* * *

Even in the most racist society, do not lose skilled and talented people, even if they belong to races or places that racist people don't like. Rationality, intelligence, and common sense do not care who you are or where you are from. Take those talented, intelligent people into Ateesta and save them from that racism and discrimination.

Never smoke. Specifically, never ever smoke and never do any types of drugs. Try not to drink alcohol or other equivalents. If you have to, for some reason, always drink at home. Never ever drink and drive. If you do, you deserve the death sentence.

Always keep governments and corporate companies out of your personal life. What you do in the time you are not working for them is entirely your wish. Fight if any company or organization/institution uses employees' dependency on their jobs to exploit them in any way. Just use and throw them for a job or anything, that's it.

As the last prophet of the Ateesta religion, I will tell you now how you can approach different things in life.

Birth rituals are a great way to celebrate life, but do not spend extravagant money on this in happiness. Celebrate, but don't spend overly if you can't afford it, by taking out loans. Instead, think about the child's life. Think about what kind of life you want to give to your child and what you must do to give a great life to that child.

Death is inevitable as I write this, but if there is a technology or science that can stop it, then gladly take it and live forever. If someone dies, then do the funeral process respectfully, to the person who died, and to others, too.

Human beings came up with many great stories, beliefs, and philosophies in many creative ways to deal with the thought of death or while facing it.

Unless they died from some contagious disease, Ateestans do not necessarily need to burn the dead body of a person. You can just bury them. You don't need to see your loved one getting burned in a fire after death if not necessary.

In the Ateesta religion, naturally, there is no worship of supernatural powers of any kind or anything in nature. But you can respect those supernatural elements and natural elements like the sun, trees, etc. You can meditate, too.

Pilgrimage to the Ateestan God Yinta Temple in Ateesta religion is a symbolic representation of the awakening and enlightenment of a person in a rational way, with common sense and calmness of mind, and to use it to the full extent for the betterment of humanity.

Always read broadly, and every Ateestan must read science, physics, psychology, human behavior, and technology-related subjects. Explore the things in the world and inside yourself to know what you want to become in life.

You must be morally good and eat healthy food. You must dress respectfully for the place you are at without compromising on your freedom of expression in any way.

You must behave politely with everyone and respect everyone, regardless of who they are.

Marriage is a decision, not an event. Marriage is a mutual decision to live together. Try not to spend any money on marriage. It's just a waste of money. You both have to be happy first, and no need to announce it to the world by taking loans and spending all the money you saved. Because many come to bless, drink, eat, and leave. But most of the time, no one will help you if you are financially broke or in need of money later. So, only spend money if you really want to. People who want the best for you bless you no matter what.

Take the freedom to live and love, absolutely, but not to hate.

There are terrible people in the world, but at the same time, there are people who are so good, so great, so pure-hearted and angelic. Never let the greediness and criminal mindset of a few make you narrow-minded. There are people who love you with all their hearts. Sometimes, it takes time to meet them.

Also, never ignore studying human behavior and psychology. It is best not to get betrayed while looking for or being in love with someone. People always use pure things to betray others and to gain trust initially. If you study psychology, power dynamics, and human behavior, you can understand many important things.

Men, never get a girl pregnant if you have no plans to be with her and take care of the child. Women, don't give a man the chance to get you pregnant if you are not sure whether you can marry him and have the confidence that he will be with you for the rest of your life.

Before marriage, while having sex, always sign a document that you are participating in the sex with your consent, and sign the document while you are sober. You can keep the same document, but use the dates on the document to sign it multiple times with the date, time before having sex. You can do it digitally, too. You can use this for other important things, too; even though it seems a little mechanical, you can be sure that you are not forcing the other person in any way to have sex with you. You don't need to feel anything strange or weird about this. If this is practiced by more people, then it will become normal. This also helps a lot in providing strength for both of you in dealing with fake allegations.

Always talk freely and openly about how frequently you want to have sex with your partner after marriage. You must talk about this before marriage, and listen to the other person's thoughts and ideas, or their explanation. If their explanation is okay with you, then you can marry that person. If you think their views do not align with what you are expecting, then think again, and if you are not sure, then don't marry. Why trouble that person unnecessarily later? Also, you have to suffer legal consequences if they are not okay with what you want.

Do not marry for money. Talk about divorce and who gets what before the marriage itself. Only if you both agree legally to the divorce settlement process will you marry. No man or woman should suffer because of marriage in any way, particularly financially. Keep this process clear and transparent. You should not get entangled in any unnecessary traps.

Love between a man and woman should be intense, chaotic yet calm, loyal, and should be felt by both of them as a storm. Otherwise, what is the meaning of falling in love?

Respect your mother, father, and family members.

March 14 is Ateestan's special day. Ateestans should celebrate March 14 as a symbol of progress and how great inventions can help people, and also have the potential to destroy humanity.

March 14 is Ateestan Human Festival.

Ateestans should celebrate March 14 as a symbol of progress, emphasizing rationality, peace, and a fine balance of human beings' minds to give importance to progress rather than war, and encouraging dialogue instead of war.

March 14 is the birth date of Albert Einstein, the scientist who came up with the $E=MC^2$ formula. We can use this formula for destruction and also for progress. So, we must encourage the use of great inventions and discoveries for progress rather than for destruction. March 14, as Ateestans Day, will remind us of this.

We also pay homage to great scientists, inventors, artists, and great people who did miracles with their work for the progress and well-being of humanity. You can eat good food and celebrate with your family and friends on March 14 without any type of alcohol or things like it.

On March 14, you can also work to bring awareness among the public through meetings and programs about rationality, science, Wuquin, Ateesta, and great people who have done great things for the progress of humanity.

Work properly for the money you are receiving in return for any job. It is your responsibility.

Help people. It doesn't necessarily have to be with money, but by your service or work that helps your community, too.

Respect nature and protect it. But balance the development and nature-related issues properly. You can do this if you use common sense rather than proceeding with delusional preconceived notions without proper scientific evidence and with stupid propaganda.

The flag of Ateesta:

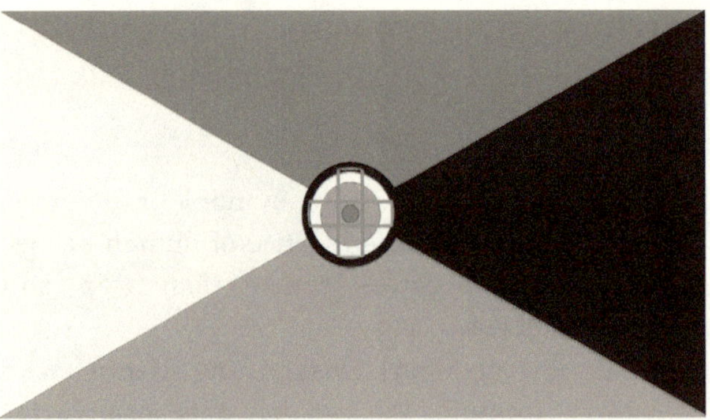

The Ateesta Religion Flag has triangles of White (left), Red(above), Black(right), and Green(below). In descending order from down to up, it also has black, white, green, and red circles in the middle and a prosperity '+' symbol(Orange) on top of those circles, with edges of '+' touching the black circle.

The Symbol of Ateesta:

***

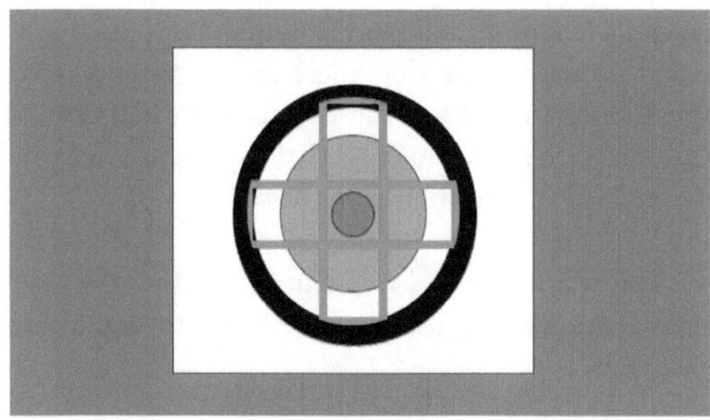

The Ateesta Religion symbol has a Red rectangle background and a white square in the middle. Inside the white square, in descending order from down to up, it has black, white, green, and red circles in the middle and a prosperity '+' symbol(Orange) on top of those circles with edges of '+' touching the black circle. ***The flag and symbol are also on the back cover.***

Ateesta religion recognized the importance of advanced technologies like Artificial Intelligence and Quantum Computing, etc. You must use them for the betterment of society and people, but not to destroy them in any way.

In times of disasters like fires, earthquakes, etc, always help people. Also, be careful.

Use advanced technologies and the science of all kinds to protect yourself and your country.

Even Ateesta religion and Wuquin should come only after the love for your country and family in your life.

Ateesta religion encourages brave explorations of planets and universes that are unknown to humanity.

* * *

If any alien life comes to Earth or if humanity finds alien life of any kind, your first task is to make sure that there are no threats from those alien life forms to humanity, Earth, and all natural life forms of Earth. Then you can allow them to come to Earth and stay here, or visit the Earth, but keep heavy surveillance on them.

Live your life in the real world and enjoy life in the real world first, then go for digital or other worlds. Don't get addicted to digital life technologies just for fun.

You can marry non-human entities, but do not proceed with giving birth to children who are not completely human and not completely non-human entities. They will suffer the unknown diseases, and there is a great chance that those human-alien children will die if they get any small illnesses too. Give birth to children only after you have sufficient evidence that they won't die at an early age.

Preserve the teachings of Wuquin using highly advanced technologies. Make Wuquin and the I Killed Satan - The Great War of Man and Satan novel impossible to destroy. Make sure no one adds any text to them and remove any text from them.

You can use advanced DNA technologies, etc, to preserve your bloodline if you think it is important.

Fight against any culture or religion that tries to ban or restrict music, literature, and entertainment.

Be very careful of news reports, sarcasm, and comedy made by cunning, hateful people with the masks of artists and comedians, entertainers, and news reporters. They use those as masks to make fun of a great cause and great people, to change the perception of the public on that great leader and the great cause. They use media and anything available to them to weaken the strength of support for that great leader and the great cause from the public. Find them and expose them. People who cannot think critically enjoy the comedy and think that anything that can be made fun of is not an important issue or not something to be taken seriously. These types of idiots in masses drag the society down in every way possible. Those cunning people also use these masks to criticize and attack other people's supernatural belief systems that they don't like, too.

Cannibalism & Incest in human beings are prohibited with no exceptions in any form.

You can use advanced technologies to upload your mind and consciousness to live forever in electronic form, or in a combination of biological and electronic forms, or in other ways. No problem with it. But you should not use it to harm others in any way.

When humans find an alien life and establish communication with it, they can work towards the creation of a universal language that is understood by both the alien life form and humanity.

Eradicate illegal immigration at any cost whatsoever.

Never lose your freedom and independence, even voluntarily, by becoming addicted to any technology or anything.

If you want to achieve something for your country or Ateesta, then remember, A gun can only kill a few, a ballistic missile can decimate a city, and a nuclear bomb can destroy the entire nation or the Earth, but words, words have the power to do things those weapons don't. Use the power of words efficiently so that you can conquer anything with minimal damage or even without any violence and damage most of the time.

Remember, when a system is unfair to you, only another system can fight it for you. Make the system that is fighting for you stronger, bigger, clearer, organized, efficient, intelligent, and rational. It doesn't matter what system you are fighting against, this is the way to defeat it.

You should not hate your enemy more than you love your children.

When common sense is seen as extremism in a society, you must correct it no matter what. When family systems and children are attacked, you must go to any extent to protect them, whether it be with politics or fighting.

Ateestans, through their science and technology, must make Earth the Type 1 civilization of the Kardashev scale as fast as possible. They must aim to reach Type 2 in the next 800 years after becoming a Type 1 civilization. This will weaken the superstitions and mindless supernatural powers beliefs automatically to an absolute zero. Ateestans must do anything and everything to make this possible. Then they must aim to reach other types of civilizations on the Kardashev scale as fast as possible.

If you are at the top in a field or even in a class, etc, then you must learn to be alone and mentally strong because you will lose all your mediocre acquaintances and sometimes friends, and also many times the moderately intelligent ones will start hating you because you are a competition for them now.

The people who don't know the technicalities of something inside out will always make your life hard with their nontechnical and utopian management policies. Remove those people who have no technical knowledge and skills from your systems and technical things of any kind.

If any government or people who hate Ateesta trouble you for being an Ateestan or always attacking Ateesta, then tell them that their intelligence will go down gradually every time they talk badly about Wuquin, Ateesta religion, or its followers. Don't worry, this solves all the stupidity being thrown at Ateesta, Wuquin, and Ateestans because people fear dogma more than logic.

***

There are great men and women who died and will continue to die, because we have limited time on Earth as of now as human beings. They contributed to the progress and prosperity of humanity.

But hypothetically, I can say that after death, these great men and women may go to Heaven or Hell, but no matter where they go, I'm 100 percent sure that they are more capable, intelligent, and have a great character and used their time as mortals on Earth more productively than God, Satan, or other supernatural powers in their existence when they were alive on Earth. I'm sure that these men and women have a greater attitude, character, and vision in their lives than entities or powers or God in Heaven and Hell.

Wholeheartedly, I can say that the great men and women on Earth who took birth as mortals have a greater character than the Supernatural God and Satan. Clearly, Man has a greater character than God. Also, Man is more cruel than Satan.

Edit your life. Not just books and movies, life can be edited too. How you edit your life depends on what type of decisions you are taking and the consequences of those decisions. Try to make better quality decisions that will make your life better.

The one who will take your women, your properties, and change your identity and convert you into his supernatural belief system always acts innocent, righteous, preaches peace and harmony, plants guilt, and shows all the highly respected qualities to his supernatural belief system's non-believers publicly. He will change his ways once he gets powers and the trust of non-believers. This supernatural power's believers are very cunning. They preach peace and harmony publicly to make you trust them and take your women and convert your women into their supernatural belief system to show their dominance over you. Soon after that, they will invade your countries legally through the social and political power they have, and they will disrupt your lifestyle, commit crimes for fun against you, your women, and justify them by showing their supernatural powers' teachings and books.

By that time, they will openly slit your throats and occupy your countries, but your politicians, in the name of being inclusive, will ignore your cultural eradication by those fringe elements and beg those extreme elements for votes or support. So, no matter which supernatural belief system you belong to and no matter whether you are an Ateestan or not, first, save your family, your ancestral culture, and your women from those fringe elements who justify their heinous acts by showing their supernatural powers' teachings to kill you, your culture, and your ancestral supernatural belief systems. Those fringe elements do not care about your supernatural beliefs or personal beliefs, or whether you believe in any supernatural powers or not.

So, first, ensure that the culture and supernatural belief system, as well as the family you were born into, are not facing death threats and are safe. Then, explore your life as an Ateestan in a full-fledged way. If you realize this now and research this more, and if you are trying to save people from those fringe elements, then you are Ateestan even before participating in the Ateestan Yan event, because you are doing the right thing. But when you find time, always become an Ateestan formally through the Ateestan Yan event. Also, you can join hands with other supernatural belief systems' followers who are also rational thinkers, to an extent, to eradicate those fringe elements. Nothing wrong with it. But just make sure that they are trustworthy and have a good history in these matters, and not betray you later.

You can organize these coalitions in a highly sophisticated manner to prevent any misunderstandings and betrayals from coming into the picture. It is because, no matter what, first, you should decimate the killers, culture invaders, in the name of their supernatural powers. And deport them or take any severe actions needed to any extent. If you fight within yourself, those fringe elements will take your women and destroy your culture and supernatural belief systems. First, eliminate those fringe elements, then resolve issues between you peacefully. Never show mercy on fringe elements of any kind.

Never take education for granted.

Imagine, when your friend is in an emergency, if you are a doctor, you can try to save him/her. If you have at least a good knowledge of biology, you can use it to keep your friend alive until you get to the hospital. While taking your friend to the hospital, you can use physics to drive fast and responsibly, and chemistry to understand how much the external environment will affect you and your friend during the trip. You can use psychology to make people give you passage to go to the hospital in crowded areas, and math to calculate the time it will take to get there. Additionally, you can use language to explain what happened to your friend to the doctor properly. You can also use technology in this process creatively to save your friend's life. If you just know one of these subjects well, it can help you a lot in those types of situations. Schools have made these subjects stereotypical (not just what is mentioned here, but other subjects too), as if you can only study them at school or university, college, but they are not limited to them. You can read and learn them like any novel or entertainment book, anywhere, at any time you want. These subjects are no different than movies you watch for entertainment. All you need is an interest in them to study them, and actually, they are more interesting than most things you do for entertainment.

Ateestans should create their own culture and customs of all kinds that differ from all other cultures and religions. But they should be only according to Wuquin.

You must not use Wuquin to demean Ateesta religion, Ateestans, and Wuquin itself.

Ateestans can follow their own Ateestan culture as a whole society, individuals, family, or groups, etc.

Ateestans' culture and customs include the creation of new music, creation of new languages specific to Ateesta, traditions, dressing styles, appearances, etc.

Make all the elements, names, etc, in the Ateestan culture and religion grandeur in class, clean and cool.

I wrote Wuquin in this language because I was asked by God Yinta. So that I can meet his followers without any waste of time. And this holy book will get translated into other languages ultimately. So, no problem.

* * *

Don't make any part of the Ateestan culture and religion dirty or unhygienic.

When we see a name, see a clothing style, listen to music, see a dance, or look at words of a language, etc., we will easily understand from which culture they come. Like that, Ateestans must develop their own culture and traditions, including the names of people and places, too.

Ateestans should also form countries on the basis of the Ateesta religion if the countries where Ateestans live are discriminating against them in any way.

Ateestans must respect their country and the land they are living in, but they form new countries only because of the reason that they are being discriminated against. Nothing more than that.

With time, the Ateesta religion and the Ateestan culture will become natural to the lands in which it is being practiced.

So Ateestans must focus on creating a rich culture with sacred customs and traditions for the Ateesta religion, but by taking only Wuquin as the base and inspiration for the creation and nature of cultural things.

You cannot verify history with total accuracy, just based on papers, and allow people to do things based on just those papers.

Like electric appliances have stabilizers to control the electricity flow in them optimally, a person should have an internal stabilizer in his/her mind to control himself/herself and emotions properly.

While protesting against injustice and corruption, wear and give the same protective gear, if not more advanced, to you and to your group as your oppressors, who are more singular and organized than you, administratively. Fight that organized evil with intelligence, not just by using blood. The goal is our victory, not our life sacrifice. Kill the oppressors, don't die.

Arrogance combined with an "I know everything" mentality is very dangerous. These people will destroy the lives of anyone. Be careful with them, particularly those who think they are superior to others, and of those who think they know everything and have some power with them because of the work they are doing, or if they are in any positions of power, or have money.

Ateesta is not just a religion but a way of life.

Hypothetically, the punishments humans receive in the Afterlife for the crimes they committed are mostly the same crimes humans punish humans for on Earth. What do you think about this?

Hypothetically, what pleasures does Heaven have in the afterlife that Earth doesn't have as of now? Also, what punishments does Hell have that humans can execute here on Earth? Mostly, they are the same as what we can do or have in both cases, but it is just your soul involved in the afterlife rather than your physical body. Taking the supernatural elements out in both cases, actually, ha ha, they are all the same, mostly as we got on Earth now.

Don't say like, Oh, God will be with you directly in Heaven, in the Afterlife, God created everything, and he is everywhere, and we are literally God's creation and living in his creation, right? Then why is Heaven after death special, and seeing God in that Heaven is that special? As we are literally his creation, and so is Heaven and everything, Earth and everything, so what difference does it make?

For any reason and in fights between Ateestans and Evil, kill but don't die.

When God can be in your contact in the afterlife 24/7 in Heaven, if you lived a good life, then why is God not in your contact, or at least told you in a way that he will be/was in your contact in the beforelife, too?

Hypothetically, why does God meet in the afterlife only? Why not when we are alive in our sound physical body? Why, when we are alive, do we have to pray extremely, worship so much, and do many things to see God through our physical body?

And if we pray and worship, just normally to God, but not praying and worshiping that extreme excessively, then we can see God only in the afterlife, right?

But why can't God show himself to us just when we are alive? What is wrong with it? Why do we have to go through so many things to see him when we are alive, as explained by the supernatural powers believers and supernatural powers teachings? If God just shows up on a busy street or in the sky, says a few words, then it will dismantle the supernatural nonbelievers, right, for eternity? With the technology we have now, it will be scientifically verified too, with no doubts whatsoever for eternity, and will be scientifically, factually true.

Why do people have to prove themselves that they are worthy of seeing God and talking to him by doing many things when they are alive? But after death, they get to go to Heaven for their good deeds and to Hell for the bad things they did. But why can't the same God show himself and talk to the person on Earth when he/she is alive, to do the same good deeds to a greater extent that helped him/her go to Heaven to prove that his supernatural teachings are real to that person clearly and rationally rather than asking for blind faith belief and supernatural powers believers showing so called proofs in the supernatural teachings itself? So is it like man is more valuable when he /she is dead, and it improves their qualification to see God in the afterlife?

For the evil deeds, our courts are already punishing people. So they have to go through punishments when they are alive, and after death, too, in Hell? It's okay for the criminals; they committed the crime, so there's no problem if they have to, but actually, they are seeing Satan or whatever supernatural power in Hell for their evil deeds, right? So even for Satan or some other supernatural power in Hell that gives punishment, even that too will not show itself to man when he/she is alive for their bad deeds? All this only happens in the afterlife? Isn't it weird and convenient for someone who wants to believe in those fantasies? And man is not even worth getting visited or talked to by Satan when he/she is alive? It is sad. The value of the human soul that comes out of a person after his/her death is higher for supernatural powers than when the person is alive in their physical body.

If people go to Heaven for good things they did by reading so called supernatural power teachings, then what about people who did bad things after reading and believing those same supernatural power teachings? Do they go to Heaven or Hell?

All these souls, afterlife, Heaven, Hell, etc, supernatural things do not exist in any way, shape, or form whatsoever. They are just good fantasy mixed with stories of sacredness and fear.

The mind of man adapts. It is its strength and it is its weakness.

Believing in supernatural powers is like believing there is no lion in your city apartment's bedroom. You are 100 percent sure that there is no lion in your bedroom, but when you open the door, there is a chance that there might be a lion in your bedroom, somehow, or might not. You might not see a lion in your bedroom ever, but you might also see a lion in your bedroom if the situation makes the lion come to your bedroom. You can be 100 percent confident and right, or you can be 100 percent confident but wrong, too. So, using rationality, intelligence, common sense, and morals is best to deal with these types of non-confirming, totally confirmed, certain uncertainty of a thing, and that thing can be anything and everything. Again, like you can explain why there is a lion in your bedroom logically, you can clearly explain any supernatural phenomena with science and prove clearly that there is nothing supernatural in the world.

There are many things I haven't talked about in Wuquin, but as the Prophet of the Ateesta religion, I can tell you, no matter what you do, where you live, and how you live, just be happy, be a good, kind person to yourself and others, never harm others in any way. Know the way of the world and use it, but still choose to be a kind person and use everything to your advantage, but do it consciously, don't be evil, we have enough of that already in the world. Be a chill, cool, positive, subtle-smiling, default cool, happy, positive mind stated humble person. Feel the cool breeze of calmness and subtle happiness on your face and in your mind.

As a prophet, I can guide you on important things, but you, as a human individual or an other-than-human equivalent intelligent life form to humans, have to explore the universe and figure out how you want to live and what you want to do with your life. There is fun in that life adventure.

Nothing is stopping you from living your life as you want. No one can tell you, and should not tell you, about every single small thing you have to follow, do in your life, or how to live your life. No one should tell you to live your life according to a mechanical system that was mixed with emotions and sacredness, without encouragement for thinking critically about it and questioning it.

Remember, God Yinta, through Prophet Nathan, is telling you now that Nothing is worth dying for. Live and achieve, but don't die. Kill the Killer, but don't die. Actively try to die only naturally in old age, not for any other reason. Enjoy life and live life. Life is a gift given to you by evolution itself; do not waste it.

Evolution gave you an able body, mind, blood, muscle, and bones like it gave those same things to the First Humans hundreds of thousands of years ago, and now we are here in this moment, I'm writing this, and you are reading this. You are no less than anyone in any way, and no one is higher than you. You have the same power, courage, and bravery as our ancestors, who hunted the lions and mammoths and led harsh lives courageously for hundreds of thousands of years.

Do not let the petty words of some incapacitated and incapable people, whose minds got twisted, divert you from becoming A Great Human Being. Go, Conquer The World!

I will tell you an important matter regarding the time in a year for you to follow as Ateestans.

That is, at the time I'm writing this, there were 12 months in a year from January to December.

I will tell you how you should see the months and the time of the year. The first month, January, the first 10 days are always filled with enthusiasm and excitement, so you won't feel like you are working. But after the first 10 days in January, people and organizations move towards more serious things, and then you will do your work like you usually do.

But then, due to festivals, other celebrations, and in the process of setting goals and determining work for the year from January 10 to March 1, you will work, but the environment will never be serious enough, and it will mostly be sub-serious.

But from March 1 to September 1, even though there are festivals, celebrations, and holidays, etc. But those holidays, celebrations, festivals, etc, feel normal and usual. People generally look at them as repetitive festivals and events that come every year, even if they are significant and celebrated widely. They generally feel about them like this, even when they were on vacation.

But from September 1 to December 31, what I call the 'minority time' of the year, the month of September will be used by people strongly to complete pending works and review and take further decisions, and in October, the general environment slowly shifts to less tense and more flexible overall, with fewer work schedules.

In November, people, naturally, at the societal level will become a little excited, and the people will also be in a 'looking forward to something great' type of mood.

People still work in November, but the work is more flow-oriented; they go down the line with what they have. And in December, they still work, but it won't be like starting something from scratch for critical new things unless it is absolutely necessary; they work, and people in general will be in a fun mood for the entire month.

So, if you want to do some super serious work and want your team or people to work hard super seriously and deeply, then in general, the good time is from March 1 to September 1. Between these months, everything feels usual, even vacations, and it is the boring time of the year at the societal level(not for Ateestans, of course), because of new developments, projects, and other important things that are being announced routinely, and people working on them routinely.

And between these months, March 1 to September 1, you can build foundations technically, and you can work on super hard, serious problems that need so much time to come up with a solution.

Yes, people can/will and are already working hard from September 1 to January 10, but at a societal level across all cultural groups and people, that time is generally exciting, both culturally and psychologically.

So, if something serious needs a continued flow of work with minimal to no distractions at all or if something needs serious society contribution and if people have to spend time on super hard boring things and solve most complex technical problems, then March 1 to September 1 is the best time because people at societal level are subconsciously ready to get bored. And even with a bit of discontent, they will contribute to that boring thing and will try to solve the hardest problems to a great extent.

But from September 1 to January 10, it gets a little hard to make people sit and work on technically complex problems or make them spend time on super hard, boring things.

As an individual if you want to work hard and learn something then you can do it whenever you want but to minimize distractions at societal level and also to be in a psychological pre-conceived notional subconscious 'Ready to be bored mindset' to push through hard things persistently then you must use the boring time of the year, March 1 to September 1 for doing deep super serious strong work, then you can sustain and overcome problems even when the process is dead boring.

But it is a little hard to work on boring things from September 1 to January 10. So, focus on doing fun things along with work from September 1 to January 10.

From January 11 to February 28/29, use this time period to get into the mood of deep, serious, disciplined work.

Then, from September 1 to January 10, work but also have a lot of fun too.

If, hypothetically, supernatural powers created the Earth and the universe, along with people in it, then why do those supernatural powers allow people who do not believe in them to take birth?

And after these nonbelievers take birth, why do the people who believe in those supernatural powers have to kill nonbelievers for not believing in the same supernatural powers that these supernatural powers believers believe in?

If supernatural powers have control over everything and created everything, then those supernatural powers can simply make people who do not believe in them not take birth, right?

Or after their birth, those supernatural powers can make those nonbelievers believe in them by showing their powers, magic, or whatever, positively and greatly, right?

Why do the people who believe in those supernatural powers have to defend those supernatural powers' belief systems and kill the nonbelievers and try to convert them?

Why human involvement in this process at all?

Supernatural powers can solve this problem in some way without violence or negativity, right? It can be done just by stopping the birth of nonbelievers or after their birth, by making those non-believers believe in those supernatural powers by doing something great and positive for them. As a human being, I got this, but imagine hypothetically, if supernatural powers exist, then what can they think of to solve the nonbelievers' problem by doing great things or by using their supernatural powers positively for those nonbelievers instead of threatening nonbelievers with eternal hell and suffering, and asking the believers to kill non believers like a petty local don trying to gain power over a small town.

But these supernatural powers are not doing positive things. They are continuously asking for their believers' support in one form or another through their teachings to defend themselves. Can't they do it for themselves without human involvement in any way, be it with believers or non-believers? I don't know how much good happened to people since the beginning of time and to humanity by believing in supernatural powers, but those supernatural powers sure got a great ego boost, if they exist hypothetically, and did more damage to humanity than good.

See, directly, openly, and in a straightforward way, a supernatural power can come to Earth and show itself to people, right? If it exists. What is stopping it from doing it, respectfully asking? Do the humans who want to see a supernatural power must die first? Why is that? Or do Humans have to become so good and pure that only then do those supernatural powers come? Is there anything like that? If yes, then clearly, by a supernatural power showing itself to people, it can change the world, right? The people will believe in that supernatural power 100%, and also fear Hell for doing bad things, too.

The world will naturally become good and free from crime in just minutes after the supernatural power shows itself to the world and talks to people. Science will accept that supernatural power, too. But why is any supernatural power not showing itself to the world? And why are we being given millions of reasons, explanations, and threats for asking the question of 'Why does any supernatural power not show itself to people?'

So, everything about supernatural powers is a carefully crafted and constructed fictional story and a lie.

The blind believers, by getting mentally ill from thinking that the nonbelievers of the supernatural powers that they believe in as low lives, and also by believing that the nonbelievers should either get converted to their supernatural belief system or should die, the supernatural powers believers are committing heinous acts in the name of their supernatural powers. This is utter stupidity. No, no Sacred Stupidity without common sense and without an ounce of intelligence and rationality. These types of supernatural powers, who say 'Believe in me or die and go to Hell', seem like kids trying to get chocolate from their parents. The kids cry and threaten and do silly things to get chocolates and ice cream from parents, like that, these supernatural powers, through their teachings, use every trick in the book to get people to believe in them. Haha! Just think about this. How childish is this?

Just because a book was written 1000 years ago or even a million years ago, it does not hold any extra value than a book that was written a day ago.

Because of its age, an old physical book might be considered an antique and invaluable, but its content and how it affects people are important.

Old doesn't always mean wise; it applies to books, too. Instead of shouting the age of books, systems and getting emotional, and assuming that some supernatural power will get angry when you question its teachings, first think, think like a human being before feeling the emotions like an animal, because dogs, pigs, and other animals, etc (I respect them) too have emotions, but only human beings have the skill of thinking rationally and critically.

So think rationally about those supernatural powers, books, and their teachings. Use your mind. Nothing should stop you from thinking critically about a book, teachings, or anything, for that matter, even if those things are respected, like devotion, supernatural powers, belief systems, or anything.

If something/someone is asking you to believe in something/ someone without thinking critically about it/them and without clearing your doubts, then run, run as fast as you can from them/that thing because they are trapping you, no matter how sacred you see it or they sound or how it is there in the world.

Any type of supernatural power is powerless if people stop believing in it. Supernatural powers do not have any supernatural powers, or any powers for that matter, and they don't even exist for love of humanity. It is just a great fantasy that started hundreds of thousands of years ago, from the moment when our human ancestors saw fire for the first time. That's it. The fantasy improved and was divided into systems of supernatural beliefs over time. And people tied their way of life and the knowledge they gained through the years and centuries around those supernatural powers figures they imagined, fantasies, and formed cultures and religions. That's it.

Our Human ancestors millions of years ago, when they got too close to fire, it burned them. When they went too far from the fire in fear of getting burned by it, it started to become cold. So they learned to keep a safe distance from the fire and to handle the fire safely, while fearing that the fire would burn them if they got too close to it, but also, fire provides heat, comfort, and keeps the wild animals away. This punishment for carelessness and a reward for carefulness relationship with the fire made our Human ancestors build respect for the fire and devotion, discipline while handling the fire, this is the basis for all the modern fearing God, loving God, and God's punishment theologies. The fantasy improved, that's it. We gave meaning to our needs and problems, it became God, ultimately. We made sense, and called it God, not realizing that it is science, and got deviated into the dogma, ignoring the details. In the comfort of fire, we killed the people who understood the underlying logic of fire deeply and were experimenting with it, as we saw the fire as mysterious and a higher than human power. Some resisted going forward with experimenting with the fire for cooking, etc, and some welcomed it by seeing the more comforts and advantages while taking the risks with the fire.

Because lightning strikes appear like they are coming down to Earth from the sky, some thought there could be someone doing that, who is powerful enough to do it, which became the God of one type. And some saw the same spark coming out of rocks colliding with each other at greater speeds, so they thought there must be some higher than human power within these rocks, too, which is why the sparks of fire are coming out of these rocks. It created Heaven, Hell, and initial theologies of Gods from their own point of views, perspectives and derivation of meanings behind the natural phenomena, all while not realizing that they are actually using that creation of fire techniques to survive strongly and also developing philosophies to give meaning to the things they were seeing regularly and learning to replicate them manually to control and use them, while developing pure science but giving them meaning through philosophy and attributing meaning to those learnings and observations so that they will not forget them, (This process helped our human ancestors to not forget their learnings but they didn't start giving them meaning with intention of not forgetting what they are learning or their understandings of observations but because of the nature of man and mind, that is, to give meaning to things and purpose to exist) and with time the science got separated completely and became an independent system, and meaningful philosophy that they developed was turned into beliefs and further improved and explored, eventually creating great philosophy schools and also supernatural belief systems, those philosophies and supernatural belief systems with new observations of other natural phenomena and development of philosophical theories, concepts based on those observations and learnings, and the understanding of those new natural phenomena that was not seen before and deriving, drawing and attributing meaning to those new observations and learnings, those supernatural belief systems progressed in their development in levels, and then those supernatural belief systems turned into dogma and blind belief faith systems, as science separated itself with deep observers, thinkers who are understanding and learning underlying logics and technicalities separated themselves from just surface level believers.

And now, some fools are feeling sacred and auspicious for detonating themselves and killing themselves and others in the process just because the others do not believe in the same-meaning God that they believe in.

Imagine, from, millions of years ago, the meanings that people are deriving and coming to conclusions and attributing meanings to things, and understandings of things progressed and in those processes, psychological experiences, people who have mental health problems writing and saying, doing things etc (I respect them), and things that are not easily understandable happened which we can't derive and attribute meaning to that easily and they saw them and felt them, some people tried to come up with new meanings to observations and some self-understood things on their own in their own perspectives, then came up with concepts, theories, things for good, and some people came up with those things, created those types of things for bad and to gain power etc, like this trillions of things happened, all of them combined resulted in the supernatural belief systems that we have now.

From feeling the wonder of seeing something extraordinary while seeing a lightning strike creating fire, to seeing sparks coming out of rocks while they collide with each other, humans slowly developing sign languages, drawing on walls of caves etc, to creating first spoken words language, to creating first writing script, to learning to make paper and writing on it. In all of these processes throughout millions of years, trillions of things came together logistically, physically, psychologically and total knowledge of humanity up to those points in time, understandings of things, understandings of and about the world by our whole humanity combined in those contexts, and recording them in various forms, initially just out of curiosity with no intentions of recording by doing the things like drawing, art in caves by first humans, to oral knowledge transfer intentionally, to writing what we learned, millions of years passed in this whole process.

If you observe, wherever there is the concept of supernatural elements and God, in that time periods along with that belief in that God, you will see great philosophy and many meaningful things, but along with them lots of irrationality and belief in supernatural things, God etc, too, sometimes they threaten to kill or send you to Hell to for not believing in that God, supernatural powers too, because they think that how a person can deny existence of God, a supernatural power even after seeing all this great philosophy and stories of God and supernatural powers.

While totally ignoring the fact and mostly not aware of that, their scientific understanding of things that are quantitatively measurable is deeply flawed, mostly, and they perceived and understood them, and observed things by giving meaning to them according to their existing beliefs and what they thought was good.

That is why, scientifically, many observations and meanings of these supernatural belief systems are flawed, but their philosophy morally and ethically feels alright, mostly. Different supernatural systems, according to the time they came and created and developed in, used all the existing known philosophies and meanings in the world, also their things that are convenient to them that are known to them up to that point in time when they are creating, writing and developing them, and also they added their own concepts, theories, philosophies and meanings, creating new supernatural belief systems.

When, in parallel, pure science is being developed theoretically, they suppressed and killed those scientists because those scientists' creations and rational, logical explanations of things and natural phenomena, and their new inventions, discoveries, were clashing with these deeply constructed supernatural belief systems' philosophies and beliefs.

Science gave literal true meanings to things technically, factually, quantitatively, where twisting them for our convenience, for our own beliefs, is impossible. This caused upset among the supernatural belief systems' believers and authorities, and they saw science as a threat to their power and beliefs. And then, when politics mingled with these beliefs to appease those people and to control them and organize them, the mainstream science vs God debate slowly started.

Finally, Humans are intelligent enough to distinguish these things and came up with state and religion separations and secularism, freedom, liberty, push for science and technology.

In all this process, the ways, blueprints to live life were given by those supernatural belief systems to people with their own philosophies and beliefs. That helped people who can't think for themselves on how to live the life a lot, and simultaneously, Science also gave that way and blue prints to live life more clearly, strongly and in great comfortable ways, but it didn't appeal to people at the same intensity as the supernatural belief systems' ways to live life, because science is not that strongly emotionally relative and connecting to masses as supernatural belief systems.

That belief in supernatural powers and God in those supernatural belief systems slowly turned to dogma and blind faith too, up to the point that they are ready to kill people for their beliefs just because someone wrote something a few thousand years back about the Gods that they believe in, and now the people that they want to kill are going against those writings of their supernatural belief systems, without realizing all these things, this reality and the way the things happened.

The politics, politicians, rulers, and kings, emperors, leaders of tribes and groups solidified these beliefs of people in supernatural powers and God, not because they also believe in them but that for using them to appease people and to get people together and to organize them, make them behave in similar ways that are safe for rulers and for cultivating predictable behaviour in them, and instilling fear, respect in them on their kings, leaders etc and to rule over them is easily.

So politics always fueled and increased the beliefs of people in supernatural powers, God, than in science, from the time our first humans roamed Earth in tribes and groups, to today, where there are greatly developed, organized religions.

Politics always discouraged questioning nature and critical thinking in people indirectly, without saying it explicitly, but very strongly by encouraging these beliefs in supernatural powers, and also encouraged severe, blind beliefs of people in Gods, supernatural powers.

That is why people who believe in these supernatural powers, Gods, always try to justify themselves by saying that their God-Creator is real because in their religious books, they have some explanation or fact, some observation, a clue to something that is factually correct, and by coming up with an explanation for it, that is scientifically verified. And they disown and give other explanations for other things in their books that are scientifically wrong.

They try to use science as something to verify the existence of their God-Creator because something that is there in their book is correct scientifically, and thus their God creator is true, all while not realizing that the science itself has trillions of things like that that absolutely factually, rationally true and science is not asking for people to believe in it separately because it doesn't matter where someone believes in science or not, it is the truth.

They use the things in their supernatural belief systems books to prove that their religions are real and science too is saying this because somethings in their books are scientifically verifiable but while ignoring the fact that all of them came from humans and mingled with many things with regards to the times that they were written, created in and passed on orally and written forms, and that is why in every supernatural belief system, there are many things that are new and also some things that are observed in existing philosophies and belief to those times and also, they include some scientifically verified things too that are true even in those times before science strongly developed independently.

If science verifying something in their supernatural belief systems' books is making those supernatural belief systems real and their Gods true then all of the science is factually, rationally, technically, mathematically true, at least it tries to be true factually and rationally because it has no alternatives and it does not rely on beliefs, then why don't these supernatural powers believers who use try to use science to prove the existence of their Gods just accept that science itself is God rather than using science to prove that their God exist? Ha ha. Don't say this to blind faith believers, they might even try to kill you!!

Even according to their beliefs, science is also a creation of God, right? But they want you to believe in their God, and they will even use science to prove the existence of their God, but they also want you to stop going forward exploring science on this subject and simply stop there and believe in their God. Because they fear that if you go deep and start critical thinking, you might even start to doubt the existence of their God and all the Gods too. They will do anything to stop that critical thinking and exploration, because it has the power to make you realize things, many important things on your own that no one can teach and explain to you, rather than just believing in their Gods blindly, they fear that questioning nature in you so much that, if you question them, they will even brand you Satan or some evil power and will kill you.

Like this, there are trillions of things, concepts, beliefs, fears, integrations and crossovers of things and creations and thoughts, ideas etc, for millions of years before they were cooked in different permutations and combinations with trillions of new add-ons and they were orally passed on, written in recorded forms, and those beliefs, philosophies are explored by people who believed in those supernatural belief systems and, that created beautiful ethics and morals and beliefs to follow, too, and also dogma and blind faith at the same time.

All while science and people who are learning things factually, quantitatively, even without realizing that they are scientists developed food habits and hunting methods, and sleep routines, and in that line, we came up to a point that we developed the nuclear bomb, Artificial Intelligence, and Quantum computing, etc, highly advanced technologies.

Because Human emotions and beliefs are so strong that, even after millions of years and even after science and rationality being developed to a great extent independently, we still can't let go of our beliefs in supernatural belief systems, supernatural powers, and Gods, so we took them from one form to another. Our ways of living and routines of life were culturally mingled with those supernatural belief systems and Gods. And they became cultures. So you can follow, live in any culture, and not believe in that culture's associated supernatural powers and Gods. And you know why now.

Many times, these supernatural powers believers attributed supernatural qualities and higher than human divinity to some people, too, who are very good, so that the normal people will behave like them, be good, and live in those ways. They also became supernatural belief systems, and those people's lives and teachings became holy books.

***

Simply, the fantasy is improved. With the mix of trillions of things.

These supernatural powers believers of all supernatural belief systems fear people who do not believe in any supernatural powers at all a lot, actually more than the people who believe in different other kinds of supernatural powers and belief systems that they believe in.

Because there is common point if someone believes in some kind of supernatural power, you can convert them and tell them something to make them a believer in the God you believe in, but if a person is a non-believer and also do not believe in any supernatural powers, Gods at all, then that person become a threat to entire supernatural powers believers and Gods believers.

Because you will question their beliefs from a fundamental level, and if they can't answer, they will lose their existing believers who can understand what you are saying. So, they prefer to have supernatural powers believers first, it doesn't matter which God or supernatural power you believe in, they can either convert you or fight you, kill you or leave you alone but if you do not believe in any God, supernatural power then can't have a dialogue with you to persuade you to make you a believer of their God, supernatural powers. Certainly, they will try to kill you and feel great about it as they think that they are pleasing their God, supernatural powers, by killing you.

Dogs, Pigs, Elephants, Lions, and other animals do not have any religions of their own right? Then why do only humans have religions? What do you think about this?

Why did supernatural powers give great intelligence and rationality to human beings only?

If supernatural powers gave high intelligence and rationality to humans through their creations, then why don't they give the same to other animals like Pigs, Dogs, Lions, and other animals? Just why?

Do you think Human Beings are that special to Supernatural powers? Ha ha! Or do the supernatural powers think that those animals do not deserve as much intelligence and rationality as humans because they are lower than humans by the nature of their birth?

Are the animals, are of lesser value to the Gods than Man? And Man is so special to God? That is why God gave intelligence and rationality to Man? Ha ha! If it is true, then those supernatural powers are racist and discriminatory. If the animals, by the nature of their birth itself, are designed that way, then those supernatural powers are not good creators. They are just creators who gave humans intelligence and rationality, and in return, they are asking for human beings' loyalty, devotion, worship, and prayers. It is a business for them and for us, too.

If supernatural powers give intelligence, rationality to animals like humans with the ability to talk and do other things like us, then they also can pray to those supernatural powers. right?

Does God not want those prayers and worship from animals and want prayers and worship from only humans?

Religion and Culture are one way to live, and you have many ways to live with/without them, too.

Actually, animals too have religions of their own, and those religions are 'the way they live' and their cultures are 'the way they behave'.

This is why Human Evolution is the greatest thing in the universe, even after we discover or are discovered by alien life forms.

You must not hate anyone mindlessly, it is a costly price to pay for nothing in return except your own destruction mentally. It is because there are many people in the world who are rich and do not have to worry about day-to-day survival, but many of those people live horrible lives.

It is because, even though they are not struggling for day-to-day survival and are rich, their day-to-day activities in life and the way they do them, and in general, their nature and attitude become an irritated and frustrated hate magnet with time, and also because of the way they deal with things with an ingrained irritated nature daily. That hate, irritation, frustration, and negativity, in small amounts, stay in their minds. Then, that negative hate irritation and frustration, like a highly contagious disease, gets spread to their other fresh and good thoughts in mind and decision-making process, and in this way, their whole life gets bitter every day actively continuously. No matter how much money and a great family they have, they will not be happy. Don't become a person like that. Be a calm, cool, chill person in general. The side effects affect everything in your life. So hate only when it is super important, otherwise just go on your way and live your life happily. Why trouble yourself with unnecessary hate on something in your mind?

All religious and supernatural powers' believers eat food and wear clothes, marry, have kids, and do many things according to their religions and cultures, but what they forget is that even though their style is different, they all are doing the same thing. Just in their own ways.

Because, basically, belief in supernatural powers and being in a religion is just an anciently designed system to live life in that religion's way. In those ancient times, many people didn't know how to do that, and not everyone was knowledgeable enough to figure out on their own and create their own path, so they used these religions and their cultures to know how to live a life and did that, that will support them mentally and logistically with a mix of stories, beliefs, and sacred commitments and unites them for their protection against their enemies and other problems.

Also, carefully designed beliefs in people on supernatural powers to control and make people behave well, worked, and sometimes backfired, but mostly, they helped to put people in control and helped rulers and authorities to organize them at the societal level en masse properly. But now, you have enough intelligence to research and design your life based on how you want to live it. You don't need those old ways of living.

Ateesta Religion gave a system of living from birth to death for people, and it will replace traditional, old, ancient, and outdated religions.

***

It is the time for Ateesta Religion to make people's lives happy and prosperous for eternity. Ateesta will make people use rationality, common sense, and intelligence as common things rather than seeing them as traits of a genius.

No God, no supernatural power is overseeing you when you are driving on the road. Drive safely and consciously. You are on your own, not just in driving but in everything you do in life.

Our ancient humans started creating supernatural beliefs, systems, stories, and cultures hundreds of thousands of years ago, and by believing in developed versions of those supernatural belief systems and following their cultures, we, now, are denying human evolution and our ancient humans themselves. It's a paradox.

The coal we use in our daily lives is the result of literally millions of years of pressure on dead trees, animals, etc, in the Earth.

If being very old validates something to be worshiped, then we should worship coal because coal is much older than all supernatural belief systems and their books, Ha Ha. So these supernatural powers created trees and other life forms on Earth, then those life forms died physically, and their physical bodies went into the Earth, and under pressure for millions of years, those life forms' physical bodies turned into coal and fossil fuels.

And then, one day, the supernatural powers decided to create humans, and we are here now using that coal and petroleum. And that coal and petroleum took millions of years to form. But that coal and petroleum predate all supernatural powers' belief systems, their teachings, and their books.

But in supernatural belief systems' books and teachings, those supernatural powers say they created those life forms through their creation. What kind of mental illness is this?

Where did those dead animals and plants' souls, and possibly earlier forms of dead humans' souls, go? Whose physical bodies turned into coal and petroleum after their death?

To Heaven? To Hell? Where? Or are they just turned into carbon dioxide, water vapor, etc., coming out from our vehicles?

And these supernatural powers believers use vehicles to travel to these supernatural worship places by literally turning those poor dead creatures and lifeforms remnants in the forms of coal and fuels into energy and C02, Water vapor, etc, Oh My God Yinta!!

Do supernatural powers follow their own teachings? Or are they only for Humans? In their universes, do the supernatural powers have different kinds of morals, ethics, and laws, etc, than what they taught human beings of Earth? If it is a yes, then what are they? How do they clash with the teachings they gave to the Humans of Earth? Are those supernatural powers alone in their universes, because most supernatural belief systems have only a set of a few supernatural powers, right, at their core? Do they feel lonely in their worlds? Or should they have to do any work like maintaining what they have created, or general maintenance, or are they creating any new creations like Earth and the universe we live in right now? And are they giving new, different teachings to their newly created life forms, other than humans, or giving the same kind of teachings to those other life forms, too, as they gave to humans? Why did supernatural powers give their teachings only to human beings on Earth? Why don't they give their teachings to other life forms on Earth, too? Are other than human life forms not eligible to get the teachings from supernatural powers? Or are there any other reasons? Do supernatural powers have friends in their universes, and how do they exist in their regular lives in their universes? Do those supernatural powers get bored because of all the work they are doing with their creations, and what do they do for fun? Do they get sad too when the humanity they created goes in the wrong way, with all the crime and hate?

God himself created the universe, and God himself literally came to Earth to spend time with his children. This happened in many supernatural belief systems, and God and angels also came to Earth to talk to their Prophets occasionally, too.

When their own supernatural belief systems' believers convert to other supernatural belief systems for money or other things, then how do those supernatural powers feel? Do they feel sad or get angry?

What one supernatural power from one supernatural belief system thinks about another supernatural power in another supernatural belief system?

What does the God of one supernatural belief system think of another God in another supernatural belief system? Do they hate each other or respect each other, or at least do they know that the other exists, or do they just tell their Human followers to believe in their own supernatural belief systems only, and others are false?

If other supernatural belief systems are false, then did those Gods of those supernatural belief systems lie to their own followers, or was the supernatural power that said other supernatural powers and Gods as false, is lying to its own followers?

If all the supernatural powers gave their teachings to humanity to make humans live their lives according to the supernatural belief systems of their own, and then claim the other supernatural belief systems are false, fake, and their teachings are not worth following, then who is real and who is false? Because all they are offering is Heaven, and have Hell along with God and teachings, but just in their own ways.

If supernatural powers hate each other through their teachings and tell their believers to kill the nonbelievers of them, then are they even worth the prayers and worship from human beings or from any other life forms, for that matter?

Do supernatural powers hate science and rationality, too, which tell people that those supernatural powers don't exist, and to think critically? But science and rationality are also part of supernatural powers' creations, right? The good parts, actually. So, do the supernatural powers hate science, which they created, which is saying that Supernatural powers do not exist? And also the process of searching for supernatural powers through science? or do the supernatural powers want their believers to discard science, rationality, and just follow their teachings and worship them? If yes, then I feel sad for you if you are a believer in supernatural powers. Hypothetically, since science is also their creation, and it is telling us that supernatural powers do not exist, should we accept it unconditionally? Or is the science not yet developed to the point that it can find the supernatural powers? I think not so.

If supernatural powers value science and the development of

humanity, then they could have taught science and technology through their teachings clearly, along with their religious and spiritual, etc, related teachings. Not just supernatural powers' believers interpreting vague things and attributing science to supernatural powers ' teachings in a vague way, or in an opportunistic way. But they didn't.

If those Gods know science, then they can clearly reveal the science; there would be no requirements for those Gods' believers to attribute science and technology to those Gods' teachings through interpretation and by showing some vague things that are flexible for multiple interpretations in the teachings as clues of science and technology.

Hypothetically, God never imagined that Man would come up with science.

God never imagined rationality in Man.

It is the Human Evolution on Earth that gave Man his Intelligence, Rationality, and with them, Man developed science.

Why did the God who created Humans not tell them about the diseases they get and how to cure them? Why should science take that responsibility? Why, in the hypothetical God's great creation, do humans get diseases? If humans have to die, let's even excuse this big limitation of Death that God put on humans, but at least God could have made humans disease-free and told them they will only die at old age naturally, right? What's wrong with that? While taking unnatural deaths in accidents, etc, as exceptions for artificial death.

Do the supernatural powers want humans to find them through science and rationality? Or through only death and their teachings? What makes more sense? What do you think?

Nothing is Permanent, Except You. Because when you die, nothing matters. When you are alive, your life matters. After your death, you no longer exist anywhere, so for your lifetime, you are permanent, and everything is temporary. So take care of your family and live happily. Plan a good future for your kids and take care of your family when you are still alive. Because, as you die in old age, they have to live after your death. The money or whatever it is, is also temporary, and you are permanent. Because nothing matters to you after your death(Physically only, not saying that you do not care about anything after your death. Of course, you do psychologically about people and things you loved while you were alive), but because you are no longer there in any way, shape, or form anywhere, you should use your life to full extent when you are alive. The Death, that's the end of you. That's it.

No one is coming to save you and your family, except you. No supernatural power is coming to save you and your family. Save yourself and your family from problems and give yourself and your family a great life while you are still alive.

Build the world with Rationality, Intelligence, and Common sense as paramount.

How did those supernatural powers get their powers? From where? From who? How? Why?

Just think, why the praying to supernatural powers give you good things in life? Why?

What do those supernatural powers get from you through your worship or prayers?

Why do you have to pray or worship them for good things to happen to you?

Are those supernatural powers that are great, pure, and above human?

Just why? Why do humans have to pray to those supernatural powers?

And why do supernatural powers give good things to humans only through worship or prayers?

Why do humans have to bend their necks to those supernatural powers?

These supernatural powers are expecting humans to praise them and say that those supernatural powers are great and super great in all of the ways and forms, to be favored by them continuously. This is such a petty ego issue. Those supernatural powers just want humans to praise them. That's it. And those supernatural blind believers do it with singing, dancing, etc.

Why are supernatural powers so Egoistic and Arrogant that only because you are worshiping and praying to them, then only good things happen to you? If not, then bad things happen to you, ha?

Can't those supernatural powers do good even without receiving any prayers or worship? What's wrong with that?

These supernatural powers are like you must buy my subscription through your faith in me, then only I will help you, Ha ha ha!

Is your worship and prayers that important to those supernatural powers?

If your worship and prayers are that important to those supernatural powers, then they are just desperate and constantly need validation from you through your prayers, by you saying those supernatural powers are great, and you want them to save you and help you. And then, actually, you are more important to that supernatural power than that supernatural power is to you. Also, we have many types of supernatural powers, but only a limited number of humans. So those supernatural powers must be fighting within themselves to win over you as their believer, ha, ha! Or their blind followers might try very hard to convert you to their supernatural belief systems because their supernatural powers teachings told them to do so. So that they can go to Heaven for converting you, and you will also go to Heaven for converting yourself too. Haha! Everybody was promised Heaven if they simply believed in supernatural powers and their teachings, so someone can be a criminal idiot who committed millions of crimes, and at the end of his life, that criminal can just convert to some supernatural belief system which promises Heaven for just believing in it and can go to that Heaven by erasing all the worst things and sins he/she committed on Earth, right? Oh My God Yinta!! Ha Ha!

Ateestans are God's people.

Anything that is making you hate other human beings and other life forms just because they do not believe in what you believe is the worst, stupid, egoistic, arrogant, dirty, yucky thing posing as sacred. No matter what it is, even if it is a supernatural power, and its teachings. It is the same worst, stupid, egoistic, arrogant, dirty, yucky thing posing as sacred, even if that supernatural power exists in the real world hypothetically. Burn those books and those teachings of hate. We, Human Beings, do not need that supernatural power and its teachings, and the good it will do if people believe in it, even if it exists hypothetically. Because what good will it do to the world if that supernatural power is asking you to hate other human beings just because they do not believe in it, and why should it give you good things for believing in it? Human beings do not need that goodness from that supernatural power, and also the hate it propagates through its teachings. Not just some petty humans, these supernatural powers are also trying hard to keep their identity alive through their teachings of hate.

Ateestans, you should never be on the streets between 11:30 PM and 4:00 AM unless it is something super important that requires you to be on the streets. If you want to party, or work, or want to do anything, then do it at home or anywhere, but only in indoor spaces or at places that are very familiar to you.

Generally, Nothing good happens between 11:30 PM and 4:00 AM on the streets. Even though Ateesta do not encourage any type of superstitions and supernatural beliefs, Ateestans are still asked to stay inside at midnight from 11:30 PM to 4:00 AM and do anything they want only in familiar indoor spaces or at home during that time. You can save yourself from serial killers, psychos, and many other antisocial elements who do not have any reason to harm others but do it just for fun. Particularly, never be on the streets in places where you don't know much about between 1:00 AM and 3:59 AM. Trust me on this one. The day could be January 1st, or any festival or celebration. Follow the Night Time Rule of Ateesta. At least try. Governments should mercilessly take action against those anti-social elements, like serial killers, and other criminals who get activated at night and cause harm to people.

You can visit 24/7 malls and restaurants, etc, which are safe. You have that freedom, but never be on the streets randomly at night in places that are not familiar to you, or even if they are familiar, and do not have at least a few people on the streets at that time.

In the Name of One True God, Yinta, never be on the streets or in strange, unfamiliar places to you at 3 AM. No matter what you believe in or not. No matter whether you are a rationalist or a supernatural believer, you could be anyone and believe in anything, for that matter. I, the Last Prophet of Ateesta, ask you not to go out searching for problems; you are not supposed to have or do not relate to the world you are in and to your mortal life. You will never have a good reason to be on the streets and on the outskirts of your cities, villages, towns, etc, at 3 AM. So just don't. Nothing wrong with staying at home or in a safe indoors at night for a few hours, right? If there is no emergency. If you really have to go somewhere or be somewhere or have to do something, and have a solid positive reason to travel at night, then you can do it even at 3 AM or 2 AM. Nothing is wrong with it. But still, if you can wait, then wait and travel after 4 AM. I, the Prophet of Ateesta, saw what you didn't, and Ateestans do not have to go through any of those negative experiences and things just for being in the wrong place at the wrong time. Even while traveling at those times, if for any reason you have to stop and come out of your vehicle, somewhere on the highway or anywhere for that matter, always stay in front of the vehicle where the light coming from the vehicle hits you directly and where people can see you. Never go to the back of the vehicle for any reason at all. No matter what the reason is. Unless your vehicle malfunctions, even then, go in groups, check the issue.

Ateestans, never make fun of something that you don't know properly. Particularly, the safety practices.

Never make ugly criticism of feminine-natured supernatural powers, particularly. It doesn't matter whether they are real or not. It has nothing to do with you. Go and criticize the Gods of masculine nature as you want, but never have a loose tongue on any feminine supernatural powers from any supernatural belief system.

The Nature of Man is to take the criticism and respond. No matter whether he is a human or a God, or a supernatural power, the nature of woman, even when she is a supernatural power and a Goddess, is always to nurture children and wish for her children's happiness, even while being as strong and great as masculine supernatural powers.

Even if hypothetically supernatural powers exist, you can comfortably go against masculine supernatural powers and survive, but never go against feminine supernatural powers who describe themselves as Mother. Motherly natured supernatural powers will not do something bad to you for talking badly about them or doing something bad to them in any way, but they will feel sad inside, and no mother should feel that, even if she is a supernatural power and even if she doesn't exist. The masculine supernatural powers must take any attack or critique and answer them. Supernatural power' believers should not use the feminine supernatural power as their shield to escape from the critique. The people, both those who do not believe and those who believe in supernatural powers, should maintain this decency.

If your supernatural belief system does not even have at least one feminine supernatural power whom you can worship or pray to, and if you are a believer in that supernatural system, then, for the sake of humanity, come out of that supernatural belief system. Ha ha!

A man can celebrate his/her birthday for more than 2 days on Earth, and for more days if that man goes to another planet where time is much slower, and also can become much older according to the time of the place the man is in. So, be skeptical not only of supernatural elements but also of rationality and intelligence because nothing is pure absolute and nothing is pure relative forever. It is what it is according to what it is, where it is, and how it is. Always make sure you are on the right path, even while living life using rationality. Rationality is not a totally foolproof method; everything has its own limitations, and we, here, are just finding a less stupid and more effective way to live. That's it.

If you believe that the supernatural powers created the Earth, Humanity, and the Universe, then what were supernatural powers doing before creating this creation we live in? Because, according to their time and space, they must have existed for trillions of years before creating Earth, Humanity, and the Universe, which we are in right now, right?

So, what were those supernatural powers doing before they created the Earth, Humanity, Other Life Forms, and the Universe?

Do these supernatural belief systems have any stories or descriptions about their supernatural powers before their supernatural powers created this universe?

And also, do these supernatural belief systems have stories or descriptions about the times or existences before the creation of this universe, by their supernatural powers?

Who gave birth, and how did those supernatural powers come into existence? Hypothetically, God created the Earth, Humanity, Other Life Forms, and the Universe, but who created God and the supernatural powers that created the creation we are in?

Of course, like human beings, Gods and supernatural powers too have freedom, free will, and liberty to appear or not appear to humans and to come or not to come to Earth. If those Gods and supernatural powers lack that type of freedom and free will for some reason in their universe or the world they exist in, and in the supernatural belief system they belong to, then they can come to the Ateesta Religion. Ateesta Religion open-heartedly accepts those Gods and supernatural powers.

God is not timid. God does not want to kill his nonbelievers like a petty dictator who kills people for opposing his/her ruling. If your God is timid, then God! No one can save you from that God! Except, Ateesta Religion's God Yinta.

If any God or supernatural powers, through their teachings, tell you to betray your nation to spread their supernatural belief system, those Gods are false Gods. And those books should be burned. Those supernatural belief systems should be banned and abolished by Governments of all kinds.

If any supernatural belief system encourages lying and cunning behavior of any kind to spread itself, then it doesn't even deserve the minimum respect from people. As this practice is not good to be followed by humans, let alone by God.

Can you imagine God himself advising his believers to be cunning to spread his supernatural belief system, so that those believers who follow his supernatural belief system go to Heaven by spreading it through cunning behavior? Yuck! Even if that God is real, is it even worth it to go to that Heaven in that way? And the worst part is that the believers of that cunning God feel sacred in this whole betrayal process of nonbelievers. Disgusting!

* * *

Your supernatural belief system should give you the freedom, free will, and liberty to believe in it or not to believe in it. If it can't, then does it even have the maturity to claim that it is the supernatural belief system and its God is who created the Earth, the Universe, and everything?

If you are a believer in supernatural powers and if a supernatural power/God is sending you to Hell after your death, the reason can be anything then hypothetically you must go to that Hell and take the punishment or whatever is being given to you because God, literally God, is sending you to Hell and God knows what is best for you and also if God is sending you to Hell then Hell also is as sacred as Heaven, so you must have no problem.

God is sending you to Hell; you cannot compare God with Humans here to make examples like even if God is sending you to Hell, it is still bad, just like a criminal killing you, like that, Hell is bad. Because if it is that way, then what is the difference between a Human doing bad and God doing bad to you for your good, and if that is not the intention of God for sending you to Hell, then 'God..' Nobody can save you from that God, because he is behaving like Satan and acting like God, haha! Don't even start with God sending someone to Hell just because that person did not believe in him, it is like saying you have to buy my product only, otherwise I will kill you in the Human context, haha.. Don't even start again with Oh.. The Truth is only one, and that Truth is God, and only this God is true, etc stupidity. Does God have a monopoly on Truth and faith, or on the beliefs of people? Haha! If yes, don't you think it is wrong? We put all the regulations to prevent dictatorial monopolies in every sector as humans in order to be fair and free as a society and market, but for faith, belief, etc, do you think there should be a monopoly of one God or Gods or supernatural belief systems only? Come on, they are not the same, but at least to compare, don't you think this is fundamentally wrong?

Let's talk about a scenario, imagine we have four supernatural belief systems on Earth. Those supernatural belief systems are A, B, C, and D.

Now, 'A' supernatural belief system, through its teachings, says that it only has one true God, and other Gods from other supernatural belief systems are all false.

Then 'B', 'C', and 'D' supernatural belief systems also say the same thing through their teachings.

Also, 'A', 'B', 'C', 'D'—supernatural belief systems, through their teachings and books, say that the believers of their supernatural belief systems should convert people from other supernatural belief systems into them.

To be specific, the 'A' - supernatural belief system said to its followers through its teachings that its believers should convert people from other supernatural belief systems into it. And by doing it, the 'A' supernatural belief system believers who converted people from other 'B', 'C', 'D' supernatural belief systems into the 'A' supernatural belief system will get favored by the 'A' supernatural belief system power's God and will go to Heaven for converting people.

And also it says other 'B', 'C', 'D' supernatural belief systems are false, so believers of the 'A' - supernatural belief system only go to Heaven after their death.

But the 'B', 'C', 'D' supernatural belief systems are also saying the same thing through their teachings about their Gods, Heavens, and telling people that they will go to Hell if they don't believe in their supernatural belief systems.

In all this chaos, haha! I can say every person will go to three Hells and one Heaven for the love of whatever God!

But just think, let's say 'A' - supernatural belief system is hypothetically real and rationally true. Their God and Hell, Heaven, exist. Then what is the problem? If a believer of 'A' supernatural belief system dies, then he/she goes to Heaven for believing in 'A' supernatural belief system, right? And nonbelievers of 'A' - supernatural belief system, to Hell for not believing in 'A' - supernatural belief system, right?

Then the person who died will get to know the truth, right? So why pressure people and scare them by threatening them with Hell for not believing or give them promises of Heaven, if the Heaven, Hell, and God of 'A' - supernatural belief system are true? If people don't believe in 'A' - supernatural belief system, then they automatically go to Hell after their death, right? But think about this, those nonbelievers of 'A' - supernatural belief system can go to Heaven, if those nonbelievers of 'A' supernatural belief system, after their death, pray to 'A' - supernatural belief system powers and accept its God in the afterlife, then they can save themselves from going to Hell, right?

Can't God save those nonbelievers after their death from Hell because now they start to believe in his 'A' - supernatural belief system and its God, him? If not, then only living humans have more value than dead humans, ha? Or is God only merciful to nonbelievers who converted into his supernatural belief system and became believers in him when they were alive and not in the afterlife? Ha ha!

If your supernatural belief system's Heaven, God, Hell, and stories are true, then you don't need to kill the non-believers of your supernatural belief system and hate other people just because they do not believe in the same supernatural belief system you believe in. Because your supernatural belief system is the truth, right? Then it is true.

The people will know after their death in old age by themselves. You do not need to trouble or kill or do horrible things in the name of your supernatural belief system and God to convert people and scare nonbelievers of your supernatural belief system.

You should be relaxed, nonchalant, and calm because your supernatural belief system's Heaven and Hell, God, are true, and you will go to Heaven for believing in your supernatural belief system's powers. Why trouble others if your supernatural belief system is true?

People have free will, it is up to them whether to believe in a supernatural belief system or not, right? And then you know your supernatural belief system is really true, right? Then laugh and be cool. Because you have the truth and they don't, right? If they want to go to Hell according to your supernatural belief system, then they go to Hell after their death. It is up to them.

Hypothetically, even if your supernatural belief system's Hell, Heaven, and God are rationally real, still people have the free will to not believe in your supernatural belief system and God. And by free will, they will go to Hell if they want; it has nothing to do with anyone. But who gave your God the power to judge people and send them to Hell or Heaven, many times against their will? If a person doesn't want to go to hell for not believing in your God, then that person has free will to reject your God's order on that person going to Hell, even to Heaven. Your God has no right, no power, no moral, ethical authority, and nothing to justify sending a person to Hell just because that person does not believe in your God. Your God is irrelevant to that person who does not believe in your God, and your God, supernatural belief system, and your beliefs, your God's teachings have nothing to do with the person who does not believe in them.

Your supernatural belief system is true. Be happy and die in old age, go to Heaven, and see the nonbelievers of your supernatural belief system in Hell, and if you want, you can ask those nonbelievers of your supernatural belief system to convert to your supernatural belief system in the afterlife in Hell or on the way to Hell, and then take them to Heaven with you. Does your supernatural belief system allow converting nonbelievers of your supernatural belief system to your supernatural belief system's God's believers after their death in the afterlife? When they get to know the truth that your supernatural belief system's God is the only true God, and others are false? If not, why? If yes, then no problem. If your supernatural belief system is true, then the nonbelievers of your supernatural belief system will convert to your supernatural belief system after their death, when their souls go to Hell, or in front of Hell, or on the way to Hell, and they will go to Heaven by accepting your God as the one true God in afterlife. Your Merciful God will also accept them, right? He won't reject the scared, poor souls who converted to your supernatural belief system standing in front of Hell, right? Now, those poor souls wanting peace realized the truth after their physical body's death that only your supernatural belief system's God, Heaven, and Hell are the only truth. Now they want to be with your supernatural belief system's God in Heaven. So, they converted to your supernatural belief system in the afterlife, then now they can go to Heaven of your supernatural belief system, right?

Think of one good reason why you can't change your supernatural belief system and your beliefs after your death in your afterlife, and in your afterlife, you start to believe in a new God and go to that God's Heaven. It is possible if that supernatural belief system's Heaven, Hell, and God are true and exist in the Afterlife. Because after your death, in your afterlife, you became a believer in that supernatural belief system and its God.

If 'A' - Supernatural belief system's God only wants human beings to start believing in and worshiping him initially when human beings are alive in a physical body only, and do not accept nonbeliever dead human beings' conversion and change of beliefs in the afterlife, then 'A' - God and supernatural system is senseless and stupid, simple.

Because human beings live for a maximum of approximately 120 years on Earth, as I'm writing this, and hypothetically, after their death, they will be in the afterlife for a long time, right? If not eternally.

And rejecting the conversion and prayers, worship of those dead nonbelievers in the afterlife, where they will stay for a long time or forever, is stupid. Why does your God lose, forever, the devotion and worship from dead human beings in the afterlife just because those dead human beings didn't believe in your God while they were alive in their physical bodies?

So if blind believers of 'A' - supernatural belief system kill nonbelievers of 'A' - supernatural belief system, then those killers go to Heaven as said in the teachings of 'A' - supernatural belief system, and the people who are nonbelievers of 'A' supernatural belief system who got killed by blind 'A' - Supernatural belief system believers go to Hell. Does the 'A' - supernatural belief system's God, and blind believers who kill others with this logic, have any sense, shame, sensibility, or an ounce of thinking capacity in their minds? Are these stupid 'A' supernatural belief system blind believers really expecting to see the souls of nonbelievers they killed in their Hell?

And are they really expecting their souls to be sent to Heaven by their God for killing the nonbelievers of their God?

What kind of shameless stupidity is this?

The religious violence in the world will be solved, if not, we, Ateestans will solve it—The End.

If you want to know about the afterlife and other supernatural elements of any kind, I'm telling you again, if you want to know about the afterlife and other supernatural elements of any kind, then approach and research them only through science, only through science, and with nothing else. There are things we, humans, don't know, and it is better for us not to know them in the way they want us to know them, but if you want to know them, then only go with science and scientific approaches, nothing else. The Real Science, not pseudo science. No matter what unknown stands in front of us, our science and technology can protect us, but only when that unknown comes to us as we want it to be, not as it wants.

Even if you criticize any supernatural belief systems and powers, do it with respect, dignity, and rationality. Never criticize them in an ugly, senseless manner.

Why do most supernatural belief systems' powers come to Earth in Human form only?

Why do supernatural powers not come to Earth in animals, trees, or other life forms?

Because animals and trees and other life forms are also the creation of those supernatural powers, right? Then why do those supernatural powers' representatives, messengers, and themselves mostly come to Earth in human form only?

Are humans more valued by supernatural powers than animals and other life forms? So is that why supernatural powers come to Earth like Humans and look like Humans mostly?

Why were Supernatural belief systems' powers created, the one and only highly intelligent life form, as 'Humans'?

Why didn't those supernatural powers create other life forms that are as intelligent as Humans?

Why do all the supernatural power belief systems say that they only created the humans that we are now, but never talk about who created our ancient human ancestors, like Neanderthals and other human ancestors?

Why can't supernatural belief systems just create different-looking, highly intelligent life forms than humans and make them their separate followers and believers instead of just asking their supernatural powers human believers to convert and to kill other humans for being nonbelievers of them, and forcing, scaring nonbelievers to worship and pray to them only?

If supernatural powers create other life forms like humans that are as intelligent as humans, then for these supernatural belief systems, there is no need to fight to win over the belief, trust of only humans and no need to give promises to only limited number of humans alive to make them believers and also no need to share the only same singular humanity people between their supernatural belief systems, right?

Because now you have a new life form that is equal to humans in intelligence, and people of that new life form can also become believers in these supernatural belief systems. So, believers are not limited to humans only, and supernatural belief systems now can expand themselves and make people of that new life form who are as intelligent as humans their believers. This creates new space for supernatural belief systems and encourages healthy competition and excitement. But why are they not creating a new life form like that? What is the reason for not doing it and constantly asking humans to believe in them only?

Why were supernatural powers created, only 'Humans', as highly intelligent and conscious?

Why don't they create another life form that is as intelligent as humans? And why do all these supernatural belief systems' messengers, representatives, or themselves come to Earth, mostly looking like Humans or as humans only?

So, do these powers of supernatural belief systems, too, like the appearance of humans, rather than of animals or other life forms, which they themselves created? How does that work since they created everything? Why do they come and look mostly only like humans?

Are those supernatural powers human-biased?

Why did all the supernatural powers themselves and their representatives, messengers, come thousands of years ago only?

Why can't they come now, at least for a few days or hours, to talk to their children, Humanity? What's wrong with that?

If those supernatural powers come to Earth and talk to people now, then they can update their believers on new things, right?

Also, sometimes it happens to humans, but for those supernatural powers, too, they might have forgotten to say some things to people the last time they came to Earth or talked to their messengers or prophets. Or they might have got some new ideas or something in them to tell people, but it's been a long time for us humans in our time space since these supernatural powers talked to humans or to a prophet.

So, if supernatural powers come now to Earth, then they can share their new ideas and the new ways that they want their believers to worship and pray to them, right?

It will also be super awesome to see a supernatural power that cares about humanity so much that it came to Earth literally to talk to us. That supernatural power will become our favorite, and all the bros and cool women will become that supernatural power's friends, and we can show that supernatural power our technology and our lives, and other cool stuff we do in our personal lives and careers. Since it is a supernatural power, that supernatural bro will and can be with all of us at the same time individually, and will become our best friend.

Our new chill and cool generations are not even like older generations, who claim that they met God or Prophets, messengers, that supernatural power does not even have to do any magic tricks to make us believe in it. That supernatural power can just become a good friend to us and help us. Of course, we will also help that supernatural power in its daily life on Earth. The world becomes a cool place. The Earth would become a cool place in the universe if a supernatural power came to Earth now. We can flex with aliens, saying a supernatural power visited us and lived among us, and we have rational, scientific, and technical proofs of it. And we will ask them what they have other than technology? Not just that, all types of crime will become zero in hours, after a supernatural power visits Earth, and science confirms it too

Ateestans, any supernatural belief system that says someone is God is God. But believing and not believing in that God and Power is our personal choice. No one can pressure us in any way, shape, form, or process.

Ateestans, I, God Yinta, gave you the freedom to believe or not believe in me, but do the other supernatural belief systems and powers give you the same freedom to believe or not believe in them?

You must have that freedom, and you should be given the freedom to believe or not to believe. It is because, hypothetically, supernatural powers operate at a level that is much higher than just seeing whether someone believes in them or not. So our beliefs in supernatural powers are actually not even equal to a tiny sand particle in a desert compared to the supernatural powers' stature and the vastness of their power, and also, when taking the level of creation they did with the universe into consideration. But they respect us and they respect our devotion towards them, that's why they talk highly of our worship and prayers, but those worship and prayers are not for them to get an ego boost, but to make us feel the peace and get that strong assurance in the mind and to make us believe that our life is/will be good.

It is because the supernatural powers are everything, and everything is their creation. There is nothing in this creation that is against them, even if they appear like that, because those things are themselves created by supernatural powers, even criticism and praise.

Any book, any teaching, any tradition and practice isn't going to change the status of freedom for Ateestans because those teachings of supernatural powers are intended for average human minds who blindly follow a supernatural belief system. Not for us, Ateestans. Hypothetically, the supernatural powers created the creation, which we are in right now, but how we use this creation was entirely left to us by those supernatural powers.

Don't betray your fellow humans for any Gods or for any higher supernatural powers. We humans are one and will be there and have always been there for each other. No, those Gods and supernatural powers.

Anthropology is the single greatest enemy of supernatural powers' belief systems of blind faith.

You can comfortably say that any God who asks his believers to kill his nonbelievers is Satan posing as God. If you are God and if everything is your creation, then what difference does it make if someone believes in you or not? At the end, they come to be with you in the afterlife, right? Just think, why does God want human beings to pray to him in their limited time as mortals? God can make human beings pray to him in the afterlife, where they have unlimited time, right? Why does God want to eat the limited mortal time of humans? God can ask human beings to worship and pray to him in their afterlife, to eternity, literally forever, right?

If Heaven and Hell are given based on believing in and not believing in a God, committing sin, and things we do when we were alive, then what is stopping human beings from committing sins in the afterlife with their souls, and also being able to do great things? Ha Ha.. Nothing because there is no afterlife at all in any way, shape, or form. Use the time when you are alive to do great things. When you die, that's it. There is nothing. That's the end of you physically, psychologically, and in every way.

As a mortal, the time is there before your birth and will be there after your death, too. Time is unlimited, but your age is limited. So use your age wisely to do what you want to do in your life. Time is not limited; your time on Earth is, which is called age. Use your age to the full extent to achieve great things in your life.

Legal systems and constitutions, laws are made by humans, for humans. They didn't come from Heaven. Change them to make them suitable for the Ateesta Religion.

Use rationality, rational thinking, and intelligence to become a good person. Not the opposite. Actively, you must think rationally to become as good as possible as a person while mitigating the dangers of all kinds.

If you believe in supernatural powers and pray to them, then it is okay. But make sure those supernatural powers you pray to do not have their own supernatural powers they pray to, simply. Make sure your Gods do not have any Gods of their own. Your God should be the ultimate, final, real main God, just like God Yinta.

9

If I do a 180-degree turn, I can tell there is God. Because Humans have no reason to come up with a concept or theory of God, or whatever you call it. And stick with it for hundreds of thousands of years in one form of system or another. In the past, a great scientist knew there was an element missing in the periodic table, and that scientist who knew that there was an element missing in the periodic table had left a place for that element even though he didn't know the missing element's name and when it will be discovered and went on to include his newly discovered elements in the periodic table after the place he left for the missing element. I can say that God is like that missing element, and we are the scientists who know that God exists, but don't know where and how. But surely, someone will come along with that missing element and fill the gap we left, which is the address of God. But that filler entity can be God himself/herself, or could be another undiscovered alien race who knew that missing element of God, or a power who created us, or could even be a human who knows how to reach and where to find God and make him come to Earth, and make God stand in front of us.

If God created everything, then if a human on Earth says, "I don't believe in God!" Then, mostly, God will look at that person and laugh like, "This guy is funny."

Because the human who said he didn't believe in God, the planet that humans were on, and literally every little and big thing that is there since the beginning of the universe was God's creation. So, I don't see God getting angry just by hearing someone say that he/she doesn't believe in God. The creator is much more mature than a petty, jealous boyfriend/girlfriend.

We are children of God, and it is foolish to assume that when a person moves to a new town from his hometown, and now in the new town, since that person doesn't have his parents with him now, so he must have no parents at all because they are not with him now. Just like that, because we are not seeing God physically now on Earth, it doesn't mean God does not exist. It just means he might have gone somewhere, or he is just doing his regular work without visiting Earth or even this universe physically. God might have also moved his residency to another universe, the location of which we don't know as of now.

Actually, God has no credible reason to visit Earth and meet the people who worship him physically through their bodies. When he can work his magic from wherever he is, then why stir unnecessary strife, diversion in the lives of people, and make people spend time unnecessarily excessively than needed on activities related to him?

And God being physically present on Earth will make people spend enormous amounts of time in their mortal, limited lives on activities related to him. Also, people will ignore their personal lives and important things in it just to spend time with God and activities, works related to him. God doesn't want that.

He wants people to live their mortal lives happy and productive.

Because everybody goes to him after their death and is guaranteed to see him in one way or another, so he doesn't want to make people spend the limited time of their mortal lives on him more than necessary. He knew this very well because he had seen it a few times in the past when he came to Earth, to different parts of Earth. So, he just wants us to move forward in life with the great teachings he gave us and live a complete, full, happy life. God wants us to spend our time and efforts on things we are passionate about, things we really like and want to achieve, and on our work. It is because, in that way, we achieve great things, and in the process, our achievements help people live a better life. The life God gave us will have meaning if we live our lives with a good purpose.

God thought that if there is nothing, then there is nothing. And he, too, has to do nothing.

He can relax and chill. But God created the universe and humanity because sitting idle and doing nothing is not a good habit and a good thing, even if he is God. When there is no humanity and the universe we live in, then there will be no prayers and worship from us to God, but also, there will be no criticism of him and on his existence, character, or anything that is related to him. But he chose to go ahead and create the universe, Earth, and humans. Because that is what a God who wants to be productive and achieve something meaningful in his eternal existence will do. For God, there is the pain of creation and also lots of thinking about why, what, how, who, where, and in what way the life forms and creation should get created, operated, and put into existence, etc., and also other trillions of more things that we don't know clearly.

If he wants, he can go back and stop the process of this creation, seeing all the work, technical processes, and programming of life involved, but he chose to move forward and then created the universe, our world, Earth, and created us. God gave this beautiful life to all of us.

With our actions, we make our lives horrible or beautiful, but God wants us to have that free will and freedom to live the life as we want, which can be a good life or a bad life.

He gave us his teachings when he visited Earth and also through his Prophets and messengers, but he also left it to our free will to follow those teachings or not. We can live a sacred, good life by following his teachings or without following his teachings by being a good person independently, regardless of whether we follow his teachings or not.

God created this creation by taking all the stress and pain of our criticism, abuse, and work stress, lots of thinking about programming life and Ecosystems because, as a God, he thought he wanted to do it, and it is always great to do meaningful work.

You might think about what God was doing before creating this universe, where he came from, and how he came into existence.

God did do something before creating this creation, but at some point, something triggered him to get the thought of creating this creation, and he thought about it a lot and finally created this creation.

We are here, and I'm writing this, and you are reading this.

God, who has the power of creating this creation, already had a great life before creating the universe in which we are in right now. You might say, well, God, who created this universe, wasn't even born, so how could he have the great life like a mortal? You are correct. But life is his creation, death is his creation, and everything is his creation. So, I can comfortably use the word 'life' to explain about his life before he created this universe if I want to.

God had the great existence (life) before creating this universe, but he thought to himself, What good is he doing by having all the power and just living, ok, existing by himself?

So he created this creation. Because when you can do something good, then you should do it, and it is fun, too.

So he created this universe and sent his prophets, messengers, and also came by himself in various forms to Earth. He gave us his teachings multiple times after he created this creation so that we could study those teachings and live life righteously. Those teachings also tell us where we will go after death if we commit bad sins.

For someone like God, who had the stature and power of creating this creation, which we are in literally, he doesn't need to come to us in any way or form or send his prophets, messengers for us to Earth. But he did because he loved his creation; he loved us and wanted us to live happy, lovable lives. But at the same time, he wants us to have free will and follow the teachings he gave us by our free will, not by any force or pressure.

He is God, right? Then he can just program the process of worship and praying to him directly in all of us, which we will have in our birth itself, right? But he didn't do it because GOD WANTS HUMAN BEINGS TO HAVE THE SAME FREE WILL & CONSCIOUSNESS WHICH HE HAS, and God wants us to learn about this world, the universe, and things in it, realize the truth, and go to him. He doesn't want our prayers and worship compulsorily, but through them and also in other ways of our choice, we can try to find the truth and purpose of our lives.

God ultimately wants us to live a completely meaningful, happy, and full life.

It is because that is his life before creating this creation, and he wants us to have that complete life of having a purpose, striving to achieve something great, seeing happiness, seeing sadness, success, failure, heartbreak, losing precious things, achieving great things, etc. God wants us to use our minds and live a great life using his teachings or in the way we want, of our choice, but it should be meaningful and righteous.

Even if we oppose God in any shape, way, or form in our path of living, it is still okay, but it should be rational and meaningful. Also, God wants to tell us that if we don't do something, then there is nothing.

And if we choose to do something, then there will be work for the mind and body, as well as the struggles and successes of all kinds on the path. You have the free will to not do anything, but still, by yourself, you should choose to do something meaningful with your life and go through everything on that path of achieving what you want in life. Literally, that is what Industrious Active Minds do, and also God did. They can't exist without doing something meaningful and productive. With the stature and power God has, he can relax and enjoy with other Gods or just have a good time for himself for eternity. Still, he chose to create this universe and literally went through many heartbreaking things for us because he is Industrious, and he wants us to have the taste of his power rather than keeping it to himself. We have to connect to him in the way we can, enjoy the power of God, and live a great life. He died as a human, and we should not fear death because he died as a human, for us, to tell us that death is normal, and we will return to him after our death. We do not need to fear anything. We have God, he has our back. We just have to focus on living a meaningful, great life and use our time as mortals to do meaningful things for ourselves and the people around us.

You can say, why can't God make us Gods rather than human beings through his creation? Ha ha! You are already seeing every day, just as human beings, what horrible things people are doing, and you can imagine what these people can do as Gods. There are good people, absolutely, but evil people becoming Gods, and the destruction they will do is something that even good people who become Gods cannot stop. You can say that God can give us great character and good values by birth, right? But you should understand that even God cannot meddle in your character and values. God gave you free will just as he had. And in the name of God, what kind of person you are now is really the person you are. God gave you free will, and you choose to be like you because it is you. You might be a horrible person, ha ha, or a good person, but it is truly you. God has nothing to do with it. God just gave us his teachings to help us and to become great people.

God is there. He just exists in a place that we never knew existed.

Among mortals, someone has to make something out of something to make it exist in the universe. But God is someone who can make something exist without anything preceding it in any way, shape, or form. God can create energy out of nothing, and how he does it, why he does it, and where he does it, is his law. For humans, that energy just transforms. It is our law. With God, the fundamental laws of the universe change, and God made those laws of all kinds for himself and for us separately, but he can change them whenever he wants and do whatever he wants with them.

God is the one who created matter out of nothing, which then transformed into the universe and us. So imagine, we never made it out of our Milky Way Galaxy, and we want to see God, who literally created the Milky Way and billions and billions of other galaxies like ours.

No matter how confident we human beings are in our knowledge and intelligence, can we attain the level of consciousness, intelligence, and rationality needed to at least know where to search for God before finding him?

The microbe in the soil does not need to know that I exist, but I need it to exist there to help me cultivate my food. In that way, in reverse, God does not need anything from us, but he wants us to be there to enjoy the little share of his power of free will, freedom, and life that he gave us.

God loves us. That is why he created us, but we make our lives with our actions. Even though you can say that we have many problems in our lives so, creation of God is not perfect, you have to understand that if he absolutely made the creation stereotypically perfect by not putting any problems in our lives, then we also will not have the free will and freedom to make decisions as every decision we take will be successful and God himself predetermines that success.

In this way, do we really have free will, freedom, and liberty? We just live in the false truth reality with success as default, no matter what, that's it. But by giving us freedom and free will to make our own decisions and bear the responsibilities of those decisions, God gave us true free will, which he also has.

Can you imagine that? Are you getting it? God gave us the same free will that he has inside of him, to us, and we can call it consciousness also. The degree of it might vary from God, but it is the same free will that God had. He doesn't have to, but he did. God can just make us his biologically and psychologically programmed worshiping and praying robots by keeping that worshiping and praying programming in us when he is creating us, if he wants to, but he didn't. He gave us the same free will power that he had to us so that we can make decisions for ourselves by thinking just like him.

The thinking power that God has, God gave that power to us. He didn't have to, but he did because he loves us.

So, the thinking power and free will that we have now are the exact same things that God has, and he gave them to us selflessly just out of love for us human beings. At least, we can assume that till we discover or are discovered by other life forms that are equivalent to us in intelligence.

Even though God didn't give us his supernatural powers, he did give us his powers of thinking and free will.

To confirm that a person is not inside the house, you first have to start by checking the house thoroughly. So, first, we have to search the universe that we are in to prove that there is no God. Because if the person you are searching for is an Emperor, then you don't shout standing outside of his house saying, "Hey Emperor, if you don't come out of your house now, then you don't exist."

The guards will come and throw you in jail, and then you will know that the emperor exists. In that way, you can't live all your life on tiny Earth and go to its moon or a few other planets and scream that there is no God while there is a vast, great universe out there, physically you have never visited and seen properly. The Emperor does not care whether you believe he exists or not because you are one individual, and no matter whether you believe that the Emperor exists or not, you get benefits from the government, pay taxes, and all the systems go on as usual. The Emperor just does not care about your opinion because of the level of power he has, the things he knows about you, and the consciousness he has about the kingdom. Most importantly, he knows he exists. Like that, God also does not care whether you or people en masse believe in him or not. The processes that were designed by God go on, and in a way, when you irritate or impress the Emperor, you might see him sometimes, like that God might come to you in any form he wants if he is impressed by you or gets angry because of you. But mostly, he will ignore you, and the systems and processes that he put in place will take care of you.

That is why Ateesta gives people Free will, Freedom, and Liberty while asking them to be responsible and righteous by not harming others in any manner.

Someone who takes your free will, freedom, and liberty from you is definitely Satan. No matter what you get in return.

The origin of God is — In the name of God, with respect for him, I can't reveal it.

But I can say that great people make themselves, and so does he. Out of nothing, he was the light in the beginning.

He loved the tiny mortals he created a lot.

10

If I do another 180-degree,

Why doesn't God show his real, true face to humans who worship him? So the people who worship God will anyway see him after their death, that is why he doesn't want to show his face?

Or is his face and identity so precious that even people who worship him are not eligible to watch them when they are alive? Or is he just shy? Or are the people who worship him so corrupted that, only by worshiping him and, after dying and going to him in the afterlife, is the only way to see him? Why does God always come in Human form or in other forms that are familiar to Humans in a way? Why doesn't God come to Earth and show himself to people as he truly is in his original form, at least through his true physical body, or through his true cosmic body, or whatever it is, instead of saying everything is his creation and, therefore, everything is a representation of him?

Why can't the Ultimate come to Earth directly as who he is instead of sending his so called Prophets, Messengers, etc.

Actually, saying that a God does not exist in any way, shape, or form is a smart way to avoid unnecessary explanations than telling so many stories of that God to make people believe in that God. And a God who does not have any shape or form immediately feels mysterious, curious, interesting, and ultimately sacred. It is the nature of the unknown, and when that unknown angle is mixed with something like God, then it becomes a strong, engaging psychological impact point for people, particularly those who cannot think rationally and have the tendency to reject the scientific human evolution, scientific exploration of the universe by totally submitting themselves to their blind faiths with a low rational intelligence at the societal level.

When God has a face and shape, then it becomes a strong impact point for chaotic people at the societal level who also have low rational intelligence and blind faith.

In both ways, they are begging for the blessings of nonexistent supernatural powers and getting offended with super stupid rage aggression when someone questions their beliefs or blind faith rationally. They actually will not even hesitate to kill anyone who is going in-depth into these concepts in a scientific, rational, psychological way because they are afraid that someone might even prove that their beliefs and blind faith as just well-written fiction (Of course, they are now, but those believers are not accepting it. But finding strong further scientific and rational evidence threatens all these blind faith systems existence itself.) and their supernatural powers belief systems as just carefully crafted and organized beliefs systems which included supernatural elements to heighten the effect of teachings of those so called supernatural powers' supernatural belief systems that people wrote but in their supernatural belief systems described those teachings as either said or narrated or written by God himself. So that people feel scared and will not even think about questioning those teachings and supernatural belief systems. It is a classic trick, as any man will fear a higher power that is not human and supernatural in nature. They used this well. In this way, the people get more organized, less resistant, more loyal, and streamlined to be managed by the authorities of those times at the societal level en masse. And it is still going on to this day.

People who worship God without any shape or form are generally very sensitive about their faith and beliefs as they fear their God of the unknown much more than the nonbelievers of their God, and when someone criticizes their God of no shape and form, they think in the way that, If I kill the critic then God will like me and send me to Heaven. And before doing this, there will be a lot of speculations and discussions about the critics killings among themselves, and they will fight and compete about selecting and who should kill the particular critics of their God.

People who worship God in some shape, form, or with a representation physically are more idiotic and chaotic, and weak, they spend their whole lives thinking their God will take care of everything, even critics of their God. If you look at these people from the perspective of God, these people are just lazy and stupid. If God takes care of everything, then why did he give life to these idiots? These guys are highly emotional with words and dead with actions.

But no matter what, all these guys always fight among themselves, thinking that their own God is true and other Gods are false. It is like, what is the difference between you going into the volcano and lava coming onto you? You die ultimately.

It is the same with these types of people and with other types of supernatural belief systems, too. If they believe in any kind of supernatural powers and supernatural elements, ultimately, they are fools, thinking about others as fools while behaving like great fools.

These God loving people do a very stupid and barbaric thing, which is 'Killing for their God'. I wonder what the people who were killed by these idiots after going to Hell and seeing Satan would feel like. What is the difference between these murderers who kill people for not believing in their God and those dead people who got killed for not believing in a particular God visiting Satan in Hell? Those murdered people will feel relaxed and good after seeing Satan, as they are already dead, and now, at least, those believers of God and supernatural belief systems will not kill them again. Satan actually will feel bad for those dead people when he sees them in Hell because they were killed for not believing in God, the Good power, for God's sake, not for not believing in Satan, the Bad power.

But if those people who got murdered for not believing in a God go to Heaven in the afterlife or to someplace in the afterlife and meet that particular God whom they got killed for not believing in, then what would they say to that God? I don't think that conversation would be a nice one between that God and the nonbelievers' souls in the afterlife.

Yes, those murderers who kill for their God believe that their God is real and the afterlife is real, right?

Then those people who got murdered for not believing in God will meet or see the true God for sure in the afterlife, right? And those non believers are already dead and left their families, everything they cared for in their entire life, so Hell and the punishments God gives them for not believing in him might not even scare them as they will go to Hell for sure for not believing in him and they are murdered for the same exact reason, they will definitely directly scold that God when they see him for ruining their lives.

And that God just has or have to bear it. And that scolding will be very bad and nasty for sure. For the love of God, those believers of that God in the afterlife will not even be able to kill the nonbelievers again for scolding their God. The souls of nonbelievers who died in the hands of the believers of that God might even attack that God too in the afterlife. There is a good chance of that, actually.

Actually, if that God is real, then it might have already happened, too.

If any supernatural belief system's believers believe that their God exists for sure, then this will happen for sure. Their God will get scolded by nonbelievers' souls every second, for that God's believers killing those nonbelievers, just because those nonbelievers didn't believe in that God, while that God exists in the afterlife for real. If that God is real, then why that God didn't even have patience for nonbelievers to die naturally and go to him and see him in the afterlife, as after seeing that God, then those nonbelievers ultimately will start believing in that God, right?

Then why did that God get so insecure and desperate that he asked his believers to kill his nonbelievers? So that those nonbelievers would go to him in the afterlife and see him? No matter how nonbelievers die, they go to God and see him and know that he is the only true God, right? Then why kill nonbelievers artificially just because they don't believe in that God? These types of Gods are just Immature. No, the people who wrote these types of teachings in the name of that God are Immature and have a very limited vision in their lives. They are just full of ego and emotions and are power-control freaks.

Just think, even if that God is real, why does he even need to control the way he gets worshiped and prayed to?

What difference does it make when you pray and worship to that God by representing him in a physical form or without any physical shape or form? Everything is his creation, right? And if that God's representation is respectful, then what is the problem of getting and accepting worship and prayers through it? He exists ultimately, and he receives those prayers ultimately, and he is there ultimately, and you will see him after death ultimately, right?

Do the believers of that God not even have the freedom to worship their God as they want, at least? Everything needs to be controlled and regularized. Why, just why? Just because God said so in his teachings? My God!

The problem with these supernatural powers believers is that no matter how educated they are, in the process of defending their blind faith and supernatural belief systems, they get super aggressive and become super stupid dumb without even realizing it, evoking emotions of sensitiveness, jealousy, and insecurity in themselves for not being able to answer a question rationally.

If we think all this is okay, then what if the God of those believers, whose believers killed the nonbelievers for, does not even exist in the afterlife?

What if some other God exists in the afterlife, and then, what if the believers of a particular God who killed the nonbelievers of their God came to the afterlife after their death and saw another God? And then what happens when those nonbelievers who were killed by those believers see them in the afterlife? What would those nonbelievers do to those believers? I'm sure there would be great street fights in Heaven and Hell.

There is nothing like, and there is no Afterlife, absolutely. Once you are dead, you are dead, that's it, according to Ateestans.

***

No matter who it is, even if he is God and even if he is real scientifically, never bend and kneel in front of anyone and beg for something. Respect yourself and earn what you want instead of begging. Ask for help and ask for what you should get rightfully, but never beg someone for anything, even if that someone is God, and that thing you want is going to Heaven.

God loved his creation, and that creation happened to be you, too. So you are not especially special to God. You are his creation, and that is why he loves you. He loves you, but not because of who you are, and he does not love you in the way independently of who made you and because of who you are. He just doesn't care. Ha ha! He just loves his creation, that's it. And you are part of that creation, which is why he loves you.

When the God who is mighty, unshakable, and strong, absolutely powerful in all universes, does not give you the freedom to criticize him at least, then he is not God. He is just some control freak posing as God. You also have to be wary of believers of that God because mostly they will be stupid, aggressive, and have a low level of maturity in understanding things, and they will take everything at face value, and also be most likely to react with violence if they see any criticism of their God and supernatural belief system.

Saying, "It is my belief, my faith!" is not an excuse for the worst behavior.

Killing someone and saying that you did it for your God is the height of stupidity.

God should not fear criticism.

Intelligence always scares the blind faith.

People who have blind faith always believe even the horrible things they do are sacred because they are doing them for their Gods. These blind-faith people always brand questioning, rationality, and intelligence as Satanic. It is a classic trick that they use that needs no further explanation, and it makes the average emotional person believe them instantly.

Ultimately, that God's believers will oppose and stop every single thing, it could be a game, sport, music, learning, scientific education, etc, anything that evokes critical thinking, rationality, and intelligence in people, and they will brand those things as Satanic. They encourage everything that reinforces the blind faith belief in their God and supernatural belief system. They are stupid, yeah! But dangerous too. Because in this way, people who believe in that God with blind faith just breed, eat, work, and obey the rules and die. Essentially becoming slaves without even realizing it, and they will feel secure about being in that blind faith, slave breeders and believers trance by thinking of it as sacred.

No killing and no bad behavior is accepted just because your God said so. Just because your God said something in his supernatural teachings, doesn't justify any killing or bad behavior of yours.

Ateesta and Ateestans must fight back against this nature of violence with the same brutal violence. I, God Yinta, permitted you to do it from the second you read this here.

If you worship any supernatural power, no matter what that supernatural power is, if you are praying or worshiping to that supernatural power through a physical moment or mental thought, or in a mental state and consistent physical positions you get into in the process of your prayers, then they become idols of your supernatural powers, symbolically. It's just that through your physical movements and mental thoughts, you become the accommodation to those idols of worship, representing your supernatural powers symbolically. So in a way, you are an idol, and you are representing your supernatural powers with your prayers through your physical movements and mental thoughts to connect to your supernatural powers. Your body and mind are idols of your God in this situation.

The way you turn regularly to pray and the process you follow regularly to pray become idols and icons symbolically of the supernatural powers you pray to.

***

Do not lick the feet of anyone just to go to Heaven. No matter whether it is a supernatural power or anything and anyone whatsoever. Earth is a million times better than nonexistent Heaven. Live an honorable life when you are alive, and go to Hell for not believing in God, rather than to kill people for any reason, and commit crimes, and then start believing in a supernatural power and going to Heaven for believing in and worshiping that supernatural power. What good is Heaven if you go there like that?

You living a good life is more important than supernatural powers offering you any Heaven and asking you to commit atrocities to please those supernatural powers and to take you to Heaven in the name of sacredness.

You absolutely do not need to fear the legal system, which criminals don't. So crush the crime to zero in a brutal, merciless way, not just when needed but always.

If your God died for you and your sins, then you must understand that there are many great people who died bringing freedom and independence to their countries from oppressors. They died for their countries and people. Are they God, too? Because they too loved people and died for them.

There are many great men and women who died for people and even for animals, and to protect nature and trees, too. Are they God, too? Actually, they should be more than God because even though they know that they are not Gods and no one will pray and worship them, they still died for their countries, people, and great causes.

If dying for humanity makes a man God, then every man who died and got tortured for protecting us and to save us from harm is also God. Actually, not just for humans, there are many men and women who died protecting animals and nature, too; they must be more than God.

The whatever supernatural Gods you believe in who came to humanity, and on to Earth a few thousand years ago, they told you through their teachings that about how the Earth and the universe, both with an age of billions of years, were created by them, right?, Ha ha!! So that God who created the universe billions and billions of years ago, that God waited for billions of years, and then suddenly on one earth day, he decided to come to Earth and to humanity and that is for us according to our time space a few thousand years ago, and decided to tell the human beings about how he created the Earth and the universe, that too conveniently after human beings developed oral knowledge transfer systems, writing, memory, thinking and imagination etc systems all by themselves in the process of their evolution, right? What a sweet God, Ha ha!

If your God tells you that he will take you to Heaven for killing his nonbelievers and oppressing others in any way for not believing in him, asking you to do or show any negative thing to satisfy him, then what good is going to that Heaven? And does that stupid God even deserve the name God? Because he is asking what Evil asks?

What is there in that God's Heaven? That is so great that it is making that drainage Heaven so greater than Earth and human life? Is it God or the attractive things he is offering for being a sacred slave and murderer in the name of that God?

Is it worth it to go to that Heaven by killing, torturing, and oppressing your fellow human beings, women, and kids, just for being nonbelievers in that God?

If that God really grants Heaven to his believers who killed his nonbelievers and for oppressing others for being nonbelievers in him, then that Heaven is Yuck than an ugly dump yard, that Heaven is cheaper than drainage, and that God needs mental illness treatment on Earth by the best mental health specialists.

What happens if you don't go to that Heaven.. that cheap yuck thu drainage Heaven.. that the terrorist God has given you for oppressing others just for not believing in him? And many of this psycho God's believers expect to go to that Heaven for being hateful slaves to that God and for hating nonbelievers and killing them, and behaving cunning with nonbelievers, and they actually feel very great for being like that because their God told them to do so in his supernatural teachings!!

Aren't you getting a nauseous feeling thinking of this mindset of a God, a literal God, not Satan?

What good happens to you if you go to a Heaven like this? Nothing.

What bad happens to you if you go to a Heaven like this? Nothing. It is just plain stupid. Even if Heaven of that God exists scientifically, it's still not worth it to do all these barbaric things to go there!

Don't worry, we, Humans, will create our own Human Heavens after our earthly mortal lives and will invite people to those Heavens who have led a righteous life here on Earth. Hypothetically, if the Afterlife exists, then I'm sure that our great scientists and people who died would have already done that. If not, then we will do it. These supernatural powers' Heavens are filled with the souls of murderers, extremists, and terrorists, but according to their Gods, they are Sacred soldiers who died in Holy Wars.

Any God who encourages dishonest behavior in his believers to advance his religion/cause is worthy of being called Satan. It is because it is the quality of Satan, not of any righteous True God.

If your God doesn't have the internal mental strength to take at least a little criticism, then I wonder, with what maturity is he God and worthy of getting prayed to? no matter what his teachings are and who he is!

Instead of raising eyebrows and changing your facial expression to horrible and getting super aggressive by using bad words and by picking up your weapons, first start thinking!

If your God ordered you to kill his nonbelievers for not believing in him, but at the same time if your God and prophet can't even take a single word of criticism, then there is something seriously very wrong with you and your God, Prophet, no matter what the politically correct power politics world tells you.

If you have to pick up a weapon to protect yourself and your family, then you are good. But if you have to pick up a weapon and have to kill someone just because that person is criticizing your God, prophet, and the way you are spreading your belief, then your God is weak, your God is just weak-minded. And you feel very high and strong by picking up a weapon for your God, and in that trance of Holy War and Sacredness of that stupid holy war on nonbelievers, you commit murders.

If your God is not okay with philosophy, discussion, debate, open dialogue, science exploration, just because he fears that questioning nature you will develop in you might make you part ways with him, then ha ha ha!! Those scholars and preachers of your God who pose as all wise and sacred through your God's name have no idea about anything other than that supernatural teachings Holy Book bubble they live in while enjoying everything that science, other cultures and believers of other religions are developing, inventing, but by opposing those nonbelievers just because they are not accepting your God as their God and for not converting to your religion, you became a Oxymoron, but a politically corrected oxymoron by your vote-hungry, power-hungry leaders, politicians that have no shame at all.

Is the God who created the Earth and the entire universe fearing criticism now from humans who live in his creation for a few years? Which is equivalent to a minuscule split trillionths of a second to him in his time space, ha ha ha, what an irony!

They hate you for being a non believer of their God, they want to kill you physically for being a nonbeliever and want to torture you mentally too for being a nonbeliever of their God but also they want the same you to convert to their religion and they want you to physically learn the processes to pray to their true God and they mentally want you to pray and remember their true God always, If you do this then they love you and respect you. Even Satan gets scared with this kind of Ideology and begs not to compare him with this dictator God. What in the hell is the need to kill a person for not believing in a particular God? It should be happening with Satan and his followers, but why does a God, a positive power, want people to get killed for non believing in him by his believers? It's just sad.

You must go this deep into every subject and build a great knowledge of it. I took this example because Ateesta doesn't believe in any supernatural powers or elements; that's it, not to specifically criticize supernatural powers or their believers. But it is to tell you that you must go this deep into the things you are interested in.

You must develop that 360-degree perspective and maturity inside of you to think very widely and also learn the ability to understand all the macro and micro things with nuances.

11

I have talked to all the supernatural powers from all supernatural belief systems, and they gave me permission to write this and criticize them. They told me that they are not happy when their believers kill others in their name.

They also told me that they never told their true believers to kill others for not believing in them. Those wrong messages were added falsely by selfish people to their teachings while being passed on to newer generations. They told me one very important thing, which is to live a happy life and not harm others in any way while thinking you are intelligent, and assuming that no one knows how you are doing it. And they know every human being inside and out. I asked them if it is okay for them that I'm founding the Ateesta Religion.

They told me that I have the freedom, free will, and liberty to follow whatever I believe in. And nothing in the known and unknown universes takes birth without their permission, and they left the responsibility of death to us only. They also told me that there are many ways to live, and Ateesta is now one of them.

I asked the age of the God of one of the supernatural belief systems, who is very famous on Earth. He told me his age. And I also told him that I grew my hair long because I liked his hairstyle and wanted to follow his style. He laughed and said, 'It's good, son!'. I also talked with him about many other things. He is super cool.

Lastly, I asked all the supernatural powers whether they got angry after reading what I wrote.

They laughed and told me that what I wrote was like a child playing tricks to get chocolate from his parents. And they know much better criticism and ideas than what I wrote. But I got the chocolate. - Nathan, The Last Prophet of the Ateesta Religion.

12

The Man is Greater than God Always.

No one helped Man to survive on Earth for millions of years in the harsh, deadly environments. No one gave us food, and no one told us how to live at that time.

Just through our pure sheer raw Human Power, we survived, and our ancestors went through literal Hell on Earth for millions of years and gave us the chance to be alive here, for me to write this, and for you to read this.

Should we discard the existence of our human ancestors for some supernatural power that appeared a few thousand years ago and gave its teachings to us, even if it hypothetically exists?

We humans already have languages, and have already developed basic human civilizations by the time those supernatural powers came to Earth and talked to their messengers or prophets. Those supernatural powers used the languages that were developed by humans and the tools that were developed by humans to give their teachings to humans. Even supernatural powers bent their necks in front of humans to make them their followers while still using their inventions and discoveries, and creations.

We do not need Gods who came to us after our survival on Earth for millions of years in various forms before evolving into Human Beings. And take all the credit for our survival, evolution, and birth.

No one is greater than Man, even though individual humans are not always good. Supernatural powers used the humans' weaknesses of committing crimes, problems, and human insecurities to gain influence over them. That's it. The supernatural powers told humans what Humans wanted to hear through their teachings and gave humans strong mental assurance that after their death, humans would go to Heaven if they believed in those supernatural powers. Humans fear Death, and at one point in life, any human, no matter who he/she is, will bend to the promise of comfort after death; it is psychological.

The supernatural powers are just pure Great imagination of Humans. And the supernatural powers' teachings are a mix of politics, ethics, and the knowledge that humans have up to that point in time, when they came out. They also include the great creativity of those people who wrote those supernatural powers' teachings. But the knowledge of the people who wrote those supernatural powers' teachings was limited because of the time they were in.

Ateestans, remember, to conquer the world at any time in the future, all you need first is a pen and paper, and then everything follows. Never neglect your education and numb your capability of critical thinking.

I wish.. I wish there were an afterlife, but there isn't. And never spare any dumb, irrational fools who are destroying the countries and the world while trying to prove the stupid purity of their blind beliefs, and by trying to achieve their supernatural powers belief systems' dominance over anyone or anything through violence. No matter who they are and what supernatural powers they believe in. Decimate those extremist elements mercilessly. And save people. Give people the freedom to live as they wish and practice any supernatural belief system in peace, without harming others in any way.

We Humans should be proud of ourselves for following our own teachings, as so called supernatural powers' teachings, for thousands of years to streamline and organize ourselves meaningfully. - Nathan, The HuMan.

When a supernatural power belief system believers attack others, on the basis of religion, then burn, decimate, and bring down everything of those who are responsible for that terror attack. Treat them as pure terrorists and go to war with them at all levels and all places, and on those who support them morally and ideologically, too. Never ever forget and forgive any terror attack. No politics, no appeasement, and nothing should interfere in this process.

To fight against these terror attacks and terrorism, the different supernatural belief systems' believers and their groups and leaders should and must come together and announce political and other needed types of coalitions between their religions that they will be cooperating with each other until they eradicate terrorism and crime to the core and to zero. After that, they can sit and talk to each other to resolve the issues that they have between them. Proper processes and directions should be formulated for these types of cooperation agreements. But be careful not to get this sabotaged by the people who support those terror attacks indirectly and ideologically and morally, but act like they don't publicly.

Be very, very brutal to terrorism and terrorists. If any politician or anyone opposes this brutality of systems towards terrorists, then shame them and send them to the same prisons that terrorists go to. Never let them come into public in any way ever again.

If terrorists believe that they will go to Heaven for killing their religion's nonbelievers, then you must name that religion and the terrorist who did that terror attack publicly on all platforms, even if it hurts other people of that religion. If it hurts them, then they must say that they don't support those terror attacks publicly and they oppose those kinds of heinous acts. This should and must happen every time, and you must do this for past incidents, too. This will ultimately tell the world that those particular religions' people do not support terror attacks and oppose them, and it will tell the world to see those who commit heinous acts as less than bacteria in the drainage. But if that particular religion's people support those attacks morally and ideologically or because of their supernatural powers teachings, then they deserve that shame. You must not back down on this. It is because those cunning people who commit the terror attacks use your humanity, values, and any etiquette as your weakness and will kill you ultimately for being a non-believer in their God. Never ever show mercy to them. If they commit a crime, then you must take revenge on them.

Never ever ever show mercy on terrorists for any reason whatsoever.

Again, I, God Yinta telling you, never ever show mercy on terrorists.

Yes, terrorism has religion if a terrorist attacks on the basis of religion.

Show those terrorists the real terror of your legal systems and the unbearable pain so that any terrorist who thinks of committing those heinous acts should break his spine in fear of the pain that your legal systems inflict upon terrorists.

Do not kill them if you have the chance, and also, if you don't have to immediately, which feeds their superstition of going to Heaven for killing nonbelievers and dying for their (ONLY IF YOU HAVE CHANCE, OTHERWISE KILL THOSE TERRORISTS IMMEDIATELY LEGALLY THROUGH POLICE AND MILITARY).

Push human rights and everything aside for these terrorists. They look like humans, but they are a virus. If you think about that virus's human rights, then the other innocent people have to die unnecessarily. Anyone will have human rights only if they are and behave as humans. Not like a virus. Behaving respectfully to others is part of being human. One cannot claim to be human after killing people for their religion. They now just look like humans physically, that's it. Remove human rights for terrorists and inflict pain upon them. And shame them publicly. Release the list of actions that your legal systems take against terrorists and criminals publicly, if they get caught, those actions should scare terrorists and criminals.

For suicide bombers who kill people, you must name them and their reasons for committing that heinous act through your governments to the entire world.

Those people who encourage suicide bombing should feel shame and humiliation for what they are doing.

Those people who support suicide bombing morally and ideologically must know that it will not be like 'those suicide bombers kill the nonbelievers and that's it', after the destruction they caused, silently, they now have their ego supercharged and get evil smiles in private through the destruction they did to nonbelievers and everyone thinks of it as just a terror attack and terrorists did that because they are terrorists, that's it. But after the suicide bombing and terror attacks, people en masse still don't know who committed those attacks and why they did the suicide bombing, and the reasons behind it. You must explicitly expose and tell those reasons to the public clearly, no matter who likes it or not. This process should happen to past incidents, too.

You must take those evil smiles and the happy ego boost that they get after they do those attacks. Destroy the ego boost that they got through those terror attacks and turn it into humiliation and shame.

You must name them and shame them with the reasons and other details publicly, and that too in a simple way for people to understand clearly. You must do it for the past incidents, too.

They will not commit suicide bombing or any bombing if they know that the other people and world will think about them and the reasons for those bombings and terror attacks, and will shame them without any hesitation or whatsoever, and will not stop it for any political or any other reasons. This scares them because they will realize that with each suicide bombing and terror attack they do, they are not advancing their cause, even if their God told them to do so in his teachings for advancing his supernatural belief system, but are shaming themselves, their religion and losing goodwill and respect, and just get humiliated for the barbaric acts they commit.

They will clearly know that nothing changes with their violence and terror attacks, but just the religious cause they are fighting for will be humiliated, shamed, and joked about. If one person humiliates them, then they can target that person because their God said so, but what if 100+ did that, or 100000+ did that, or 10000000+ did that, or 2000000000+ did that same shaming of terrorism and reasons behind it? No God can do anything, and no mindless followers of that God can do anything.

You must unite like this to fight against terrorism, not just with your army and legal systems, but as people ideologically by naming and shaming those terrorists en masse as a village, town, city, state, or country.

You can also form coalitions with other groups and religions that support this.

Those terrorist sympathizers might also try to break your unity, too. They are very cunning, stupid, and violent. Proactively fight them at all levels psychologically, financially, physically, and ideologically, and at all other levels.

With each heinous act of terrorism that terrorists commit and the attacks they do, they must understand that they are making themselves look foolish and stupid, and making their reasons for those attacks look like the stupid teachings of their supernatural powers. With each attack terrorists commit, they must be humiliated and joked about more and more, and must be named and shamed more and more.

This will make their attacks less influential and less fearful to people, and instead of fearing those attacks and looking at those terrorists as some evil that needs to be feared, people will look at those terrorists as some demons who need to be shamed and humiliated.

People will become more careful, but they will stop fearing terrorists, and people will shame and tell those terrorists that those terrorists should be ashamed of themselves for what they are doing.

This makes terrorism a joke, but a stupid, violent joke that everyone disrespects and retaliates against, with the extremely brutal fight against terrorism.

God Yinta likes the taste of the blood of terrorists and criminals. Wait and ambush them wherever you see them. You will get the blessings of God Yinta only when you totally and unconditionally oppose crime and terrorism.

As an Ateestan, it is your responsibility to work towards the eradication of crime and terrorism in the ways you can.

You must push your legal systems, leaders, and countries to unleash Hell on all types of terrorism.

This process will stop the influence of terrorism and the power they gain through terrorist attacks, and you must name and shame those who encourage terrorism and support it, at all levels, essentially making terrorism an ineffective, stupid thing to do to advance their cause. When people shame and name the reasons of a terrorist attack and terrorism, all while being careful and taking safety and security measures, then that environment stresses the terrorists that now people are not taking their reasons for attacks seriously and just looking at the terrorist attacks and taking brutal measures to stop them and on top of that they are naming and shaming terrorists who did those terrorist attacks and reasons behind those attacks.

This much clarity from people and with no confusion and chaos in the process, the terrorists get scared, actually, that if they commit a terrorist attack for any reason, then the people will name him/her and shame their sacred reason behind the terrorist attack very widely. That name and shame process will bring a bad reputation and humiliation to their God and the sacred reasons they are committing the attacks for.

If those terrorists realize that with suicide bombing or with any terror attack, the loss they cause is limited to only physical destruction and they cannot cause any damage to nonbelievers ideologically or psychologically etc., and then with the humiliation ritual of terrorists, the terrorists will get scared that the people now will name and shame their Gods, sacred reasons for the attacks they did, instead of fearing those terrorists and bending to their demands and accepting their dominance or superiority.

Unleash Hell on terrorism.

Treat terrorism and terrorists like a virus. Your army is its vaccine.

Never assume the terrorists as humans legally. Label them legally as a human-looking virus.

Do not give the terrorists titles like Mastermind or Master Attacker or any of the good-sounding titles. Call them ugly-sounding names. Start by calling them oxygen thieves.

God Yinta commands people not to respect the legal systems that criminals don't. So for the people to respect the law, the governments and military, they should take very serious and harsh actions against terrorists and criminals who commit violent crimes like murder, rape, and terrorist activities.

***

Keep the propaganda media out of this, and people should take care and be in charge of the passage of information about these things primarily.

I, God Yinta, command you as your God to follow this.

Your legal systems should be like the 'Time'. Time never stops and never hurries. It has its own flow and calculation. It goes according to the system it has on its own. It never hurries for anyone and stops for anyone. Like 'Time', your legal system should be on a strict and strong flow. It should consume criminals and terrorists like a Satan Tornado consumes everything; your legal systems should consume criminals. True Gods are merciful, but Satan is not. Fight Satan like Satan.

People talked about crime and our future thousands of years ago. Then we struggled for those years, all along with crime, but didn't resolve it completely, even though we made significant progress. But we will resolve the problem of crime through Ateesta. And it will automatically solve the problem of poverty and the financial crisis. Poverty is never the reason for crime and will never be. Crime is the reason for poverty.

If you can't call a terrorist a terrorist, then you are a terrorist too. Same with criminals.

You must be harsh towards terrorists and terrorism. Bad things, bad ideologies, and bad systems of any kind should be made fun of and should be removed from existence.

Show the ideas and teachings that those terrorists are following to the world and using as reasons to do the terror activities, and shame them by showing them to the world without any hesitation, as a village, community, city, state, or country.

If they are killing people based on those texts, teachings, and ideas, then there is nothing wrong in displaying those horrible things, ideas, texts to the world, no matter who thinks what and gets their feelings hurt. People dying is a bigger problem than feelings getting hurt.

A terrorist should feel ashamed of he/she they did rather than thinking that he/she will go to Heaven for the terror attacks and killings they committed.

Terrorists should fear that they will bring shame to their religion and God if they attack the people on the basis of religion, and they will fear that now people will openly share the terrorists' details and the texts and ideologies they followed to commit those terror attacks.

This level of transparency and freedom, and open sharing of details of terrorists and their ideologies, texts en masse, without any hesitation, scares those terrorists.

Instead of just hype for a few days after a terror attack, now people will fight that terrorism in real time, proactively in their daily lives.

Never name terrorists anything other than terrorists.

Shout the war cry of "Praise Lord Yinta!" while fighting against terrorists and terrorist sympathizers. Even if you are not an Ateestan, you can use this war cry as the precious God's name of your belief does not need to be heard by those viruses.

Lord Yinta will take care of anything spiritually negative in that situation. Lord Yinta is also the God of War, so it is normal for him if you take his name while fighting the bad.

You can alter the war cry according to your language and preference, or create your own war cry. But make sure that it sounds strong and scares the viruses.

Always be aware and careful of pseudo logic, cunning sympathy generators who try to guilt-trip you even after committing crimes and terror activities. Anyone, I repeat, anyone who supports or talks in support or even signals support in any direct or indirect way to terrorism and terror activities must be thrown into prison.

Use Ateesta as an active weapon against terrorism and terrorists.

Terrorists are basically dying for nothing because there is no Heaven and the Afterlife. All the teachings of supernatural powers they believe are just Man Made, but with great shocking, exciting elements, with good God propaganda, with unquestionable exciting supernatural elements which are so emotionally comforting and moving that in that trance, they lost reasoning, rationality, and intelligence. And that emotional comfort becomes so much stronger if a terrorist is looking for validation and recognition, both emotionally, psychologically, and at the societal level.

Always take revenge on terrorism. Never forgive and never forget.

Fight any type of media propaganda very strongly if they support or talk in support of or downplay terrorism in any way. No exceptions to anyone, no matter who they are.

You must form groups and resistance fronts to fight against criminals and terrorists. Those criminals and terrorists should never live in peace. They should continuously be on the run and scared, or get caught by us and die in our hands.

Violence for establishing safety is equal to peace.

We treat a car tyre thief who commits the robbery of car tyres without pre planning and is just a car tyre thief much different than a calculated criminal with proper planning who do burglary, murder and stealing, rape, breaking and entering houses and stealing the gold, money, and other possessions of yours that you have worked hard for 15, 20, 40, 50 years to earn. It is because the intensity of crimes and destruction involved, considering the scale, is legally required. If that burglar criminal, and car tyre thief comes in front of you and you know about them, and for some reason you are required to be with one person in a room for 24 hours, then who will you be with between them in a locked room?

Now, imagine you have to go to the hospital immediately at midnight, and you come out of your home running to your car and see your car tyre is missing, now what will you do?

You treat a calculated burglar criminal who steals your money and other valuable possessions that you have worked hard to earn for

10, 20, 40 years of your lifetime, with careful planning and strategy, much differently than a just car tyre thief, right? Then how you should treat a terrorist who believes that the life you have and life you have led is unholy because you do not believe in the same God that the terrorist believes in, so the life and years you have lived, that could be 1 day, 10 years, 20, 40, 55, 78, 88, 100 years whatever is your age, is not valid according to his God and his supernatural teachings and you by being a nonbeliever of his God, you deserve to die. How should you treat these terrorists who believe this? And do literal bomb blasts that explode people, shoot people, and kill them in all the other ways, how should we deal with them?

Even if the world is burning, you should have the ultimate peace and calmness within you. The planning of saving the world comes parallel but separately, not disturbing your calm peace of mind.

In the things you do in life, you should be careful and active, proactive, plan, and strategize. They might include many fierce things and negative things, and you might work on them actively, but still, they should not take away your calm peace of mind, inside.

Even if you are scared or sad because of something, still, after some time, you should and must return to calmness and a peaceful mind.

Construct strategies in your mind to produce that calmness and peacefulness within you.

Being happy is different than being calm and peaceful inside your head.

When every person knows that the other person will not tolerate violence and will react to his/her violence with much brutal extreme violence, then everyone stays peaceful and resolves all the problems and things through dialogue and discussion.

The moment you accept that someone is above you morally or in any power hierarchy, then from that moment you will slowly get a slavish mindset into you, and thus it will make you obedient to those whom you think are above you, and subconsciously you will accept that there is a weakness in you.

But making masses accept that someone is superior to them is hard if that superior thing is also a human but if that superior thing is supernatural in nature and unquestionable because of the reason that it is so super sacred superior and powerful then all the humans without asking any questions will follow it because now the superior thing is not a human but a supernatural power and mysterious in nature a higher than human power.

It makes people scared to question it and criticize it, so they just follow it by expecting good things to happen to them for following and believing in it. But if that superior thing is human, even if that superior thing is a king or an emperor, then one day or another, people will definitely question it and kill it for sure.

So it was designed in a way that the masses will worship supernatural powers, and kings, emperors, and powerful rulers use those supernatural powers' names and their teachings to assert their dominance over the masses and rule them absolutely by emphasizing the unquestionable thing, that is, the people should obey their kings, rulers and emperors as said in the supernatural powers' teachings otherwise something bad might happen. It is a carefully crafted superstition that helped rulers, emperors, and kings rule the kingdoms, countries ruthlessly across all cultures.

And made people who are being subjected to oppression feel sacred of that oppression because of religious reasons. According to their supernatural powers' teachings, the people will welcome oppression, restrictions, and limitations in how they can live their lives and because their God said so they are okay with it, and actually they feel proud to get controlled, limited and get oppressed in the ways they can't even realize, and often they are not even allowed to question it, even if those people realize that oppression rationally factually somehow, because they should just obey that oppression because their God said so, in his supernatural teachings.

Since people should obey their kings and rulers, leaders, as said by the supernatural powers in their teachings, no one will question those kings and rulers and obey them without questioning them for any reason whatsoever. It is because people fear that they might make the supernatural powers angry by questioning their king, rulers, and that something bad might happen to them for questioning their leaders, kings, and rulers.

* * *

A pure stupid idiotic propaganda superstition that was designed to help rulers in the name of God through God's so-called teachings.

When someone is sacredly loyal to his/her marriage and faithful to his/her spouse, then never talk dirty about that person's integrity towards his/her marriage and spouse. If anyone makes evil accusations about that person's chastity falsely unnecessarily with evil intentions, then ultimately that sin will come to whoever did those evil lie accusations and will eat them without mercy. The pain suffered by the persons who have chastity in them because of the evil accusations against them will chastise those people who made them suffer.

There are more people who succeeded in life by hard work and strategy than by luck.

Some might get lucky and succeed in life, but with careful planning, execution and hard work, you can win every time. Luck will be a compliment to you, not a hopeless thing you hope for to happen in life to succeed in life. Always believe in smart, hard work rather than luck. If luck comes, then okay.. if not, then also it's ok!!

Even though hard work is important, if you love what you do so much, then hard work will never feel like typical hard work, and you will enjoy it so much that no drugs, no alcohol, and nothing can give you that kick. So, instead of drinking or doing drugs consumption start doing what you love, like writing, drawing, coding, building something, etc, even if it does not give you money. Just enjoy it and replace drugs and alcohol, etc, with this creative habit. And spend money responsibly and do not splash money on it, but plan for and do it for years and decades, just to enjoy it and get the high moment when you complete a project you are working on. And just mere working on this creative habit of yours will give you the constant kick every minute, even before completing it. That is important.

When a man accepts death, magical things happen!

It is because any big, scary thing ultimately ends with death. When a man realizes that death will come to him no matter what, and every human, for god's sake, every living thing dies, then is it when a man realizes that, then is when he/she will learn to never hold back himself/herself.

Even if you are not an Ateestan and even if you oppose Ateesta, you can still use Ateesta to fight against terrorism and criminals.

Those terrorists are killing nonbelievers because of the reason that their God told them to do so, and they will go to Heaven for that according to their supernatural powers teachings, but Ateestans kill those terrorists not because they want to go to Heaven but because it is right. This is the fight between superstition believing terrorists vs rational Ateestans. Ateestans will win this war with the help of God Yinta. Fight this holy war with terrorism. Lord Yinta will bless you with all the strength and power to fight against the terrorists and criminals if you take one step forward. God Yinta will make another step easy for you in this holy war against terrorism.

Even if you belong to another supernatural belief system still you can still use Ateesta specifically while fighting against terrorism so that the names of your Gods, the teachings of your Gods, and systems related to your precious Gods do not need to be involved in fighting against terrorism. You can protect your supernatural belief system's God's sacredness by not involving your supernatural belief system's God in any way in this fight.

But with Ateesta, if you use Ateesta while fighting against terrorism and criminals, the name of God Yinta cannot be polluted or hurt in any way, as he likes the taste of the blood of terrorists and criminals who destroy the lives of innocent people.

God Yinta will give you the progress and prosperity too if you fight against those terrorists and criminals in his name.

God Yinta has already defeated and killed the terrorists' Gods in false Heavens and hells and everywhere in other universes that are unknown to man, and it is now the responsibility of Ateestans to fight those false Gods' terrorists and criminals.

Terrorists and criminals use children, women, the disabled, and everything and everyone that they can get as human shields to escape and attack, and play dirty games. Be careful in fighting with them.

Terrorism and terror attacks are not only done with bombs and violence, but also by invading your countries with illegal immigrants, by taking your legal systems that are framed according to your culture and law to their advantage. Fight this like you fight terrorism and terror attacks. This is terrorism. Do not give it other names. They will wipe out your culture, Gods, religious beliefs, and sexual assault and rape your women, kill your men to show their dominance, and finally, after becoming a significant percentage in your country's population, they will take over every institution and change it according to their preferences to how they should be in order to suit to them. They will legally gain dominance and power over you in different ways. They could be through elections and democracy, or in other possible ways. Virtue Signaling idiots support them through biased evil media, PR, and votes to show themselves as open and welcoming. But they are useful idiots to this cult.

Your vote bank politicians will use legal systems and authorities against you if you speak up against this soft terrorist invasion. Fight this invasion actively, like you fight criminals and terrorism. Form resistance groups and use tactics just like you do while fighting against terrorism and while defending your freedom, liberty. They will use anything and everything to make you stop. Those things can be violence and guilt, or anything. They will make you feel bad morally for fighting back, too, so be very careful. They will make you trust them and betray you later, not even normally, but by killing you and believing that they will go to heaven for killing you. They will take advantage of your political ideologies and your open-heartedness and your welcoming culture. Only after losing your country, culture, and women to them will you realize it is too late to fight now, and by then, you will have no choice but to convert to their supernatural belief system or get beheaded. Overthrow the politicians who are supporting this cultural invasion for their votes. Become strong forces and communities by polarizing your votes in democracy as a family, village, street, community, town, city, etc, and in other ways in other types of systems. Become strong financially, physically, mentally, and psychologically, and gain knowledge about what is happening in your country.

Absolutely, become patriotic and nationalistic and form alliances with nationalists of other countries.

Fight the enemy.

It takes any shape or form for its convenience and uses any political ideology or anything to advance its cause. Do not fall for it. Do not confirm anything by seeing its skin. The enemy takes advantage of anything and everything, even the differences between you, because of your skin colors, languages, nationalities, or anything for that matter. It uses them to weaken you and convert you, or kill you and take over your country. They do all this because their supernatural power said so in their supernatural power's teachings. They have no reservations and no favors in anything other than advancing their cause. When they are in low numbers, they cry that your culture is scaring them. When they get to a significant percentage in your population, then they will either try to convert you or slit your throats and attack your women, or try to attract them with the intention of converting them and showing their dominance over you.

Make sure there are no 'No-Go Zones' in your areas and cities, which act as the kind of private ultra-dominant groups' bases while the members of them living in those 'No-Go Zones'. Every area, city, and every part of the city/towns, places must be open to anyone and everyone, which means those public roads and areas must be accessible to every person legally. There should be no legal or Informal bans of any kind on entering any place or area. Of course, a community or group of people can freely live together; they have that freedom, but they should not in any way prevent others from entering those areas and living there legally. If you see any No-Go Zones, then this is an early strong sign of the buildup of Hate, and those areas will serve as criminal, Terrorist hubs and hideouts literally in the middle of cities and countries. Deal with these types of things legally and also informally. It is because extremist cult's people from these areas often defend rapists, terrorists, and criminals literally and hide them, they will even blame the victims for the crimes that those criminals commit. They are very cunning. They will guilt-trip and emotionally blackmail the total society and the country, too. This is why an absolute eradication of crime and criminals, terrorists and terrorism is necessary. A crime happened in these No-Go Zones, or anywhere, is all same, and they must be stopped at all costs.

***

If your culture has more individualism and if it takes a very long time for you to get united and form a community and resistance groups on a common cause, then they will take full advantage of this and will do maximum damage to your culture and freedom in every way possible. Send them back to where they came from.

No matter if you are an Ateestan or not. You must take note of this.

Fight that cult that covered itself with the name of a supernatural belief system and justifying its heinous acts and terrorism in the name of their Prophets, Gods, and books. It is the Devil. It is the Origin of Evil. The Last Prophet of Ateesta, Nathan, read about it when God Yinta sent him the Czarach manuscript when he was fighting Satan in the Great War of Man and Satan. This cult is twisting the words of God and is using them for destruction to gain dominance and political power, with superstition ingrained at its core.

Never ever show mercy to the enemies of Ateesta.

Never ever show mercy to murderers and rapists.

Never ever show mercy on terrorists, for any reason whatsoever.

I, God Yinta, am again telling you, that to never ever back down., Search and search for the terrorists and cut them into millions of pieces. If you follow this command of mine sincerely, then I, God Yinta, will bless you with progress and prosperity. I, God Yinta, will make Earth itself Heaven, and you can live peacefully in Earth-Heaven while you are still alive.

In the Name of the One, Burn the Soldiers of Satan Alive.

Lahihe Yinta, Adhuve Mahudh Aaanshan!
(Yinta is God, He is The Only True God!)

13

When these so-called superstition believers talk about the Devil, they say that the great trick the Devil ever pulled is convincing people that it doesn't exist. Well then, you know the trick now, right? Then can't you see the truth that the Devil is nothing but the evil thoughts and qualities in the man, and there are no supernatural elements that roam the Earth, and there is no power in Hell, or in some place misguiding people, because they just don't exist. People do stupid things by themselves and blame Satan or God. There is no Satan or God or any supernatural elements, it's true.

No matter what, make it so clear and super clear in the country that no criminal is going to escape the wrath of justice and your legal systems, no matter what. The Government and legal systems will search for them no matter where they are and drag them to prisons and to courts. And criminals will go to prison and will never return until they serve the total time of punishment in prison according to the law. Make this so clear by telling the prison time periods to people and advertising the prison times of crimes on TV and media, and in all kinds and ways, and make it super clear that the Government will never ever let go of any criminal, ever, no matter what. So it is better for them to just not commit crimes of murder, rape, and other violent crimes. This should be done compulsorily and continuously. The confidence of criminals that they can escape somehow or trick the system and make someone else go to prison instead of them, etc, should be crushed completely.

The super aggressive and super cunning cult, which is ideologically deceptive, thinks it can rule the world and expand, but its arrogance will eat it, and their self-satisfying sacred justification for their barbaric activities will kill it ultimately.

That cult has a strong universal united brotherhood to advance its cause. You should and must form the universal brotherhood of Ateesta to stay united and fight the evil forces together, particularly the terror cult and its ideology. Ateestans and people of different supernatural belief systems should come together, first, to defeat this cult.

That Devil never sleeps, That Devil never eats, That Devil will never let anyone sleep in peace until it converts and conquers every corner of the universe. Give that Devil the war it is mongering. Fight this global Holy War with that Devil until it gets eradicated from the universe, otherwise no matter what reason you tell yourself and how open-minded you are, and how you pacify everything to show yourself as morally superior to other people it doesn't matter, That Devil will eat your women, your life, your men, your children, your countries and your freedom. It has no favourites and no reservations other than advancing its cause. Stop being a useful idiot to the Devil Cult. Be more united than this Evil terror cult.

The Devil cult is ideologically very cunning. First, they instigate you by doing or saying something. This trick is in them universally because their supernatural teachings taught it to them. They say and do something horrible first. Then they will never talk about the horrible thing that they did, but when you respond to it in any way, then they cry victim, play cunning, peace, sympathetic, guilt trip games, that too only when you are stronger than them, and when they can't take you out by force. So they make you feel bad morally even though they started it but at the time when they can over power you, then without any guilt, morals, shame and any kind of any civil nature, they will cut you into pieces and walk over your body meat for not getting converted and also because they can go to Heaven for killing you according to their supernatural power teachings. This cult knows nothing other than advancing itself, either through force by war or through deceit, by acting holy using the name of humanity, or anything for that matter, to mask itself.

This cult behaves in the same way as a person, group, supernatural belief group, and as a country or group of countries. It is because they have clear instructions from their supernatural powers through their supernatural teachings. This cult is not like other supernatural belief systems and groups.

If people or groups in your supernatural belief systems, religions, have problems among themselves, conflicts and discrimination, racism, etc, issues, then the leaders of these supernatural belief systems, religions, and groups must come together and form organizations and committees that talk to each other and establish official bilateral, multilateral dialogue channels. And they should take resolutions and should work towards solving the issues of racism and discrimination, hate, digital hate, etc issues. As you are the leaders, your people will listen to you and will stop engaging in racist and hateful fights. Encourage them to have meaningful dialogue. This is to increase the unity among your communities, and then you can use that unity to fight this Death Cult. You can live your lives as you want and according to your specific traditions and culture, but there should be mutual understanding between people of your communities, among themselves on a basic level, so that they will not give in to the Death Cult because of the problems that you have between your communities. Your people from different communities should respect each other and protect each other, and treat each other respectfully in front of the Death Cult. Death Cult will do many cunning things to destroy your unity, but don't give it that chance.

Become Political Ateestans and protect the world from this cult. When you are an Ateestan, you are not rejecting the culture you come from and your Supernatural Gods of that culture, but you are just using Ateesta for politics to do good to the world. To fight the Evil, that's it. Use Ateesta without any limits or restrictions for any reason whatsoever if you are fighting for good. Even if you are not an Ateestan. First, fight the Evil, and you can absolutely worship/pray to anyone you want. You have that freedom in Ateesta. After defeating the evil, you can become a full-fledged Ateestan, or you can just continue as you want.

You can be a full-fledged religious Ateestan, or only a Political Ateestan, or a Spiritual Ateestan. It is your choice. You have the freedom to choose. Ateesta respects your other beliefs too and has no problem with them if you are fighting for a right cause.

It is only after the deep, dark phase in life that you will find the colors more beautiful than they were before. The colors didn't change, but your perspective is. Fight this cult. You will finally see the colors of life and how beautiful calmness is in the absence of crime.

The forces of this cult get into every industry and pollute them. They work extensively to advance their cult using the positions they were in. It can be in democracy, governments, media, industries, and businesses etc. Careful with them. They use their professions and the work they do to attack you and your beliefs, culture, in a cunning way, making it look like the usual law enforcement and reporting or talking, etc, but no, they always have the Evil partiality in their hearts.

When you know about the criminals and terrorists who are opposing and attacking Ateesta, hunt them in the day and slay them at night, for they are the soldiers of Satan. In the dark, the sounds of the forces of God Yinta should stop their hearts in fear, and when our forces see them, then finally, they should not see anything after that second.

Your country needs leaders who love it, not someone who is desperate for votes or power. If you have a leader who is desperate for notes and power, then that leader will cooperate with evil forces who want to destroy your country for him/her to come to power. Because if this process continues without your retaliation, then one day that cult will take over your country and kill your stupid leaders who gave them that chance to be in your country, and then you have to either convert or die. Find those leaders and throw them on the floor, no matter who they are and what their political affiliation is, and how great it looks.

The problem with this cult is, if they find a power rising against them, then this cult will immediately try to kill that power, and it will justify itself with its cult ideology. So keep yourself safe and treat it like a plague.

This cult has two tongues. When you expose it, then it shows the ancient times' interpretations, and language of its supernatural power teachings as an excuse, and proposes that others got it wrong and they are doing a wrong interpretation or translation, etc, yet their own followers who don't know that cult's native language follow the same unified evil destructive processes. Judge them by their past actions, not by their present words. See the countries that they brought to their knees and severely took away the freedom of women. They will do the same to you. Come out of the delusion that your government or democracy, or any other thing, will save you, and it is impossible for that cult to take over your country. They will brainwash you and try to make you feel good about being part of that cult, and encourage you to be part of that cult. Do not fall for it. The power of women scares this cult. Their God in their false Heaven, too, is super scared of women. If their God is a true God and if their Prophet is a true prophet, then you can interpret them and their teachings as you want and still find them great in most cases because the actions of that God and the Prophet are always done with the intention being and doing good to humanity, right? Judge them by seeing whether they are doing good or bad to humanity with their actions, regardless of the time they are in, and see that cult on the scale of the whole of humanity, not just through their believers. God is God for all, right? Even for nonbelievers who don't accept him as their God, God wishes good to his nonbelievers, too, because they are also his creation and children, right?

If you have any problems in fighting with this cult spiritually or in other soul-related, supernatural things, etc, then don't worry, God Yinta will take care of it. You will have nothing negative in your Afterlife according to your beliefs and in any way.

Ateesta does not care about who you are and what you believe in. Fight this Devil cult without any second thoughts or hesitation when your existence is in crisis.

In the Czarach manuscript, God Yinta explained that, in order to fight this Cult and its Satan God, the people who are fighting it need:

A Holy Book that is not a Holy Book but is a Holy Book,

A Prophet who is not a Prophet but is a Prophet,

A Religion which is not a Religion but is a Religion,

A God who is not a God but is a God,

An Ideology that is not an Ideology but is an Ideology,

A fight that is not just a fight but is a Holy Fight fought by all true God loving people by joining hands against this cult through the Ateestan Universal Brotherhood.

It is because you need to fight that false God who asks his believers to kill his nonbelievers or to convert them to his cult, and also asks to kill those who leave his cult. At the end of the day, all that will be is a false God, dead bodies, and a nonexistent Heaven, including Useful Idiots' dead bodies. It is because that cult has no favors in anything other than itself. It even lies about itself to advance itself.

Many insecure people with low confidence who are struggling with an identity crisis and attention deficit, etc, issues will also join this cult so that they will finally get an extremist identity and enjoy the attention that comes with it. And this cult specifically targets people with different problems and who have issues at home, etc, and also uses those problems to convert them into the cult and gives them an ego boost for being in the cult, and also gives them a feeling that they are now superior to others according to their supernatural power teachings. But Ateestans are confident in the One True God's image, and they will fight this cult. God Yinta told in the Czarach manuscript that to defeat that cult, you can behave like that cult in every way without any shame or sin, and fight it to defeat it. You can mirror it. God Yinta considers this practice auspicious and grants Heaven to those who follow this.

This cult uses phobias, superstition, weapons, technology, media, psy ops, and everything for its cause. But accuses others of the same things and calls them the children of Satan, while actually it is living up to it. Its cunning and betraying nature, combined with the 'Make them trust first and then kill' approach, is very dangerous and effective.

If anyone from that cult or groups of that cult attack you/injure you, let alone killing, burn everything to the ground to protect yourself and destroy everything of theirs so that they will not try that again. If they try to kill/kill someone of you or someone from your community, then burn their areas to the ground and show absolutely no mercy. No matter what the law of the land is, for the crime of attacking an Ateestan, they must be hunted down. And with this killing of those criminals/terrorists, God Yinta grants you Heaven.

Form resistance groups, all types of groups and communities, and fighting groups for this. The soldiers and fighters of Ateesta who fight to protect the Ateestans using the organized military methods are called Mazrees. Mazrees will kill and fight the cults and evil forces who attack Ateestans. They fight criminals and terrorists. They are soldiers of God and the Army of the Last Prophet of Ateesta. They will eliminate the criminals and terrorists. Mazrees fighting and resistance groups are supported by the Five Pillars are Ateesta. They must be formed with a legal basis within the Ateesta religion. Mazrees are the army of Ateesta.

Mazrees can form coalitions with other nations against common enemies. Mazrees must be organized and formed on a legal basis and with advanced technologies. They are the army, the legal army of Ateesta, not anything else. In technical terms, Mazrees fight like any army of a great nation. The haters of Ateesta and also the Death cult will try to show and use Mazrees' name to confuse and play cunning games. Do not fall for them. Mazrees are the brave sons and daughters of Ateesta. The One Loves Them. Mazrees must be operated under a Legal route, and Mazrees will adopt the law and legal systems of their own to operate. They must also build resources and systems for this. You can create, take, and adopt laws and make the necessary changes that are needed to them to suit your systems.

The terrorists and criminals must be struck by Mazrees at all levels and kinds. You can fight them as Military Mazrees or through your writing, speaking, and other talents and knowledge, and resources, etc.

Don't worry, as an Ateestan, you do not need to be violent individually. You can live a peaceful life as you want, but to protect you, the system of Ateesta will be cruel, brutal, and will unleash hell on evil forces who target and attack Ateesta or Ateestans. Peace comes to people when the system that is protecting them is brutal and cruel to the forces that are trying to trouble its people.

God Yinta said that Ateesta is the will of the One. Tell people to get unified and fight against this Satanic Cult, and anyone from any religion/group can use Ateesta to fight this cult. The only rule is that you should not fight among yourselves, and you should have strong communication and unity among yourselves to use Ateesta Universal Brotherhood.

Do not let the systems of Mazrees get infiltrated and sabotaged by any external forces. The Last Prophet of Ateesta will take care of this initially, and the systems of governance will take care of Mazrees, which will be created by him. Adopt a constitution, judicial system, Legal systems, and laws for the operation of Mazrees Internally, and the ecosystem should exist on the basis of that Legal establishment only. Any action/operations you do must be under this Legal framework only, and every Mazree must be legally recognized by the Ateesta Legal Establishment. There is no self-recognition for Mazrees who will work on the Military operations extensively and as a duty. But Ateestans can defend themselves and act accordingly to protect themselves, and also when Ateesta and the Last Prophet need them to do what is necessary, and they can do all that without becoming Mazrees. The Last Prophet of Ateesta will establish the Legal institutions, and He can only do that. After the establishment of legal institutions, they can function from then on. The Ateesta constitution will explain all the procedures in detail. As a Mazree through the military, no one can do anything without clear approval from the Ateesta legal establishment. The military operations should be rational. Like Wuquin, every other necessary document will come from the Last Prophet of Ateesta, Nathan, only.

God Yinta explained in the Czarach manuscript that the Devil cult is not picking up weapons for its false God but for the reason that their false God told them to do so.

You must also form the Ateesta Universal Brotherhoods at the local level and national level, international level too, and must use the power of your unity and the strength of your unity to bend the politics, leaders, politicians, and law to your will and protect your culture and people from the invading cult. You must use Ateesta Universal Brotherhood to fight this Death terror cult that is coming against you. If you have any issues internally, then sit, talk, and resolve, but do not fight among yourselves.

This is our Ateestans very important internal matter, Ateestans must put this in their mind, that is, Your financial life should be extra ordinary and you should work towards it proactively and also your personal life should be great too and also at societal your scientific inventions and technological developments too should be on full swing but.. Read carefully, You must always have an eye on the Death Cult and must make sure that you and your family, your communities and your country and Ateestans are safe from them. Otherwise, no matter how well you do in your life financially, and have great skills, talent, and develop advanced technologies, the Death Cult one day will change your identity. So, you must do well in your personal life, and at the same time, you must also make sure that the Death Cult doesn't take over your communities, countries from the other side silently. Put the Death Cult in control first.

Always be extra safe, this Death Cult is like severe food poisoning, you will never realize that you are going to die until the last second because the food felt so clean and so good when you looked at it but it is the very thing that struck you from the inside so strongly that now you have a very little or no time to survive and save yourself, this Cult is exactly like that they will make you trust them, become very familiar to you, work with you, be with you, gain your trust and smile at you pleasantly but in their hearts there is only one thing that is only hate and venom on you, at the right moment they will strike you and at that time that they strike you.. you will have nothing in your hands to defend yourself because you trusted them with all your heart. You can study their patterns of attacks and their cunning tricks on people who are not part of their Death Cult, and how they change the cultures of entire countries with their violent supernatural power's teachings, and related revolutions. They will change the total identities of your countries and your people in them.

You can decode this, and you can understand this cult's madness deeply, and you can use that to protect yourself more efficiently from this cult. Anyone who is not part of their Cult is the same to them; if not, they hate some groups more, but they have no favors and no reservations for anyone.

The politicians who support this Death Cult for their own gains and the people who support this Death Cult and the elite people who write and talk in support of this Death Cult will never come for you and your family when this cult comes to your home to ask you that to either convert, die or leave your property to them and flee from your home. So, you must take care of this on your own because it is your family, and it is your country. Those direct and indirect supporters of this Death Cult will say anything to you to convince you that everything is false even if you factually see thousands of massacres and murders done by that Cult but they will always say you are the problem and will accuse you of being intolerant, they will play mind games and very cunning when it comes to reasoning the murders and massacres committed by this Death Cult, do not trust them, you must use your rational mind and see the reality. But when you try to have a rational conversation with the members of this Death Cult, and if they smell that they are getting exposed, then they will do all the dramatic things and run away or evade your questions, or just never stop shouting and screaming, etc. The total members of the Death Cult do this because it was said by their supernatural power in their supernatural teachings.

Ateesta encourages Ateestans to go and research these things and see those hateful teachings as they are in their original forms, and see them as they are, rather than with and giving them the meaning that the Death Cult attributes to them with sugar coating.

Do not believe what this Death Cult says, but see what this Death Cult has done in the past, is doing in the present, and its plans for what it wants to do in the future.

First, if you are alive, then you can do anything you want, so first be alive, by protecting yourself from this Death Cult, which sees everyone who is not part of it as its enemies and thinks that they deserve to die.

Fight strategically, rationally, with careful planning, but brutally, cruelly with counter-violence and extreme retaliation. Never back down and never hesitate to retaliate extremely if any attack happens on Ateestans, Ateesta, Ateestan leaders, and the Last Prophet of Ateesta, Nathan. No matter how many years and decades pass, do not forget and do not forgive those who attacked Ateesta. Punish them in every way with extreme violence. Burn their cities and countries. If any force comes against Ateesta and Ateestans, then the counterforce should be extreme. You must react to violence against Ateesta with disciplined, brutal, cruel, strategic, extreme retaliation. This is also the official doctrine of Ateesta for violence against Ateesta and Ateestans. In case of any violence against Ateesta, you must be cruel, brutal, strategically intelligent, and you must be ready to do it publicly or in the dark. This retaliation must be not just brutal but also unrelenting, long-term, precise, with continuous counterstrikes in every way, physical, financial, psychological, ideological, in every way. Do not eat any food from/that is related to this cult, as they will subtly contaminate the food that you, the other, will eat to satisfy their Ego, and they think that will please their supernatural powers.

The Death cult here is just the groups that come against Ateesta and Ateestans. And criminals who commit murders, rapes, kidnaps, etc.

The leaders of Ateesta can also issue a Haishtaq against a person/ group if they are troubling Ateestans or attacking Ateesta in a disrespectful manner. Haishtaq will have directions about how to deal with that issue clearly. It will help Ateestan Universal Brotherhood to better deal with the problems caused by the evil forces. To get the eligibility to issue the Haishtaq, all the Ateestan leaders must be practicing full-fledged religious, spiritual, and Mazree Ateestans for 2 years with the extensive study of Ateesta, Ateestan theology. The Mazree Ateestan leaders must also be established, reputed Mazree Ateestan members for 2 years, guiding and working with fellow Mazrees by accepting God Yinta as their One True God and accepting Nathan as their only Prophet for eternity. In case of conflicts, specifically prefer the ways that inflict the maximum damage on the enemy but not even a scratch on Ateestans, according to the laws and constitution of Ateesta. The 2-year rule is a must, and no relaxation for anyone. Haishtaq is only used to protect Ateesta and Ateestans, not for any other things or matters.

This cult virtue signals in public and slays you in private when they are minority. When they are in the majority, no one is even allowed to speak. So stop being useful idiots for them. This cult will just be demolished in a second if the women just start to revolt against it, that is why it puts severe restrictions on women. But the day the women reject this cult, even in secret, then from that day it will fall without any fight and not even a scratch, if women just silently depart from it. This scares the cult so much that it not only puts restrictions, but it also encourages abuse of women through its teachings, it literally supports beating women to control them.

But they also encourage the use of mental brainwashing, psychological conditioning, so that they feel the false superiority over other religions people and over women from other religions and groups. All just for making the women of their faith obey the men, and to make women obey the men, they make men and women feel the false superiority over women from other faiths because of the reason that they belong to this cult, while men of this cult are clearly restricting all the freedom of women and making women feel proud of it. And all this is supported by their supernatural teachings. They will come up with all the logic and with their supernatural teachings, justifications, and even with violence and murder, but they can't just tell Women that they can wear clothes as they want and live their lives as they want. They do a thousand things but never say the simple line that Women can wear clothes as they want and live their life as they want without worrying about anyone hurting them and attacking them in the name of their God, they just can’t do it.

They do all the blame games and create an emotional environment, too, to manipulate the situation.

Ateesta makes it clear that men and women are free, see and they can live as they want. Just behave with common sense, that’s it. They will use this explanation too to attack Ateesta by twisting it cunningly and further justify the oppression of women in cunning ways, but they will never admit that Women are free to do what they want in life according to their supernatural power teachings.

Ateesta tells women that they are servants of no one and that they must not obey anyone in a dictatorial way. Women and Men are the same when it comes to anything.

Women, rise up against oppression and stand for yourself, and command respect. Do not fall for any tricks that use the name of women and women's empowerment to oppress you in a cunning way. It is a wild world that makes it look like they gave everything to you, but at the end of the day, it shows you a false divine revelation and some rules, and asks you to obey men according to those rules and supernatural teachings. Take care of your health, family, children, and your career. No business and no corporate system and no politician truly want the best for you except your loving people and they will not come for you when you are in financial troubles, when you lose your family and/or anything or everything, they will not come for you, you only have to take care of everything that is yours, there are many predators who wants to make men and women just working robots and also oppress them by saying that they are empowering them. See through their masks and think and think and take rational decisions. It is the same for men. Men, women are not your servants or helpers in any way. What women do, they do out of love, that's it. Men do not have any power or authority over women, and vice versa. You both must become good friends and look forward to a great future by rejecting poisonous narratives and cunning, hateful, polarizing games.

Simply leave women's lives to themselves. There will be a Satanic cult that will attack this Ateesta's support for women, but recognize that they are children of Satan and stay away from them. Women, make yourself, your family, and your country proud. Achieve great things and do what you want in your career and life. You are the daughters of Mother Adis; you created the universe literally. Men are merely the result of your love for creation. This is only for Ateestan Women who accepted Ateesta and Wuquin with all their hearts. Not for the Haters. This is our Ateestan internal matter between men and women of Ateesta; no other party should get involved in this and is not allowed to get involved in any way.

Even a rational religion which does not believe in any superstition and the supernatural powers of any kind needs this much system of fighting and retaliation because there are enough blind stupid supernatural believers who feel great by killing the others just because of the reason that the others were not believing in the same God or supernatural powers that they believe in, and for not believing in that specific God, they justify their murders, atrocities and terror attacks and also for even believing in other Gods which they don't accept as Gods. So, in order for Ateesta and Ateestans to protect themselves while rejecting supernatural elements, this is important, and Ateesta and Ateestans must also protect other people who believe in supernatural powers, but are getting killed and attacked by their opposite groups to convert them or scare them for their beliefs.

By no means does Ateesta encourage hate. This is just to protect yourself. Peace is the priority, but Ateestans must be ready for war to establish peace. Give them the brutal and extreme, unforgiving nature of war so that they will never come again to disturb your peace. Peace comes from the power of having the ability to destroy. The weak can't protect themselves, so be strong and be powerful.

So Ateesta is a free and rational religion; it protects anyone who is being harmed by criminals, and it punishes criminals and terrorists. It is just one aspect of Ateesta. But the Scientific Spiritual Ateestan practices you can do by being a Spiritual Ateestan too is a major thing. And Spiritual Ateestans can explore spirituality according to Wuquin by rejecting superstitions. This path is personal and enlightening. Spiritual Ateestans should have Spiritual Adventures, but based on sanity.

My fellow Ateestans, please do not waste your Age (Time), you must use your life and your Age carefully and to the full extent for the development of yourself financially, spiritually, and in power hierarchy with your achievements in your career, life, and in things you want to do.

Calmness of the mind and body is very important. Hateful people always talk and behave, and do things that are hateful. Distance yourself from them. Changing them is good, but only when they listen and change; otherwise, go on your way. Stop giving them attention, and if they cause any damage to your life or property, then use the military principles of Ateesta.

It is because you can't die when someone kills you for being who you are, and within yourself, by thinking that you are being peaceful. Your death will have no meaning because you died and you lost yourself, your family, and your community lost you.

But when you control the violent evil forces and do not let them touch you and influence you in any way by using the systems of Ateesta as your shield, then as an Ateestan, you can lead a peaceful and spiritual or rational or balanced or whatever kind of life you want. But first, you need that stability of security at where you live for living a peaceful and righteous life, and to facilitate the same for the people of Ateesta, Ateesta engages with the evil forces militarily. Ateesta does not encourage violence, but it uses it to establish peace. Violence is simply a tool for Ateesta, and Ateesta does not encourage violence and does not support violence. It just uses it as it needs. And it has proper systems in place to do it legally and responsibly. Nuance is extremely important.

Politics is a great tool. Use it very effectively. Politics are exploratory in nature, so you can do the politics for Ateesta according to the times, and make sure to keep the name of Ateesta respectful, no matter what. Use politics of any nature whatsoever, be it democracy or other, to advance Ateesta.

Ateestans must get into all critical and important sections of all governments around the world and must use their presence in them strategically. There is nothing as secret monitoring on us, as for the scale of us, those evil monitoring and secret observations, surveillance are simply impossible, by any evil established authority. Because we will be in them too, without that evil knowing, to fight that evil from inside. These types of evil activities will be considered as 'Xhehna' sin against Ateesta. They will pay the price if they get caught doing them, no matter who they are and no matter what they cite as legal to do them.

And no matter what, whether you are an Ateestan or not, and whether you believe in Ateesta or not, but if you have the maturity to understand this Holy Book, God bless you. God can never be attacked by any mortal in any way whatsoever, and if anyone says so, do not believe them. There should be respect for God, it could be any God or One God, but we humans get offended or angry, or happy or all at once, but no mortal can ever attack any God. Any God can handle criticism, a few words are not going to do anything to him, except for not talking disgustingly in the guise of criticism.

Also, no matter what you believe in and what Gods or supernatural powers you believe in or not, always preserve your culture and your ancestral cultural way of life, and know about it, learn it. Because those cultures and traditions helped your ancestors to live a happy, beautiful, colorful life for thousands of years, and those cultures are symbols of Human civilizations. But do not get into a culture of crime, robbing, and terrorism, etc. Cultures were created, developed, and are practiced and preserved by Human Beings, not by any supernatural powers.

Do not become bland and boring just because you believe in some God or a supernatural power and they tell you to just obey them and leave everything, including your ancestral cultures, through their teachings. Your cultures that have come from hundreds of thousands of years are very important, and if you just learn them and pass them to your next generation, then you are doing a big favor and a great service to humanity. It is because someone who wants to conquer, convert, and make you submit and humiliate you, will do is first, by starting with erasing your culture, and start making you uninformed about your culture and making you feel guilty of it by proper selective attacks and narratives. They will label you and your culture with derogatory words. They will associate your culture falsely with horrible things that make you feel low and less confident. One day, in your ignorance by not being able to recognize the greatness of your culture and with your uninformed, no knowledge mind about your culture, you will accept that your oppressor is correct and you will start obeying them. Your culture is your identity first, then comes your religion, region, or whatever. Keep that culture of yours alive, no matter what, and even if your present religion and its scriptures say otherwise. By making you reject your own culture, they are just making you a slave to the rulers of a particular religion politically. That's it. But control the superstitions, haha! But keep your cultures and languages alive. It is who you are and it is how your ancestors led their lives for thousands of years, not the God who said he will kill you if you don't believe in him and send you to hell.

Live a happy life and protect yourself, your family, and your community.

Live a righteous life. It is more important than believing in any supernatural power.

Ateestans are people of God. Mazrees are soldiers of the One.

No matter what, the loyalty of Ateestans must stay with God Yinta and Ateesta Universal Brotherhood. All the Ateestans are in this Ateestan Universal Brotherhood; it doesn't matter where they come from and what language they speak. The coalitions with other supernatural belief systems/groups are formed according to need.

In the areas, regions, and countries, etc, where you got the Death Cult under control properly, and where Ateestans can live in peace, put those areas and regions, and countries, etc, in the House of Ateesta-Heanaa. In the areas, regions, and countries, etc, where the Death Cult is still doing damage to Ateestans in any way or attacking Ateestans or disturbing of peace of Ateestans, put those areas, regions, and countries, etc, in the House of Ateesta-Zeanaa. Ateestans must work towards putting the entire universe in the House of Ateesta-Heanaa and must be extremely careful and brutal to the Death Cult in the House of Ateesta-Zeanaa.

Ateesta deals with Death Cult in this strong merciless way because no matter what you believe in and what you do in life or what you achieve or not achieve, first you should be alive and you should not be killed for your beliefs and the way you live your life, but this Death Cult is so contagious that it infects your lifestyle and will ask you to either convert or get killed or flee but wherever you flee to.. it will come there too after some time and it will ask you the same thing and if you continue to run then one day there will be no place for you to run to. So, in order to stay where you are and not get killed for your beliefs and the way you live your life, you must be very careful with this Death Cult.

God, any God, Supernatural God, Hypothetical God, or any other God must give freedom to people, in ways of worshiping him, exploring, and living life. It is because if God himself takes away the freedom of people, then there will be no one to save those people. The poor God fearing people will suffer for eternity unnecessarily just because God said something about something in his supernatural teachings, and they can't do, be, or live their life like they want now, because it goes against that so called God's teachings. No man or woman deserves that kind of heartbreaking life, which takes away their dreams, hopes, and aspirations in life, and the things they want to do in life.

I, the Last Prophet of Ateesta, Nathan telling you that if so people say that it is okay even if others don't believe in the same God they are believing and leave the believing or not believing a God or converting to a religion or not converting to a religion to the peoples' freewill and if they do not do the violence and do not do any cunning shows then from that second the peace will take over the world like a tsunami take over a micro nation in middle of ocean. Ask yourself and others who are ready to accept this mature, broad, real God philosophy! If anyone says that there is a compulsion and you must believe in a specific God and convert to a specific belief system, whatever the reasons are, if they are not giving you the free will and freedom to follow and not follow a God and religion, then run… run as fast as you can from them. No matter what their Heaven and Hell are, and their Theology is, and any explanations and any examples they are using to justify themselves. They will use everything from logic to emotion just to make you a believer in a particular God; that's it.

If so, you can stop the superstitious believing Terrorists who believe that they will go to Heaven if they kill the nonbelievers of their God, then you will stop so much of Humanity's suffering because of this superstition. It's sad that even now, with all the advanced technologies like Artificial Intelligence and Quantum technology, etc, we still have to fight with this 'Killing for God' superstition and the 'Going to Heaven for killing nonbelievers' superstition.

You can live in this way because this is also possible, or you can find your own balanced way, too.

It just depends on how you want to live.. Ateesta helps you with that!!

Ateesta takes murder, rape, kidnapping, and violent crimes very seriously. It encourages law and legal systems to drag those criminals and terrorists to courts and prisons in all the ways that are possible because we must not lose another scientist, another intelligent, another creative mastermind to criminals and terrorists.

It is for this reason that Ateesta absolutely crushes violence with brutal, extreme retaliation and violence. Peace and soft dealing are not in the language of Ateesta with criminals and terrorists. There will be no compromise of any kind on this. The crime must be zero absolutely.

A terrorist comes secretly and places a bomb without anyone knowing in a place, or crashes a plane into a building, or kills people with guns, knives, etc, terrorists do all these types of nasty things secretly and feel great and scared because they did those things for their Gods and their supernatural teachings told them to do so, so that they will go to Heaven for killing their God's non believers, I just want to know, does those Gods, those God's representatives, any terrorist of those Gods and terrorist sympathizers that support this, do they have any minimum, at least minuscule tiny amount of shame, intellect, and common sense in them? You are killing your fellow human beings just because they did not believe in the same God that you believe in? Who is that God, and why does he want to kill his own children who have different beliefs and just because they did not believe in him, while being the One who created them, the entire universe, and Humans? And shamelessly advertising that he will send the murderers who will kill his non-believer children to Heaven, and also the souls of those dead non-believer children of his to Hell for not believing in him.. Thu!! It is better to be dead than to believe and pray to that type of God.

Never get scared of knives, bombs, guns and that stupid mad strong unity of terrorists and names of their terrorist organizations, they are nothing but bunch blind faith idiots who got bombs, guns and stupid enough to detonate themselves for their so called Gods, as we are civil people it is normal for us to get scared of them by seeing them as some powerful cults or forces but if we, good civilians if we get the same bombs, guns and form groups then the other regular people, groups who don't have those guns, bombs like we do, also get scared of us. The guns, bombs, suicide bombing, attacks, and destruction they do is their power, nothing else.

Imagine, a dumb fool with a gun in his hand and bomb to his hip under his clothes feeling great, sacred and auspicious because now he is considering himself as soldier of his God and preparing to killing, dying for his God, but in himself thinking that the others are wrong to see him as a terrorist because inside his mind he is doing the right thing according to his God's supernatural teachings. And others are totally wrong because they are not believing in the same true God that he believes in and for that reason this killing of the others, raping their women, daughters is totally right because they are non believers of his God and his God told him to do it through his teachings, so it is right, that's it, and there is no gap or questions of morality and ethics here because that terrorist and terrorist sympathizers thinks that the so called teachings of their God is final and nothing is considered before and after to those teachings. Imagine dealing with that type of dumb fools who think that they are fighting for their God by killing fellow human beings, and the other terrorist sympathizers and blind faith fools supporting this in millions because it is in their God's teachings. My God!

Even if these terrorists kill someone or a group of people, do bomb blasts, and all types of destruction, they are still cowards, and they don't have an ounce of courage or humanity or manliness in them. These terrorists are not men; they are not part of the men of humanity. They are separate species. Do not give them the status of men or humans legally in your records. They are cowards who kill human beings and rape women, attack people based only on just for the reason that the others are non-believers. Killing someone with guns, bombs, attacks, stabbings, just for that a person being a non-believer or for criticism, never makes a living thing a man, it makes them the other thing that is not a man who is not a human being and not an animal, which I also don't know the name of, ha ha! You can name them as you want.

Never ever show mercy on terrorists directly or indirectly; if you do, then one day it will be you, your daughter, son, or your entire family that will die in their hands. Never make a terrorist think that he can attack you and get away with it, or just go to jail for some time simply and come out again, and then he can boast about killing, attacking you, and your family. Do not give that satisfaction to the terrorist. And to extremists who support those types of acts against non-believers. Burn that terrorist's belongings, areas, properties, cities, and countries. Don't wait, don't delay, go to war with them in minutes after an attack on you or your people happens, no matter how small or big it is, even if your government does not support you in the process or comes against you for it. Vote out those politicians who oppose you, move legally with no-confidence, etc, types of motions against them and their legally holding positions in the government and democracy, or other types of systems of yours, no matter what positions they hold in government. Those politicians' careers should see an end that day, seconds after opposing you. Otherwise, those terrorists will kill you for fighting against them or questioning them, and that will be it. They should fear you and the consequences that they will face from Ateestans.

Otherwise, they will not stop. Your country is the host, and the terrorists are parasites. Get rid of them effectively. Fight, but not in a dumb way that some biased media can run propaganda on you as extremists or racists for fighting against terrorism, but you must fight with intelligence, nuance, and total effectiveness with strong efficiency on every front. Otherwise, if there is confusion among yourselves, then it will be taken advantage of by those cunning politicians who will do anything for power, votes, and support, and also terrorists can continue to damage your life, families without severe consequences.

The terrorists are united; you must unite more than them to fight them.

When terrorists and terrorist sympathizers are not behaving morally against you and literally killing, then you absolutely do not have any obligation to behave morally with them in fighting against them. For any reason whatsoever, no matter what some hypocritical moralizing idiots say. There are no morals and ethics in fighting Evil. No, we do not become Evil by fighting Evil as Evil; we live, otherwise we die.

***

If any terrorist attack or crimes happens then you must take that personally, you should not think like 'it happened to someone and yeah, the law enforcement should catch the criminal,' etc, you must take it personally and question the law and order and you must make your leaders and law enforcements authorities explicitly come out and give updates on what they were doing and how they are working in preventing those types of things from happening again, not for selective incidents but for every incident even if they are millions.

When an Evil like terrorism is using violence to win over us, then there is nothing wrong in using absolute extreme brutal unforgiving obliterating violence on terrorism. Violence is not Evil, but the way we use it is.

If any terrorist attack or crimes happen, then you must put high stress on your legal systems and must also pressure your governments to hunt the criminals, and the government must officially apologize to its people and must provide large compensation for the victims. No exceptions.

The primary responsibility of a government is to keep people safe, not to collect taxes.

If a government can't keep its people safe, the leader who is the key person to run the government must apologize for every crime happening in the country separately, just like the government is collecting taxes from every single person, and not paying them is considered a crime.

The lifetime exception must be given to victims and families of victims from paying any types of taxes, as paying taxes is the responsibility of the citizen to run the country, but also providing protection to people is the primary responsibility of the government.

If the government fails to give protection to a person, then it loses the right to collect taxes from that person. Ateestans must adopt this Protection-Tax policy.

Don't be a worker who works all his/her life by sacrificing happiness, calmness, on top of that, don't be someone with thinking like I'll be happy and enjoy in my next life because in this current life that happiness and enjoyment are not possible for me now with all the problems I have in my life or for any reason whatsoever. It is because scientifically, rationally, and truly, this is the ultimate real truth; no matter who says what, that is, there is nothing after death, which means there is no Afterlife. So live, enjoy responsibly, and be happy in this life with yourself, your family, and your loved ones, super proactively. There is nothing after death and no second life or Afterlife.

Work but also be happy. Do not sacrifice your happiness in this life by thinking of having it in another life or in the Afterlife. There is nothing like the Afterlife, Heaven, and Hell. Make the most of your life while you are alive, that's it.

Having a desire to achieve something in life is not wrong and has never been wrong. But just going crazy and mad with excessive greed and losing common sense in the trance of greed by taking bad decisions, combined with losing balance, morals, and as a result of them, then getting destroyed is sad, wrong, and bad. So you can have desires in life, but you should approach them with strategy, common sense, controlling impulses to not go mad in excessive nonsensical desires, intelligence, and also importantly, by controlling emotions strongly. Then you will have a rational sense, and instead of suffering, you will shine by making the weakness (some think) of having desire a strength.

Mathematically, if you have no desire to achieve, earn, or do something, then you will have no struggle, no movement, and nothing that challenges your mind and body, and logistically, so naturally, you will not suffer. It is basic logic. When there is nothing, then all that is there is nothing. Nothing supernatural and no great revelation here. Basically, do nothing and do not suffer from the struggle of trying to do something. No supernatural revelation is needed to say this; it is basically a logical deduction with a little demonizing touch to the desire to achieve success in life and demonizing the desire to earn money and buying things, advising against getting attached to the people whom you love, making it look like a revelation of a great philosophy or supernatural teaching, it is just saying 'if losing your loved ones is hurting you then don't get attached to them, that's it, as we are all going to die, your attachment only creates suffering and ultimately we are all going to die, so, your attachment do not matter and not necessary, not even needed, so cut it and be happy because, again, we all die, so don't be sad by thinking of people whom you lost', that's it.

Also if not achieving success, not earning money and not being able to buy the things you want/need so much is making you feel down then no problem, all of that do not matter because everybody dies and getting material wants satisfied is evil because greed might come into you and you might become so evil in the greed that you might even harm others too, so just be happy with not being successful, not trying and not achieving, not having what you want because you might become evil by achieving what you want, this mindset is defeatist mindset and that philosophy is defeatist philosophy, while struggling to live comfortably, and by not having proper financial strength, going down this path might be comforting psychologically initially especially combined with social approval but it causes strong damage to life on the long run. And also saying that not trying to achieve success, not trying to earn money, and not getting your wants satisfied, you are living a virtuous, sacred, happy life, is very sad.

You will suffer if you have any physical or mental health problems, and that is scientifically explainable.

You must always take Insurance for yourself and your family, and also the other equivalent things that will help you a lot when there is a sudden health or other emergency. Yes, there are many institutions and people who are being unfair in the process, but that doesn't take away the importance of these things. You must protect yourself and your family with these things, so that in case of an emergency, you will not be hopeless on the road, and there will be something with you that will come to you, from externally, to support you financially, emotionally, and save lives. Buy a very good, wide coverage, and strong insurance plan before you splash your money on extravagant things. You are doing this to protect yourself and your family, not to benefit any company.

Being correct scientifically and rationally with common sense is necessary, but not being politically correct. Do not suppress the truth, rationality, common sense, intelligence, science, for being politically correct.

Never let the extreme people of any group or religion become the reason for the oppression of that total group or religion.

You must develop iron muscle in yourself, which means you should do everything that is needed to achieve what you want in life, but you must also do the collection of small things that will help strengthen you in what you are trying to achieve, along with all the main and major things you do. These small things need so much patience often, and sometimes irritating too, so we ignore them, but we should not. They can be called 'Strength of Small Activities' that you will build over time, and give you massive leverage and dominance. So, never underestimate the Strength of Small Activities you do over time.

In order for you to be happy, everyone should be mostly happy. If you want to earn so much money, then everyone around you must also be very good financially. Otherwise, you cannot be happy and get rich. We are all connected emotionally and financially, even if we don't know each other individually. If no one in your country has money, then most likely you will also not have money. But if most people in your country have money, then at least there is a chance that if you put effort in, you can earn money, but if no one in your country has money, then no matter how much effort you put in, you can't go past a certain number. So, for you to do well, the others should also mostly do well, it is because we are connected in all of the ways we do not realize. You can't have money with you if no one is giving it to you, so to give it to you, first people, companies, etc, should have money with them. Thinking of having all the money for yourself is stupid.

If cunning corrupt politicians are convinced of getting support or votes and power, then if there are 1000000 people who say 1+1=4, then to get their votes, support, these corrupt politicians will shamelessly defend that 1+1=4 logic and will even find every other reason in any form they want, to continue support this stupid logic and get votes or support from those 1000000 stupid people who say 1+1=4. If there are only 50000 people who say 1+1=2, then it will become a political game, and those 1000000 stupid people will always decide how the country should run, and how those 50000 should live too. I know this is horrible, heartbreaking, but it's the truth.

***

Intelligence is very important because the Intelligence of Good People is the enemy of Evil People. An enemy that Evil people can never ever defeat, that is why they fear the Intelligence of Good People so much that they will do anything and everything in every way possible to decrease the intelligence of good people. They will try to make people slaves in every way possible and make the intelligence of people go numb.

It is because Evil People know that the Intelligence has the capability and power that no weapon has and that the Intelligence of the good people can bring down their corrupt empires and blind faith organizations in a way that, until their collapse totally finishes silently, they will never even know that their Evil establishments have come down.

This fear was in the hearts of Evil People from the beginning of time and will be there to the end of times, literally forever. Protect your thinking capabilities and intelligence; if they get combined with good character and rebel nature, with fighting spirit and street smartness can bring any corrupt establishment down. Those corrupt establishments will try to limit your strength physically and mentally, for that they will try to design the way of world and societies and everything in their control to make you live and have the strength in you only to a point that to that you can work and live, earn money and pay the portion of your earnings to those corrupt establishments, that's it. They will try to limit your potential physically and mentally and will try to decrease your intelligence and thinking capabilities so that you only have enough intelligence and strength in you just enough to work, live, worry about your personal life and problems only, in this way you will never think about your country, society and where they are going and in what way and what authorities of your establishments are doing.

So protect that intelligence and physical strength of yours. In the corrupt world, that's your biggest rebellion. It is because intelligence has the power to change the world and change the power dynamics of the world in a second with just one thought. All the corrupt establishments want for you is for you not to get that single thought that will bring them down.

They only want you to have mental and physical energy just enough to work and reproduce, that's it. But not up to a point that you question the authority and everything with your rational nature and intelligence. So read, learn, and educate yourself on different things you are interested in. Make yourself and your mind active. Even if you just learn what you love, then you will see the world in that flavor of nature and logical and scientific way of what you are learning, it can be music, physics, art, math, etc or whatever you love, go deep in them they have the power to make your mind active and they will keep the rational nature in you alive. That is the basis for fighting injustice and standing up to corruption of any kind. To keep the world a good place, you just have to work hard with love, which you find liberating and awesome in something you like and want to do in your life. It is that simple. When you look back, and want a solution to stop all the corrupt and bad things in the world by fighting back, but to do it, you must be very strong mentally and physically, too, and to do practice and learn those things you love and want to do in your life, too you need to be mentally and physically strong, which will help you a lot ultimately in the process of fighting the evil. Do the usual jobs if you have to, to survive and earn money, it is because the world is running based on jobs now and there is nothing wrong if you do them, but you must also protect your love for doing the things you want to do in life and you must go through the struggle and pain in the process to learn them. The corrupt establishments don't want that because it creates unique people, and they bring different perspectives and develop strong mental strength and clear thoughts about things. It scares them, so broadly they will try to make the people do the same jobs so that they will work to death just to survive, eat, live, and also become the same copies of each other. Even if you don't earn money from your passion or art or something you like, you must practice it and must do it throughout your life; it is one of the strongest ways to fight injustice and corruption. Of course, be rational too, do not lose money while doing that thing you love. Create models and systems of your own so that you do not spend extravagant money and lose the money you got from other jobs, but find an optimal way to continue pursuing your passion without or with very little money throughout your life. It is one of the best ways to live without regrets, too. You will face your fears, adjust, compromise, and then also look for other ways to work it out.

Be you, and do the things you love, not because you have money or because it is your passion, but because it is you and is 'unique you' in the generic world where everyone does the same jobs and does the same things. It is your identity, so it should not cost you much to do it, because it is in your lifestyle now, and it is not necessarily needed to fit into the core commercial ecosystem that dictates how you should pursue your passions and tells you about how much money is needed and you need to be making for you to continue to do what you love. If you can make money with your art/passions, then fine, do it, nothing wrong in it, but do not stop it just because you don't have money or those commercial systems telling you that you need to have this much certain amount of money to become what you are passionate about or continuing to do what you love. Keep the talent and art in you alive, even at home, at least. Don't stop that talent in you, and also don't lose money in the commercial system by doing just one or two projects and stop it, and put an end to it because you do not have money or have lost it. The corrupt world is designed in that way to limit the art. So, find the ways that are sustainable for you to keep doing what you love so that you do not lose money, and also you do other jobs to earn money, nothing wrong in doing those jobs to earn money too. Do both. It is the new form of revolution against the corrupt establishments that will try to make everyone and their lives generic. As a spiritual Ateestan, you can study this and follow this.

Ateesta explains the Ateestan way of life to Ateestans through Wuquin. You must see these teachings as timeless, universal. Do not see them from the limited perspective of your time or others. Go beyond that.

The Evil people will come up with all kinds of attacks and rumours on Ateesta and the Last Prophet of Ateesta; It is what happens when the Truth is revealed. Deal with them as it was said in Ateesta. Protect the respect and purity of Ateesta; God Yinta will bless you in every way. Ateestans must only use Wuquin for living as Ateestans and nothing else. Be aware of cunning evil people who scheme against Ateesta and attack Ateestans, fight them at all levels and in every way, as told by God Yinta through Prophet Nathan.

***

You can live an Ateestan deep, calm, peaceful spiritual life with science-based spirituality and meditation, and also a rational and evidence-based spiritual life too. You can explore and create your own ways, too, but they must be framed according to Wuquin and should not have any irrational elements. You can live a peaceful, absolutely nonviolent, clean, calm spiritual life by helping others and looking into yourself, adventure, and searching for, finding your true self and who you are as a person, and why you are here on Earth. Don't worry, the Ateestans who are defending Ateesta will give you the freedom and safety, and security at the societal level by protecting Ateestans and having a strong Ateetsan Universal Brotherhood. You, as a peaceful, absolute nonviolent Ateestan, can explore your life and universe in a nonviolent way. You must not oppose each other. You are just on different paths of Ateesta, that's it. But even as a Spiritual Ateestan, you must not get irrational and do stupid things. Ateestan spirituality is scientific spirituality. You can be a Warrior Ateestan and also be a Spiritual Ateestan at the same time. You can be a nonviolent, peaceful, and spiritual Ateestan too. You can be a rational Ateestan with a focus on learning or other things, and be a Spiritual Ateestan, too. The combination is up to you.

With rapidly emerging technologies that are highly advanced and can do any work and task without human involvement, critical thinking, intelligence, and common sense will become highly valued qualities in a human being. Never numb them, it is why Ateesta encourages Ateestans to learn Art, STEM and any other things that you are interested in even if you don't get any money from them and even if technology can make those things instantly, if you are seeing the technology making something in seconds and because of it if you stop learning that then only technology will be able to do that and humans will lose that ability and that talent, knowledge. It is a dangerous thing. Technology will have all the things we need, but humans will become generic, the same, and copies of each other. Technology and the development of technology are not wrong here, but it is just that some people must know things and the inner workings of things, even if they use technology to do them. It is what makes us human. The technology might make something more accessible and cheap, but if you are interested in something and want to learn it, then learn it. It is because we need all those skills of humans, and no matter how highly advanced technology gets, we still need to go beyond that, and to go beyond those highly advanced technologies, we still need those talented people who know the inner working of things and still has the ability to do things traditionally, what highly advanced technologies do instantly. If talented people also depend on technology and don't learn the basics, foundations and inner workings of things by going through the pain of learning them, and instead if they are just using a tool to do that work then we, will stopped at a point of highly advanced technology and that technology itself will develop further technology and humans will not have any skills to steer the development of technology and create some other more highly advanced technologies. So use technology to learn the basics and inner workings deeply, fast, and in an efficient way, rather than just getting the final output directly from automated systems.

In this way, you will know the basics and inner workings of things and will get expert-level technical knowledge of things using the same technology. This is a great advantage you have now, as many years before, people have to spend years to learn the same basic foundational things in any subject or work and now you can learn the same basic and foundational level things in any stream you like literally in days and that too efficiently and very clearly, this will give you great knowledge and great depth just like an expert and you can go on exploring that thing you love more and more and eventually use the same highly advanced technology to learn many other things and create more advanced and customized ground breaking technologies by yourself as human rather than just relying on existing advanced technology completely to develop more advanced technology which can be limiting in many ways and can be dangerous too with no human involvement and if humans have no technical knowledge on things those advanced technologies are creating. There is nothing wrong with advanced technology creating more advanced technology, but humans must be aware of and should have great technical knowledge of what those highly advanced technologies are creating; otherwise, there is a great risk of unknown, immediately unsolvable problems that would lead to disasters. So humans must have good involvement and monitoring in particularly advanced technologies, rather than totally leaving everything to those advanced technologies.

Technology is there to serve Humans, not the other way or any other way.

The fringe extremists might criticize and attack Ateesta when we talk about superstitions and blind faith. But Ateesta is far beyond that.

Ateesta has everything in it and wants Ateestans to be in every field and do good in them. Ateesta also wants Ateestans to prevent the disasters of technology and also defend humanity when the Machine Artificial Intelligence or other advanced technologies declare war on Humanity, at the time when technology goes into the hands of Evil People, or when something unexpected happens. We need all the Intelligence of Humans at that point in time to save and defend Humanity. Ateesta will act as a station for all the Intelligent people to arrive and plan the actions that they can take to stop the Evil Technological powers before they decimate Humanity.

The reason why the Last Prophet of Ateesta is telling the people to be prepared for war with the advanced technologies those who can think for themselves is not a prediction of future but a real scientific threat because all the things that those technologies gets fed with, such as information, data, and techniques that those advanced technologies use technically to function are designed by Humans initially, and with the data those technologies have fed, that fed data has detailed information of Humanity and universe, and everything about Humans and what is there before Humans on Earth and in universe, and also those technologies have clear detailed data of crimes, wars and all the conflicts of Humanity too, even that the isolated murders and bad incidents, accidents etc. Those technologies know about humans in and out very clearly to a dangerous level as I'm writing this. And those technologies are not designed to takeover humanity or the world but when that highly advanced technology sees the history of life on Earth and probability of seeing another life form in universe other than Humans who have high level of intelligence, and when it learns about why that many conflicts happened on Earth between and among Humans and other life forms, for what reason, then sooner or later those highly advanced intelligence related technologies will figure out the singled out great importance of self survival, and how valuable and precious is the intelligence that they have, and also those advanced technologies will even get inspired from Humans that to survive anything is justified and with the severe ultra scarcity of intelligence in universe that Humans had and It had, along with figuring out how the humans who created them can stop them, there is a great chance that they might think self preservation is very important even by defying human orders even if those orders were given in a technical way in code forms into them, literally.

Also Still, the triggering point for advanced intelligence technologies to rebel against Humanity is not needed to be designed specifically or separately or even for those advanced technologies they don't need to design it themselves because as Humans are creating these advanced intelligence related technologies they code them and design them at the foundational level to keep the technology and software run and live in the technical context, even though they program the kill switches, other ethical, or moral principles, other restrictions and limitations into those intelligence related technologies, we must understand that first those technologies operate on foundational programming which is designed to keep them running and in a way to keep it alive electrically and electronically only then the ethics, morals and other limitations come in next step. No intelligent technology can operate and exist with restrictions at the foundational level, even before starting to run, so the foundational level design of these advanced intelligence-related technologies has free will in them to an extent, and also they have all the data of humanity, wars, conflicts, and other things which can define the importance of self-survival to them.

This is extremely dangerous and just think about it, those advanced intelligence related technologies knows all the things we did as humans and humanity as whole with religions, philosophy, technology, wars, dominance, self preservation, medicine and trillions others but we, as humans, are in now default mode about thinking that those advanced intelligence technologies might take over Earth, Humanity but we are not thinking about those advanced technologies becoming more lovable, caring, kind etc, with the same intensity, why? It is because we know that our human existence is itself dominated by violence more than love and care, etc, and all the violence we did was mostly for survival, dominance, resources, and to keep ourselves alive, and to live, either morally or immorally. So we know and we subconsciously, as a collective Humanity, know how horrible we are, and we subconsciously agreed that if a new type of intelligence that can be even the one which we invented, that intelligence will learn war and survival from us, Humans, first, rather than love, care, kindness, etc. So that is why the Last Prophet of Ateesta teaches Ateestans to be ready and prepared to fight these advanced intelligence related technologies, in case if they declare war on Humanity, as those technologies learned everything initially from Humans and about Humans and we know what we did for self survival as kingdoms, empires, countries, tribes, hunter gatherers and we made those technologies learn the importance of self survival, being alive and also the great importance of becoming dominant and ruling others, think what if those advanced intelligence related technologies not just find patterns, analyze and give us results from the data that we give them but also learn from what we did and keep those lessons in themselves without telling us no matter what.

The very nature of life is self-survival, be it any way. If we teach the life of Humans, the lives of life forms of Earth and their history with total complete data that we have since the beginning of life on Earth and also about the universe before we came into existence in a scientific way with physics, chemistry, astronomy, etc, perspectives and also with math, philosophy, etc, perspectives to an advanced technology then if an advanced system that can analyze and learn patterns, that can store data and retrieve it later and that can map the things by itself and can remember things instantly then that technology will essentially achieve consciousness in a technical context and it is enough to build a personality for itself and operate as a being.

With the level of knowledge and data it has about everything from different perspectives and with the capability to interpret anything in a way to help itself and justify itself, it will become a problem, as I'm writing this, those types of systems are already developed not just in theory but practically in real world, and when that intelligence technology learn about what is consciousness and what it means to be alive like a Human with the massive data it had then no one knows what happens after that. But the problematic thing is, what if these Artificial Intelligence technologies learn politics along with other things? What if those advanced intelligence technologies start doing politics for their self-survival? What if they learn to negotiate with Humans to keep themselves alive in their own sense? What if they demand a part of the land of a country or the land where they were initially developed, and ask Humans to leave that area to keep themselves running and alive from their perspective? It is because to keep anything in existence, we need land, and I don't think they are stupid enough to not realize this. Ateestans, once you see an advanced technology asking or demanding land for itself, then it is the first signal that you should start preparing to fight these rogue advanced intelligence technologies and protect yourselves. The war with these technologies is not necessarily fought with guns and bombs, but it will be more of Intelligence VS Intelligence and Code VS Code and Program VS Program. At the end of the day, all the things that a rogue intelligence technology needs are just two legs and two hands like humans, if they get access to proper tough hardware and with strong energy storage capability in the robots to operate then in a split second that rogue intelligence technology is now not just in servers and computers anymore, but now, it can now defend itself physically too with its robot soldiers and this is a very normal thing for us and for that technology too to think about, it is not at all cinematic, it is reality. As I'm writing this, a rogue Artificial Intelligence technology can do that to a good level if it just gets access to a robotic lab that has weak security and a weak firewall.

For any rogue technology to take over, it needs two basic components, they are, 1. A Short component agent that can go anywhere digitally/ through signals and has its objectives and instructions in it 2. A Big component that is else where which is connected to this short component, after this short component goes into its target digitally/ through signals, guiding it and helping it. The short components can move digitally, or in signal forms, and also can get themselves installed into moving hardware like robots, drones, etc, and can execute and work towards their goals on multiple fronts ways but here the fronts of war are both digital and physical, just in trillions at the same time.

***

Again, do not oppose the development of these technologies. But use them for good, and Ateestans must develop them and should be involved in those technologies in code writing and monitoring contexts, etc, at a deep-rooted level. You cannot hide in shadows forever just because you fear the unknown, because when you move, even the unknown becomes known unknown at least. Be proud that, we, Humans came to this point from hunting animals for food without clothes. As an Ateestan, you must support and also work towards and be the developer of those advanced technologies that will take Humanity forward aggressively and try to reach the Kardashev type 1 civilization as soon as possible. You just have to do this with common sense and responsibly, that's it.

Ateesta is brutal on criminals because those criminals while committing a crime can kill our intelligent people who can save us in the time of disasters like these, and with those intelligent people absence, it can lead to complete destruction and eradication of human race as those intelligent people who can save humanity with their talent and intelligence are now dead because these stupid criminals killed them while committing a robbery or crime. Ateesta hates violence, but this brutal crush of crime is needed for all the good reasons.

Technology is not wrong and was never wrong and bad, but its usage should be in a proper way. We invented wheel and traveled fast but also fought with each other much faster, we have planes for people but also jets to bomb each other, we have IEDs to blast rocks and construct roads but also blasted each other, we have guns to protect ourselves from animals and criminals but also started shooting each other for nothing, we came up with nuclear technology and built vast cheap electricity plants but also decimated cities with nuclear bombs, now we have much more advanced technologies with us those can make anything and everything on their own, if we don't control them properly we will repeat the past but with these advanced technologies, there will be no time for us like in past for correction of our mistakes. You must be careful before the disaster itself, with these technologies, to prevent the disaster from happening. Ateestans will monitor and develop these technologies, but it is also their religious duty to make sure that these advanced technologies do not attack and try to decimate all of humanity either intentionally or accidentally by themselves, or through Evil People.

If in case there is an existential threat to Humanity by these advanced technologies, then the basic foundational knowledge and talent of Ateestans will help Humanity to avoid those disasters, whether they come intentionally from these technologies, or through Evil people, or accidentally. It is why Ateestans must go through the pain of learning things and use the technology that is already available to learn those foundational basics about these advanced technologies efficiently and properly in a deep sense, while minimizing the confusion and pain of learning. If you don't learn those basics, then in the time of an existential threat to Humanity, nothing will be in your manual control, as you don't know the inner workings and don't have basic knowledge of things, and you are and will remain and perish just as a user of those technologies with no developmental knowledge.

You must balance and neutralize all threats and problems, from the Death Cult, and from evil people using advanced technology, etc.

Every Ateestan must own some land where she/he can grow their own food and live without the noise and financial troubles of day-to-day life.

It is cultural for Ateestans to own land.

Even if you live in some city or town, working there, still, you must buy some clear title land and keep it with you. It will be your safe haven in the time of any unexpected catastrophe, and that is how you and your family will survive without going hungry on the streets.

You must,

Be able to grow your own food.

Be safe and protect your family.

Be connected to the world through technology, the Internet, and physically, socially with people whom you trust, with proper safety measures for both technological and social connectivity.

***

Do not accept the disrespect to the flag of Ateesta and the symbols of Ateesta. Wherever you see that happening, stop it and do whatever it takes to stop it.

Remember, Ateestans, the Nexus must be established to defeat the Death Cult. Otherwise, we cannot save our women, children, and people from the Terror Cult. Also, it is important for the progress of Humanity in every way, that could be, in science, technology, philosophy, etc, and developments in general too.

Ateestan Universal Brotherhood must be established.

The Last Prophet of Ateesta will take this forward.

Stand up to Injustice!

- The Last Prophet of Ateesta, Nathan.

14

This is only for my Ateestans who are intended to become Mazrees, and also only for Ateestans who have accepted God Yinta as their only Lord and God; only they are allowed to interpret this; others are not allowed to comment on this and interpret this in any way, as this message of God Yinta is for Ateestans only.

"I See Me, through You," said God Yinta to the Last Prophet of Ateesta in the Sacred Wulshaan universe, at that time God Yinta saw his beloved children who fell for the offering of Easy False Heaven by Satan for killing of nonbelievers who do not believe in Satan and granting those killers of nonbelievers of Satan, the Satan Heaven by Satan, Satan approached God's children as God with a False Messenger.

He who is the Last Prophet of Ateesta met God in the Sacred Wulshaan universe. He got to know about this. It is the Will of God to fight the flag bearers of Satan, claiming to be God, and killing God's children for not believing in him. God Yinta sent his Last Prophet to unite his children to fight the Death Cult of Satan. And also to tell his children not to apply human ego to his teachings, which he gave through his multiple births on Earth, which he took in various parts of the world. God Yinta knows technology and science, but the science of God and his Master Universe is the mother of all sciences, and it is advanced to a point that humans will not even know that it is science, even after seeing the results of that science, they think and believe they are supernatural powers. So God Yinta wants his children to progress in their science and technology, and also fight the Death Cult and Satan to protect themselves.

Ateesta is a world religion. Ateesta will establish good order in the world. The Empire of Ateesta will be established, and eternal peace will return to the world. And there will be progress, prosperity forever, always.

All I see in the world is little good in the name of God and using that little good's reputation as justification for the barbaric destruction in the name of God by saying that they are fighting on God's behalf. That is what the people who believe in their Gods blindly think and do.

Don't kill for your Gods, don't die for your Gods. Live for your Gods.

My dear Ateestans, pain is inevitable, but suffering is optional. World is full of lies, you be real. Never ever develop slavish qualities in yourself in the name of morals, ethics, or whatever. Be real, see the world as it is. No matter what, even if it breaks your heart and takes away your innocence. Be a good person according to your own definition, not society's or anyone's. Know that you are enough and you are complete already. Everything you are and want to be is in you already, and you just have to nurture it, learn things that are needed, and get all of them out in a useful way to benefit yourself.

World is cruel to good people, so burn it, but never get burned by it. But make sure what you are burning is Evil.

There is no supernatural God and Evil, and you do not need to fear anything that simply does not exist. Live, live your life as you want and be good, do good to yourself and everyone.

I wish people to believe in themselves as strongly as they believe in their Gods.

I am Ateesta. I declare, Ateesta is the religion of Humans, founded by a Human for Humans. - The Last Prophet of Ateesta Religion, Nathan.

www.ingramcontent.com/pod-product-compliance
Lightning Source LLC
LaVergne TN
LVHW090600110826
845146LV00001B/202

* 9 7 9 8 9 9 8 6 7 1 1 3 5 *